The Petticoat Empire

Monique J. Libotte

The Petticoat Empire
Copyright © 2023 by Monique J. Libotte

All rights reserved. No part of this publication may be reproduced, distributed, or transmitted in any form or by any means, including photocopying, recording, or other electronic or mechanical methods, without the prior written permission of the author, except in the case of brief quotations embodied in critical reviews and certain other non-commercial uses permitted by copyright law.

Tellwell Talent
www.tellwell.ca

ISBN
978-0-2288-5927-7 (Hardcover)
978-0-2288-5926-0 (Paperback)
978-0-2288-5928-4 (eBook)

Dedication

3 Words 2 Describe 5 Sisters

Hearts of Gold

To Wayne & Kelly,
 I hope you enjoy the story.
 Merry Christmas!
 Monique

Table of Contents

A Good Book ix
The Petticoat Empire Cover xi
A Tribute to My Cousin, Sylvie xiii
Acknowledgements xv
Preface xix

La Famille Pinard 1
(The Pinard Family)

La Famille Cyr dit Vincent 13
(The Cyr dit Vincent Family)

Une Lettre pour Moi? 24
(A Letter for Me?)

Un Pays Étranger 32
(A Strange Land)

Qui Regarde? 36
(Who's Peeking?)

Le Début de L'empire des Jupon 39
(The Start of the Petticoat Empire)

Le Manteau de Bonbons 43
(The Candy Coat)

Un Appel Aux Prêtres 51
(A Calling for Priests)

On S'amuse Avec Papa 57
(Having Fun With Papa)

Les Poupées Aussi Peuvent Voyager 60
(Dolls, Too, Can Travel)

Ma Soeur, Madeleine 73
(My Sister, Madeleine)

Bière et Liqueurs 78
(Beer and Liquor)

Une Voix Feutrée 81
(A Muffled Voice)

La Bulle Éclate 85
(The Bubble Bursts)

Quand on Veut, on Peut 93
(Where There's a Will, There's a Way)

Ça C'est de la Science 96
(Now *This* is Science)

La Curiosité Peut Être Choquante 100
(Curiosity Can be Shocking)

Une Nouvelle Gouvernante 108
(A New Governess)

La Nature se Transforme en Technicolor 120
(Nature Turns to Technicolor)

Un Accouchement Difficile 129
(A Difficult Delivery)

La Vie Sans Maman et un Bébé 140
(Life Without Maman and a Baby)

Maman et Bébé Reviennent Pour de Bon ... 152
(Maman and Baby Return for Good)

Les Chuchotement d'une Corde à Linge 156
(The Whispers of a Clothesline)

Le Radio Crosley 164
(The Crosley Radio)

Dynamique Familiale Mal Interprétée 167
(Family Dynamics Misunderstood)

La Saison du Carêmes 171
(Lenten Season)

Captivé par la Messe de Minuit 176
(Captivated with Midnight Mass)

Au Revoir Monsieur et Madame Laroche 182
(Goodbye Mr. and Mrs. Laroche)

La Vie sur la Ferme, 1934 187
(Life on the Farm, 1934)

À Notre Grande Surprise 196
(Much to Our Surprise)

De Retour à la Ferme 201
(Back on the Farm)

S'épanouir à L'âge Adulte 212
(Blossoming Into Adulthood)

Leurs Dernières Années 219
(Their Final Years)

Bibliography 265

A Good Book

Picture yourself in the country
Sitting on the veranda
With a good book!
There's nothing like fresh country air
Birds singing
The wind softly blowing
And the sun shining brightly

Every once in a while
Be sure to look up
So you can see the beautiful blue sky
It evokes a sense of quietude and serenity
As you lounge on the veranda
With a good book!

It allows you to explore the world
Or different eras remembered in time;
Interesting characters you meet
As they take you to delightful places
And through exciting adventures

I hope you enjoy this book and many others
As you look back to a different time in history …
This can only ever be
Through the eyes and mind of a writer
And the many pages of a good book!

The Petticoat Empire Cover

Country Scene, by Madeleine
(Vincent) Libotte, 1940

In Loving Memory
Madeleine (Vincent) Libotte

They say a book cover is as important as the story itself. I spent countless hours stifling through hundreds of pictures I felt might be fitting for this book. Then one day I suddenly remembered a picture my mother painted when she was a teenager ... *it's perfect!*

The cover of this book is a picture my mother drew and painted in 1940 when she was seventeen. She had an artistic talent, and drawing became one of her favourite pastimes. She had a knack for capturing the essence of the subject she wanted to portray. Having spent many years living in a Quebec village, country life was her inspiration for this painting. She drew what she knew and loved! Drawing proved to be a wonderful hobby for my mother, this being pre-television times in their home.

I am most proud to have the opportunity to use a piece of her artwork for my book, The Petticoat Empire!

Monique J. Libotte

A Tribute to My Cousin, Sylvie

There are two things I know Sylvie is passionate about; genealogy and history. She was the one person I counted on most for any information I lacked about our family's history. Sylvie helped me remember who's who in our family hierarchy and confirmed some locations for me. Even though she had a busy schedule, she set time aside for me on many occasions, for which I am grateful. She provided all family photographs that are in this book. We all have stories to pass on, and there is always something to learn, cherish, and remember from our loved ones who have gone before us. *The Petticoat Empire* is a Historical Fiction, based on a True Story, (our story), and I am sincerely thankful to leave this legacy to my family. My cousin's help was most valuable and it is much appreciated. Merci Sylvie!

My cousin, Sylvie 2021

Acknowledgements

My late Aunt Pierrette for sharing the many stories of her life with me. She would have loved to read, *The Petticoat Empire*!

My late husband, Brian, who was an exceptional spouse and father. He had all the patience in the world and was most supportive and encouraging with any of my writing projects. My daughter, my son, and I will miss him forever ... He lives on in our hearts every day and always!

My late mother, Madeleine – Hands down, if there were such a thing as choosing your own mom, it would have been her! Loving, kind, understanding, intelligent, generous, empathetic, friendly, and a hard worker are words that come to me when thinking about her. Both my mother and father, in fact, were wonderful parents. Just like my mother, the life lessons my father taught me through many of our conversations were plentiful. He too, was the best. Miss them both lots!

* * *

I wish to acknowledge and thank the following people:

My son, Marc, for his insights and wonderful advice. I can't forget to mention, for his patience, because I know I drove him crazy trying to choose a cover for this book! Out of respect he would never say, but a mother just knows...

My daughter, Michelle, who has a fantastic memory for remembering dates, birthdays, and events, especially when it comes to family and relatives, was helpful in my research. Her kind words of support and advice were very much appreciated. Love you both so much!

My awesome siblings: My brother François, and my sister Louise for sharing family history with me and their continuous encouragement. Their opinions were very important to me.

My loving Aunts: Marthe, Louise, and Thérèse, for sharing family history with me, some I would not have known otherwise. A special thank you to my Aunt Marthe because she took time out of her day on many occasions to share family stories with me, which are all included in this book. Merci Tante Marthe!

My beautiful niece, Anne Marie: I reached out to her on several occasions. She put much thought into her feedback which was greatly appreciated. Merci Anne-Marie!

My BFF, Maria, who is an avid reader. She read my manuscript before it went to publishing and her positive feedback and great review were most encouraging and invaluable to me. Thank you, Maria!

My friends: Shirley, Coleen, Betty, Meridith, Nora, and Fran – I thank you and appreciate all your suggestions and advice.

Ingrid & Andrew Peacock: Their opinions helped me get one step closer to deciding on the cover for my book. I was curious to hear Andrew's remarks, which was good feedback, as he, too, is an Author. Ingrid was the last person I had a discussion with about the cover; her comments helped me finalize my decision. Thank you both.

My production team at Tellwell Talent Inc, publishing company, Victoria, B.C.:

This publishing company is highly professional and they are great people to work with. My publishing team was instrumental to me getting this book finished. Without their help I would still be sitting at my computer, trying to write a book! A very special thank you to all of you who were involved in the making of *The Petticoat Empire*.

My production team:
Jennifer Chapin, Publishing Consultant
Joy Comendador, Project Manager
Darin Steinkey, Editor
Von Langoyan, Designer
Ben Graham, Marketing Consultant

I feel confident in saying that I would be a repeat customer of Tellwell Talent Inc. should the need arise.

A heartfelt thanks to EVERYONE!

Preface

The Roaring Twenties and the Great Depression of the 1930s is a time in history that fascinates me. Although it was two generations ago, I remember hearing and reading about it. From family unity to farming to transportation and fashion, what we refer to as the good old days were simpler times.

In the years after World War I, industrial and economic growth flourished. There was a feeling of liberation in the United States. Artistic and cultural changes were on the rise as if celebrating the end of the war. America was the land of opportunity, and the American dream said anyone could succeed if they worked hard for it. Everything prospered for a time ... until ... the bubble burst! The upbeat tone of the Roaring Twenties came to a sudden halt in 1929 when the stock market crashed and caused a decline in the global economy. This sparked the Great Depression, which lasted until 1939. People faced many struggles and hardships during these times.

At the beginning of the 1920s, my grandparents were in their mid-twenties and raising a young family. Like the rest of the world, their lives were greatly impacted by these events.

We visited my grandparents often when I was growing up. When I was approximately ten years old, I recall many hatboxes in the spare bedroom of their house. Most hatboxes were filled with family photos. Climbing the steep and narrow staircase to this small bedroom with its slanted ceiling, I would pretend I was entering my little haven. There were hatboxes of all sizes and I just had to look through each one of them. Many questions and thoughts would enter my mind as I riffled through the photographs.

My mother, Madeleine, was the oldest of five girls. Pierrette came next, then Thérèse, and four years later, the twins, Marthe and Louise. Over the years, I had many interesting conversations with my Aunt Pierrette about our family's history. These photographs I had gazed at so many times piqued my curiosity, so I would ask my aunt what it was like to live in the 1920s and '30s. I wanted to understand what her life was like as a young girl and teenager. She was happy to oblige. My grandmother shared stories with Pierrette, and, in turn, Pierrette shared them with me. I was then able to put the stories to the pictures!

Some things we learn about life come from our past generations' wisdom and become a part of our heritage. Rural life in the '20s and '30s was a time when people's values, traditions, and a strong sense of community and friendships brought people together and gave them a sense of belonging. These may be years gone by, but not forgotten.

The story of *The Petticoat Empire* comes from my diaries of these stories as told to me by my aunt, some by my mother, and their three other sisters. I chose to write *The Petticoat Empire* with my Aunt Pierrette as the narrator, as it was about her and her family's life.

La Famille Pinard
(The Pinard Family)

My mother (Maman) as we called her, was born Eva Rose Pinard in 1896. She was the daughter of Amédée Pinard, my grandfather (Grand'papa), and Virginie (Levasseur) Pinard, my grandmother (Grand'maman). Maman and her siblings grew up in Sainte-Monique, Nicolet County, Quebec, Canada. My mother was a happy, mischievous, and energetic little girl. She loved to play tricks on her siblings and felt it was well worth the scolding that might follow.

Maman's father was a wealthy businessman who was also born in Sainte-Monique, in 1857. From the time he was a young boy, Grand'papa dreamed of becoming a merchant and opening his own store someday. He remembered his mother taking him to the general store in Sainte-Monique quite frequently when he was young. Throughout the years he noticed the many facets of a shopkeeper's role. He saw how the shopkeeper, Mr. Blanchet, spent a lot of time stocking shelves, pricing items, and unloading merchandise. He was a friendly man, seemed to know everyone, and had interesting conversations with many. Grand'papa also noticed that Mr. Blanchet called many of the regular shoppers by their first name or surname. *He must know these customers well, like friends,* Grand'papa thought. Mr. Blanchet even called my grandfather by his first name.

"Hello Amédée, how are you today young man? (Bonjour Amédée, comment ça va aujourd'hui jeune homme?)" he would often say.

Mr. Blanchet sold merchandise, yes, but he was also the Postmaster. The parishioners viewed the general store as the social hub of the village. When my grandfather turned sixteen, Mr. Blanchet hired him to stock shelves and unload merchandise on the weekends. Grand'papa loved his job. He was a hard worker and very much a people person. Mr. Blanchet paid him twelve cents an hour, perhaps a fair wage for a young boy at that time. He loved the atmosphere of a general store and knew that he too, would become a store owner when he got older. It was his calling, one might say.

Grand'papa's father, however, had decided that his nine sons would be farmers on contiguous farms. As a son was married, he gave them money to put towards the purchase of a farm. When my grandfather's turn came, he asked if he could use the money to open a store instead. His father declined. So Grand'papa dug a hole, buried his overalls, and announced that he would delay his wedding to go earn money to buy his store. With the hopes of marrying his sweetheart on hold, he was determined to fulfill his dream.

Because the state of Vermont was reasonably close to Sainte-Monique, Grand'papa purchased a one-way train ticket. He wanted to learn to speak English to communicate with his English-speaking customers in the future and felt the United States was the perfect place to go. Hence, he packed his belongings and headed for Vermont even though he did not know a word of English.

Shortly before leaving, however, Grand'papa found out Mr. Blanchet was thinking of retiring and selling, both, his store and house. He went to see Mr. Blanchet and told him he was very interested in making a deal.

"If you hold off selling, I will buy your property upon my return," he said enthusiastically.

They came to a financial agreement and Mr. Blanchet waited for Grand'papa to return as promised.

My grandfather found a job on a large farm and did not spend a dime except to buy work clothes and postage while in the States. He worked for one year in Vermont and, upon his return, married Virginie Levasseur and purchased Mr. Blanchet's house and store. At the age of twenty-five his dream had come to fruition.

My grandparents were married as planned; however, they left their wedding party early to stock shelves so they could open their store the very next day. They were up most of the night and had their Open (Ouvert) sign up by morning.

Because barcodes were non-existent back in those days, my grandfather devised his own barcode system which showed his entrepreneurial smarts and acumen. It helped him update prices and reorder stock. Since no one spoke English in the area, he took a ten-letter English phrase, 'cut very low', as a way of identifying his wholesale costs (marque de commerce). Each letter stood for a number.

Breakdown of 'cut very low':

Cut - represented numbers 1, 2 and 3
Very - represented 4, 5, 6 and 7
Low - represented 8, 9 and 0
xx represented 'for two'
.e for 'a half'
e on its own represented 5

For example, eoxx meant that the wholesale price was fifty-nine cents for two. Or uo.e meant the wholesale price was twenty-nine and a half cents. This system proved to be efficient.

Grand'papa's business came to be known as the General Store (Magasin Général). His large country-style store had all sorts of spacious concrete-floored back rooms plus a large attic. It was a good size with two large wooden counters, a smaller one at the cash, and a fourth U-shaped one near the back of the store. He had many shelves for stocking goods. There were two pot-bellied stoves, one on either side of the store to keep it warm. Grand'papa always kept his store clean and the shelves well-stocked for his customers.

It became the one-stop shop in the village. He sold everything from groceries to fencing wire, tools, fur coats, sewing fabrics, spools of threads, soaps, brooms and whatever residents of a small village and the surrounding farms required. One could also find such goods as baking soda, baking powder, coffee beans, salt, ketchup, tea, spices, crackers, as well as canned fruits, vegetables, and soups. Grand'papa priced the eggs that the farmers brought in and put it on their tabs. The farmers agreed to spend the monies owed to them in my grandfather's store. It was like a bartering system, a system my father would use in later years.

Whenever time allowed, Grand'maman would bake breads for the store. On those days, the aroma of homemade bread baking in the oven filled the store. Grand'maman's breads were popular and always seemed to sell quickly. It gave women a break from baking their own for a couple of days. Once a week my grandfather liked to make a dozen or two of pickled eggs for the store. My grandmother would cook and peel them and Grand'papa had a special recipe for the brine. He kept them in a glass jar on the front counter by the till, out of the sun. They never lasted more than two days, so they never spoiled. Like Grand'maman's breads, the pickled eggs were a good seller. On occasion, the family would happily eat the leftovers when not sold out within the two days.

Soon after refrigerators came out, Grand'papa purchased one which he placed in a corner near one of the counters. When in season, he filled the fridge with homegrown fresh vegetables, lettuce, tomatoes, cucumbers, onions, radishes, turnips, and carrots. The potatoes he kept in a barrel by the fridge. A sign on the fridge read: Please help yourselves, and I will see you at the till (S'il vous plaît servez-vous et je vous verrai à la caisse.) My grandfather also reserved a small section of a counter for toiletries and medicines.

A further attraction was that Grand'papa always sold his flour and sugar one cent less per pound than other stores in the surrounding area. Farmers always baked their sweets and loaves of bread, so when these staples could be purchased cheaper, it was essential to buy them. Sugar sold for five cents per pound at Grand'papa's store for years. Both the flour and sugar were sold in cotton sacks that were kept in barrels to keep them off the floor. There was also a scale in the store for when a customer only wanted a specific amount.

If Grand'papa did not have what a family needed, he ordered directly from the travelling salesmen who stopped by to display their wares and take orders on a regular basis.

When my grandfather took over the store from Mr. Blanchet, he inherited the job of being the new Postmaster. It was the only way the parish could have mail service. In the countryside, a parish was meant to include the village as well as the farms whose inhabitants attended the village church; in this case it was the parish of Sainte-Monique. A town employee went by horse and buggy (or sleigh in the winter) every day to fetch the mail at the nearest railroad station and deliver it to the store. People seldom had mail, but they came every day just in case. There are so few places to go in a small village that going for the mail was a good excuse to get out of the house, take a walk or simply get some fresh air. For young people, it was a chance to meet a potential mate they secretly eyed.

There was a small number of parishioners who could not read, so one of Grand'maman's tasks was to read them their mail.

"Come with me; we'll go in the house (Venez avec moi; on va aller dans la maison)," she'd say.

She would take them to the living room to be out of earshot of other customers. They might come back a few days later to have a reply written, also Grand'maman's task. This was privileged information; they trusted my grandmother and it created a unique bond between them. Sometimes they would ask her to explain the contents of a letter or even ask for her advice.

The revenue for postmaster was a small percentage of the postage sold. There was not much money in it, but, like Mr. Blanchet, Grand'papa too felt it was an essential service for the community.

My grandparents went on to have five children who survived to adulthood; Marie-Anne, Françoise, Antoine (everyone always called him Antonius), Onil, and my mother, Eva Rose. Between the children and the store, they were very busy people.

The ceremony for my mother's first communion took place in Sainte-Monique Church (Église Sainte-Monique) in 1906, when she was ten years old. She wore a gorgeous white dress with a bow on the back, white shoes and socks, and a beautiful veil that attached to a stunning flowered crown. Maman was a pretty girl, but on that day, she looked exceptionally beautiful.

Grand'maman said to her,

"Eva Rose, there is an elaborate dinner waiting for you at home upon our return."

My grandmother kept a few ornate white dresses in one of the back rooms in the store. She loaned them to families who could not afford to buy one for their daughter's first communion. The mothers were sent to the store by the priest or had heard from a friend that a loan was possible. They usually came a few days before the event.

"I have a pretty dress for you little one; come to the back with me (J'ai une belle robe pour toi ma p'tite; viens à l'arrière avec moi)," she would say.

The little girls' eyes would light up when they saw the dresses. Their moms would return the dress of their choice within a day or two following the ceremony.

All my grandparents' children worked in the store from the time they could count and wrap small packages reasonably well. Until then, they simply enjoyed being in the store because that's where all the action was. When not in the store they could be in the house playing if they wished. There were nannies to watch over them.

My mother said she was not yet twelve when she made her first sale of spools of thread and ribbon which sold by the yard. She wrapped the purchased items in brown paper and used the spool of rolled up string that hung on the wall behind the cash counter to tie the parcel. One never forgets their first sale.

Some years later my grandfather sectioned off one part of the store for his daughter, Marie-Anne. She was a milliner (chapelière) and decided to open a hat shop. Besides the local trade, many rich women from Montreal and small towns near and far came by train or horse and carriage to have elaborate, enormous, imaginative, and expensive hats made by Marie-Anne. Sometimes they came for a hat and ended up buying a fur coat to wear with it. Fur coats, however, were sold mainly for men. They wore raccoon coats or fur-lined coats while the women shivered in their little cloth coats. But then, times changed. After WWII, fur coats for women became more popular and more affordable.

Grand'papa's store was always open after Mass on Sundays and religious holidays for farmers who came to church. He posted a sign in the window that said: Open every Sunday from 11 a.m. (Ouvert tous les Dimanches à partir de 11 heures.) This enabled them to make purchases while they were in the village and save themselves a trip. Those who lived near the limits of the parish seldom came during the week. Grand'papa stayed open until everyone had been waited on, usually one o'clock or so, then my grandparents would have their Sunday dinner.

My grandfather eventually had a telephone installed for his convenience and the parishioners'. It was a novelty for many, and Grand'papa viewed this as an essential service too.

The house connected to the store by a small hallway from the kitchen, and we entered the store behind the large U-shaped counter where the cookie and candy jars sat. There was an open black book on the counter where any items taken from the store were recorded for inventory purposes and to calculate the cost of household and family expenses. Children asked for personal items and entered them in the book. Expensive or special items had to pass the review board (comité de révision); that being my grandparents.

Because Grand'papa was a wealthy man, Maman grew up in a large, richly-appointed home with white columns out front and a long veranda that opened onto a sizeable porch. Grand'papa filled the porch with chairs, a three-seater swing suspended from a black pipe, a table, and his favourite, a Morris chair. My grandmother liked to add the finishing touches by placing beautiful plants on the porch. A door off the veranda opened into the living room (next to the parlour), and a second door off the porch opened into the formal dining room. The store was on the corner and the house stood next to it. The public school was next door to them in the centre of a large piece of land. Across the street and beyond a stand of large trees was the stone Sainte-Monique Church that had only two steps surrounding the whole building, and the two-story rectory was beside it. As people arrived at the store following the church service, women went in to browse and shop while the men often stayed on the porch to chat and smoke.

From the outside, the store looked very much like a big house with three steps up to the porch and entrance to the store. For the men who had little interest in shopping, the small porch was an enjoyable place to wait for their mate. Often, they were not alone. There was usually one or two others waiting, so there was lots of conversation since almost everyone in the village knew each other.

Grand'maman, born in 1859, had been a school teacher until she married at the age of twenty-three. She was a grand lady (grande dame), a highly respected woman because of her experience and knowledge. She had a degree from the school in Nicolet, Quebec. She was very pretty, well-dressed, and her hair always well-groomed. She was low key and fun-loving. She taught Grand'papa how to read and write. Since his father had planned on him being a farmer, he did not consider schooling a necessity. He felt school was a place to send kids when there was no work in the dreary winter months.

"So they aren't around the house to get into trouble," he used to say.

One day, the students at the small one-room countryside school where Grand'maman taught were talking during a test. She threatened to 'give the ruler' to whoever spoke again. One student did, likely to test her, so she told him to stay after school. He did, and she explained to the boy that she dreaded hitting anyone, but felt obliged to keep her word.

"It will be as painful for me as it will be for you," she told him reluctantly.

She gave one good smack on his open hand with a ruler, as he screeched in pain. Was it for show or real? Grand'maman never knew, but it had its effect on her. She regretted it and promised herself she would never hit another person.

To that end, she raised her children to adulthood without as much as a slap and convinced my grandfather to do likewise. He was very tall and had a booming voice, so that sufficed. The only child to take a 'blow' from him was Maman. While Grand'papa was involved in a business transaction, my mother persuaded her younger brother, Antonius, to stand on the counter and jump into a double case of eggs, one foot on each side. That's four rows of six eggs each, twenty-four eggs per tier, six tiers high—an omelette worthy of the *Guinness World Records*.

Grand'papa threw his soft felt hat at Maman and yelled, "To the house! (À la maison!)"

Once his business transaction was finished, and the salesman was gone, he went to get my mother and Antonius, who had washed up and changed his clothes by this time, made them clean up the mess, followed by a stern talking-to. That was the extent of their punishment. Grand'maman's hands-off policy was her method of bringing up children, and she passed it down the generations in our family.

Maman attended a private school for girls at a convent rather than public school. The last grade was ninth, which equated to ten years of schooling. Prior to public school, she attended a preparatory course (cours préparatoire) equivalent to kindergarten. She obtained admission to an art school in Trois-Rivières, Quebec, when she was seventeen. The school burnt down that year during the summer and was completely destroyed. Maman never returned to school. Luckily, she was an avid reader which furthered her informal education.

By the time my mother was to meet my father, the fact that she was not a graduate was not apparent, as he would soon find out.

La Famille Cyr dit Vincent
(The Cyr dit Vincent Family)

My father (Papa) to us, grew up in similar circumstances. He was born Louis-Philippe Vincent, in 1898, in Saint-Célestin, Nicolet County, Quebec. Papa was the first of his family to be baptized using the surname Vincent, as the family was known. His older siblings were baptized with the surname, Cyr, and later changed to Cyr dit Vincent.

It was customary for French Canadians to use dit names, a tradition that lasted until approximately the nineteenth century. The French word 'dit' translates to 'say'; therefore, Cyr say Vincent. When families adopted a second surname, it was referred to as their dit name. They were sometimes used when one family lived in proximity to another with the same surname. The original family name and the dit name contained the same legal weight. One's dit name was even considered legal to use for land transfers. Adopted children were often given a dit name, commonly the adopted family's surname. The adopted child could keep both surnames or choose to go by only one if he or she preferred. Either was legal.

The reason for the adaptation of the Vincent surname in my family is not known. However, by the time my father was born, the name Cyr had been dropped altogether. It could have been something as simple as the farmer down the road having the same family name as my grandfather, so to avoid confusion the dit name Vincent was adopted.

Henri, Papa's older brother, hired a professional genealogist from Montreal to research the family tree. This genealogist's customers were almost non-existent during the Great Depression of the 1930s, so when my uncle hired him, he was more than happy to research our family and ancestors. Henri was aware that the name Vincent had stuck for generations, but many did not know why people called them Vincent if their name was Cyr. Many documents read Cyr dit Vincent.

According to this genealogist's findings, the Cyr family name came about because of an ancestor named Cyr. He was born in about 1745 in Beaubassin, Acadie, in the colony of Nova Scotia. He was a young man at the end of the Deportation of the Acadians (Le Grand Dérangement) which lasted almost a decade, from 1755 to about 1764.

In 1755, Lieutenant-Governor, Charles Lawrence, with the support of the Nova Scotia Council, requested that Acadians sign an oath of allegiance to Britain, making them loyal to the Crown. Their refusal to sign resulted in the dreadful order for deportation.

In September of 1755 males ages 10 and up were ordered to gather in the Grand-Pré Church to hear a message given by the Lieutenant-Governor of Nova Scotia, Charles Lawrence. The message delivered, in part, was that their land, tenements, cattle of all kinds, livestock's of all sorts, their effects, savings, money, and household goods be forfeited to the Crown and they themselves be expelled from the Province. A plan was devised to surround the Acadian churches on a Sunday morning, capture as many men as possible, breach the dykes and burn their houses and crops to the ground. When the Acadians were deported, they left crying, singing, and praying.

Some Acadians were expelled from what are now the provinces of Nova Scotia, New Brunswick, Prince Edward Island and what is today the state of Maine, USA. Some were imprisoned, others had to endure forced labour, while others were put aboard ship transports and sent out to sea to different points around the Atlantic. In many cases, families were torn apart, never to see each other again. They were put out to sea at different times and on different tides, the waves taking them to various places. Many succumbed to starvation and diseases due to the dire conditions on the ships. Others died by drowning when ships sank and were lost on the high seas.

In November of 1758, a fleet of vessels with Acadians on board left from Ile Saint-Jean (Prince Edward Island today) destined for France. Shortly after their departure, they encountered stormy weather which sent the ships in different directions. At least two ships from this fleet, the *Violet*, and *Duke William*, ran into difficulties. At one point, the *Violet* was spotted by the *Duke William* and it was reported that it appeared to be taking in water faster than the crew could pump it out. Two days later, it sank into the North Atlantic. Between 280 and 400 lives were lost. On December 13, the *Duke William* also sank in the North Atlantic, and approximately 360 people perished.

There were some Acadians who were lucky enough to escape, and Cyr, a member of our family, was one. He travelled from island to island in the Gulf of St. Lawrence (Golfe du Saint-Laurent) and back to the mainland along the Canadian coast, guiding himself by the sun and stars in search of Acadians. He wrote the names of all the Acadian women he met as he travelled. He advised them to stay where they were, assuring them he would try to get word of their whereabouts to their husbands. He left lists of wives' locations wherever he found clusters of men. Because of Cyr's dedication, a fair number of families were reunited. In 1774, Cyr married on a French island in the Gulf of St. Lawrence.

Approximately 10,000 to 18,000 Acadians were deported during the expulsion, and thousands more died. The Deportation of the Acadians led to unimaginable calamity, distress, suffering, sorrow, and death. Today, Acadian Remembrance Day is on December 13, the date the *Duke William* sank.

The Deportation of the Acadians finally ended around 1764 when they began the long process of resettling themselves in their homeland in various locations. They were given permission to return by Britain once they agreed to take the controversial oath of allegiance.

Today, many Acadians once again reside in the Canadian Maritime Provinces of New Brunswick, Nova Scotia, and Prince Edward Island, as well as in parts of Quebec and northern Maine in the United States. Some Acadians settled in Louisiana and became the earliest Cajuns.

Evangeline: A Tale of Acadie is a poem written by Henry Wadsworth Longfellow and published in 1847. It is about a fictional girl named Evangeline who searches for the man she loves, Gabriel, as they are separated from each other during the deportation. People were drawn to this emotionally powerful poem about this couple because it represents tragic, real-life events that took place during the expulsion. The poem was Longfellow's most famous work and the rural community of Grand-Pré, Nova Scotia, was made famous by it. Today, it is home to the Grand-Pré National Historic Site of Canada, where a statue of Evangeline and a Commemorative Church stand.

**Commemorative Church,
Grand-Pré National Historic Site of Canada, Nova Scotia
Courtesy of Betty McGregor**

Evangeline: A Tale of Acadie had a significant effect in defining Acadian history and culture.

Grand'papa Vincent was born Pierre Cyr in 1855. He was my godfather after who I am named. He was the grandson or great- grandson of our ancestor, Cyr.

Grand'papa was first a farmer and later became a merchant, much like my mom's father. He lived on a farm in Saint-Célestin, Nicolet County, Quebec. He married Octavie Bourgeois in Bécancour, Yamaska, Quebec. She was a grade school teacher.

Evangeline, A Tale of Acadie poem, shown on page 225

My grandfather had a young brother aged two at the time, and his mother asked Octavie if she would raise the child for her because she was now in her late forties, had raised an enormous family and was exhausted. Great-grandmother had thought she was finished raising kids and could not find the courage nor the energy to raise little Jean-Baptiste. My grandmother, who had taught school until her wedding, was both stunned and disappointed at this request.

"Give me six months to enjoy my husband's company and married life alone and then I will raise him for you."

She kept her word until the day she had to send Jean-Baptiste back to his parents' home for a while when she gave birth. Four little girls arrived at about fifteen-month intervals. Then diphtheria, for which there was no vaccine, struck! To their horror, two little girls died on Tuesday and the two others on Thursday of the same week. My grandparents were absolutely devastated. Jean-Baptiste escaped diphtheria because he was at his parents' home at the time. He moved back in with my grandparents several months later.

Grand'maman and Grand'papa became depressed at the sight of children's clothes, baby shoes, nighties, blankets—anything baby; it was more than they could bear. After having a very busy home with four little ones, they felt isolated on their farm and could not tolerate the loneliness. They sold their animals and farm tools, boarded up the house and barn and covered up the furniture since they were unable to sell it. Leaving with only their clothing, they took a train to Manchester, New Hampshire. There they rented a room in a large boarding house owned by a first cousin and whose husband was co-owner of a bakery. Both were hired at the bakery, saved money, and paid off their farm loan.

Two of their children were born in Manchester. Monseigneur Henri Vincent, the oldest, was pastor of a large parish in West Warwick, Rhode Island, USA, for many years. He was ordained priest in 1910. Antoinette, his sister, later became a nun and was the organist of the Nicolet Cathedral for many years.

My grandparents returned to Canada after a few years. They sold the farm and with the money from the sale, opened a general store in Saint-Célestin. They had eight more children, five of whom survived to adulthood. Their children were; Henri, Antoinette, Germaine, Cécile, Irène, Louis-Philippe (my father), and Charles.

Grand'papa Pinard and Grand'papa Vincent borrowed merchandise from each other's store, especially when they ran out of essential staples in winter when trains were snowbound. They did not pay or invoice each other, they simply replaced borrowed merchandise. Their fiscal years ended at different dates so that when inventory time came, one family travelled the six or so miles between villages to help the other. They always treated the visiting family to great meals. What started out as a business arrangement turned out to be a lifetime friendship as both families got to know each other well.

The store was the place to be and was the hub of everyday life. Papa told me that he did not remember a time when he did not work there as a teenager. One day he figured out their 'marque de commerce' by himself and was aware it was a secret not to be told, even to best friends. Their ten-letter code was 'catholique' (catholic).

Grand'maman was a lively, amicable, and happy person. She invited all the farm women to use her bathroom, sotto voce. Because there were no hotels, restaurants, or public places where public washrooms were available in the village, women who had ridden miles in bouncing buggies or open sleighs shopped there so they could use the facilities as well. They had muddy boots in the spring and fall, however, the nanny cleaned after each family to make the room inviting for the next one.

When farm women purchased fabrics, Grand'maman would frequently cut out her own patterns from brown paper and write directions on snippets of paper which she pinned to the appropriate piece of material. She could cut a man's suit coat, trousers, a woman's dress, children, and baby clothes, as well as shirts and underwear. It was custom to wrap purchases in newspapers so that when the day's paper had been read, mainly *La Presse* from Montreal and *Le Devoir* from Quebec, they were spread out flat and placed on piles at the end of the counters. The piles either grew or thinned depending on sales. However, sometimes the newspapers got shuffled around. Papa recalled the odd time when Grand'maman would read whatever page of the newspaper was on top of the pile and tears would run down her cheeks.

"What's wrong Maman? (Qu'est-ce qui ne va pas Maman?)" he would ask.

"It's a very sad story," she would reply.

Papa would look over her shoulder and say,

"Why, that's six months old!"

Grand'maman was a sensitive lady.

For many years, there was a piano in their house, and Papa's sister, Cécile, took lessons but she mostly played by ear. The family would gather 'round-the-piano', and my Aunt Cécile who was the peppiest of the bunch, would play. When she heard a piece of music or a new song, she would sit at the piano, figure it out, practice and then play it with gusto. She tried to teach my father how to play. However, she would hit his knuckles with a baton as her teacher did to her whenever she hit a wrong note and Papa grew impatient. During what was to be his last lesson, he quickly grasped the baton out of her hand and broke it in two on his knee.

"Cécile, you've hit me for the last time with that thing; I'm done!" he retorted as he walked away.

"That's enough you two," came Grand'maman's voice from the kitchen.

There was no such thing as central heating in those days. Wood-burning cook stoves and pot-bellied stoves were the norm. The cast iron cook stove had the oven on the bottom, the oven warmer on top, the hot water reservoir on one side, and the firebox on the other. As a source of heat Grand'papa Vincent had two pot-bellied stoves; one in the house and one for the store. The cast iron stove in the kitchen was for cooking, but also gave off heat when in use.

Papa and Charles, his youngest brother who they often called Charlie or Charlot, shared a bedroom. He recalled cold winter nights trying to keep warm.

Charlie would steal Papa's blanket and say,

"I have a spoonful of heat (J'ai une cuillère à table pleine de chaleur.)"

They would wrestle each other back and forth with the blankets. Finally, one would say,

"I have two spoonfuls of heat, now go to sleep (J'ai deux cuillères à table pleines de chaleur, maintenant va te coucher.)"

The wrestling alone, I'm guessing, helped warm them up.

My dad went to public school because there were no private schools for boys. He liked school, especially math and French grammar which, with all its exceptions is not an easy subject. He had the option to attend a seminary where he would pursue a seven-year curriculum that led to a BA. The degree was necessary for those wishing to continue at a university and go into professions such as medicine, law, priesthood, engineering, architecture, or notary. The alternative was commercial school.

Papa enrolled in Nicolet Seminary from which his older brother, Henri, had graduated. Papa did well in Latin, but Greek spelled boredom to him. During his second year, he asked to quit school at Christmastime in favour of working in the store. After long discussions, my grandparents accepted his decision.

One evening in January, things changed again when some of the school board members came to the store with a tough problem they could not solve. They wanted to build a new school, but their budget could afford only three quarters of an acre of land. They wanted the land to be square but could not figure out what each side of this square should measure. Grand'papa couldn't either. My dad overheard and explained how to arrive at the correct figure. They left happy. Grand'papa who was not a highly educated man, told my father that with his intelligence he should go back to school. My grandparents convinced him to go to a commercial school instead of back to learning Greek, so Papa decided on a two-year commercial course.

Although my father knew he would be busy for the following two years between school and working part-time in the store, he secretly had a plan. He knew Maman worked in her father's store in Sainte-Monique, and because he had a crush on her, he planned to pop in as often as time would allow.

Une Lettre pour Moi?
(A Letter for Me?)

Papa said he noticed and liked my mother, who was two years and three months his senior, from the time he was a little boy. She thought he was cute, but shy. He hid when she came to their store but watched from his hiding places. She always considered him a child since he was so much younger than she was.

Onil Pinard, Maman's oldest brother, fell in love with Germaine Vincent, one of Papa's older sisters. They were to be married in Saint-Célestin but would live in Sainte-Monique, as Onil had acquired a quarter interest in Grand'papa's store. It was 1914, and Maman had just turned eighteen.

During lunch one day, Onil asked Maman, "Wasn't that Philippe Vincent I saw you talking with in the store about an hour ago?"

"Yes."

She hoped the matter would rest there.

"What did he want?" pressed Onil.

"Oh, he asked if I would go to the wedding with him."

"And what did you say?"

"I'm eighteen," she said proudly. "Do you really think I'm going to go with a boy who's not yet sixteen?"

"You said NO?" the groom asked dejectedly.

"I said I had plans to go with someone else," which was true. Grand'papa, in his thundering voice said, "As soon as you are finished eating, you will sit down and write this boy a very polite note telling him that you will be pleased to go to the wedding with him. We have been friends with this family for years. We are now going to be joined by the bonds of marriage. You cannot insult that family. I want to see your letter before you mail it."

Silence for the rest of the meal.

Maman wrote the letter and went to show it to her father.

After looking at the envelope he asked, "Did you write it as I said?"

"Yes Papa."

"Then mail it," he said without reading it.

A few days later at the Vincent house, when Papa came home from school his mother announced,

"Philippe, you have some mail."

These were words he had never heard before.

With a quizzical look on his face, he stared at the contents in his mother's hand and in a whisper said,

"A letter for me? (Une lettre pour moi?)"

He momentarily stood in disbelief; with a smile on her face, his mother gently reached for his hand and placed the letter in his open palm. He quickly disappeared to his bedroom. Grand'maman never knew what the letter said, but she did notice that her son looked pleased. That night during supper Papa was most proud to tell everyone he would be going to Germaine and Onil's wedding with Mademoiselle Eva Rose Pinard!

Maman wasn't feeling so happy to go to the wedding. She dressed to the nines and wore a pair of very high heels, her first. Because Papa had not yet grown to his full height, it made her appear taller. She wanted the age difference to be apparent and admitted to being a little naughty.

Sidewalks in those days were wooden slats about four inches wide with a narrow space between them to let water drain and to accommodate for contraction and expansion. While walking from the church to the reception, Maman caught her heel in one of the sidewalk's narrow spaces, and it broke off. Papa took the shoe and heel and said,

"Wait, I'll be right back."

He went to their store and, according to Maman, returned in no time with shoes in the right size, the right colour, and somewhat lower heels. She was impressed, as he likely hoped she would be.

For the next several years, Papa made sure to visit his sister and new brother-in-law in Sainte-Monique while always paying a visit to the store where Maman worked full-time.

With a wink and a smile, Grand'maman Pinard would ask,

"Philippe, why don't you stay for dinner?"

Of course, my father never refused. Grand'maman would glance at him over the gold rims of her glasses as if they had a mutual understanding.

Grand'maman Vincent, Papa's mother, who had suffered from diabetes for several years became progressively worse. In 1919 the doctors had to amputate her left leg. She agonized for some time but never recovered. She asked to see Mother and extricated the promise of marrying her son, Philippe.

Maman promised but said she did not feel bound by the promise nor did she feel it was appropriate (de mise) for my grandmother to ask her this. Grand'maman Vincent aged very quickly and died a few weeks later that year. My grandfather was devastated. He no longer took any interest in the store. The girls had all gone their own way, and only Papa and Charlie remained. Although the boys helped their father, life without his wife and maintaining the store became too much for him, so the store closed.

Within a few months, Grand'papa declared bankruptcy and asked my father if he could put the store in Papa's name so he could have a clear record should he ever wish to reopen. Papa accepted. To be bankrupt at such a young age does not presage well for a prosperous life and the hopes of marrying, a pretty rich girl.

There were few jobs available in Saint-Célestin, a village of 250. Grand'papa wanted to go back to New Hampshire, perhaps because that is where he had escaped to cope with the deaths of his daughters. Papa and Charlie went along. They spoke no English, but there were a significant number of French speaking people in Manchester at that time. Job hunting started in earnest. Papa took a few odd jobs here and there: delivering the newspaper, a busboy in a restaurant and a field mower on a local farm. However, railroading was what appealed to him most. Trains were one of the main means of transportation and freight in the '20s. World War I had started in July of 1914, and the railroads had to deal with an increase of cargo as supplies and war materials flowed through. The railroads dominated land transport for war supplies at the time.

My dad moved to Boston, and although he had no experience, he was hired at the Boston and Maine Railroad. He was elated and thought it was a stroke of luck.

Because he did not want to lose my mother, he made sure to write to her often. She was still always on his mind.

For a short period of time, he worked on the session repair crew and then as a callboy. There were few phones then, hence, when an employee was needed for unscheduled work, a callboy was sent to the employee's home to notify him to report to work for a certain time. After some training, Papa became a firefighter. Several years and many courses later, he became a stationary engineer.

Railroad employees had rail passes for free travel which enabled Papa to visit his family in Canada and, of course, my mother with whom he continued to correspond. It took him a couple of years to win her over.

One evening during one of Papa's visits, he and Maman went for a stroll. It was a beautiful summer's night and the stars were shining. They sat on a park bench, and that is when Papa asked my mother to marry him. Although she felt hesitant, Maman said yes.

She told him, however, that she wanted to wear the diamond ring he had surprised her with on a chain around her neck. It was hidden under her dress or blouse for a year before she let him put it on her finger. Indecision was her reason; my mother was not convinced marriage was for her. Only one of her siblings was married. Fear of living in a foreign country she had not even visited and fear of the language barrier were the major impediments in reaching a positive decision.

Although Maman had her reservations for a time, she did love my father and the day came where they chose the date for their wedding. They married September 14, 1921 at five in the morning by my uncle, Monsignor Henri, in Sainte-Monique. Uncle Henri had come up from Rhode Island, USA. Maman wore a chic travelling suit and due to lack of time, Uncle Henri performed a low nuptial Mass. The Vincent and Pinard families and friends crossed the street to my grandparents' home for a quick breakfast before the bride and groom galloped the four miles in their carriage to the train station. The only passenger train left at seven in the morning that day.

Honeymoon trips were not in vogue then because of the lack of transportation. Newlyweds generally had a late morning wedding followed by an elaborate dinner. After a few hours to digest and rest, the wedding party was held in the evening. After a reasonable time, the newlyweds excused themselves and went to their new home together. But Maman's new home, which she had yet to see, was hundreds of miles away. She preferred the early morning wedding and to be on their way.

Papa had railroad passes for him and Maman and had planned a thirty-day trip to Niagara Falls and parts of New England to show his new bride the world. They were excited to leave. They first made their way to Niagara Falls, USA. Maman said the Falls were spectacular, especially at night when they were lit up.

Then off to New England where they visited Maine, Vermont, Connecticut, and Rhode Island. Maman said they saw beautiful places they had only dreamed of before. Not only was some of the scenery breathtaking, but the weather was on their side too. A couple of their favourite places to visit were Providence and Newport in Rhode Island. There they saw beautiful beaches, tall buildings, trollies, amazing mansions, and beautiful architectural buildings such as the Old Stone Bank, Providence Athenaeum (Library), Old State House (it was once the meeting place for the colonial and state legislatures), and Fleur-de-Lys Studio (a historical art studio).

Together they discovered new country and had a wonderful honeymoon. Once their honeymoon was over, they settled in their new abode in Concord, New Hampshire.

Papa had rented a first-floor apartment that he furnished with a leather sofa with an oak frame, a huge armchair, and a rocking chair to match. He put a writing table in the living room, an oak dining room set with a large round table on a massive pedestal, and a sideboard and chairs. The dark walnut bedroom set had a high headboard, somewhat ornate Maman said, and the footboard was a foot higher than the bed with corners that continued around the sides of the mattress. There was a large, mirrored dresser, and a highboy with two doors that opened out to reveal many small flat drawers and two deep ones at the bottom. In addition, there was a small armless rocking chair with caned-back and seat. However, Maman's showpiece (pièce de résistance) was a beautiful vanity table with small, dainty drawers and a triple mirror. Each side opened on a piano hinge so that if she brought her head forward and moved the side mirrors towards herself, she could see a sea of faces, all her own. Narcissism at its best!

A new husband, a new apartment, an unknown language, and a new country. Maman would have to adjust to a completely new lifestyle almost overnight! It not only frightened her, but it left her wondering what her future would look like.

Un Pays Étranger
(A Strange Land)

Papa was happy. He had married the girl of his dreams. He returned home after work every day to his new wife and wonderful meals instead of the YMCA and going to restaurants whose menus he knew by heart. He was in a familiar surrounding (milieu) and spoke English fluently after having lived in Manchester, Boston, and Concord for a few years. He made a large salary and had substantial savings. He had it all.

It was a different story for Maman. She did not speak English which made her feel illiterate. When she accepted the fact that she would live in the United States, Maman purchased what few books she could locate and studied vocabulary and grammar on her own, but it did not suffice. Not having heard the language spoken, it was impossible for her to speak English or to communicate in English other than in writing.

The moment Papa left for work her world became empty. It was limiting for a bright person who felt anything but isolated from early childhood. She was accustomed to a large circle of friends, entertaining, and to being in contact with customers every day. Coming from a home that had a live-in nanny, a cook, and a wash-woman three days per week, her days were now filled with cooking, washing, and what cleaning she could find to do in a new apartment. She was lonely. If Papa was gone for a day or more, she spoke to no one, heard no one. By this time Maman had been living in the States for almost seven months. My father needed a plan...

He thought of Marcelle Chauvette. She was a girl that Maman's parents had raised from the time she was an infant. Marcelle's mother died when she was only twelve days old, and her father, a poor farmer, was left with eight children and no one to care for them while he worked his farm back in Sainte-Monique.

On Immaculate Conception Day (a day when all the Catholics went to Mass), the parish priest of Sainte-Monique announced that Mrs. Chauvette had died and asked that families come forward to take a child. The conversation that day amongst parishioners quickly turned to the plight of this poor family.

My Uncle Onil and Aunt Germaine went to my grandparents' house that afternoon and asked if they were considering taking a child. Maman and her siblings were enthusiastic and told their parents they would help with whatever chores were involved. They suggested they go and get a child, but this was a big decision for my grandparents and required a lot of convincing. They did love children, but they were not young anymore. They had frequently taken in children from farms who attended the village public school when roads were unpassable in the spring or closed in the excessive cold of the winter. The local farmers would ask if they could leave a child with my grandparents who lived next door to the schoolhouse knowing they would not be refused.

After a lengthy discussion, my grandparents decided they would adopt one of the older boys. He could help in the store and they could send him to school. The horse was saddled to the sleigh and off they went in the bitter cold. As they were approaching the small farmhouse, they met another couple on the road. The wife, Mrs. Segal, held a baby in her arms. My grandparents stopped to chat.

"Are there any children left?"

"Only the baby," Mr. Segal replied, "and poor Mr. Chauvette is crying."

After a short conversation, the Segal's drove off because it was cold and they had a baby to keep warm.

My grandparents were stunned and momentarily undecided as the child was a new born. But they went ahead and took baby Marcelle anyway. She had lost a mother and found a new one almost overnight. She was a very bright little girl. Marcelle always called my grandparents Grand'maman and Grand'papa. The others she called aunt and uncle. When she spoke of 'Papa', she was referring to her natural father, Mr. Chauvette. Whenever he came to visit Marcelle, he was received as a special guest in their home, so the meals were served in the formal dining room.

My father suggested to Maman she write a letter to her parents asking if they could have Marcelle, then five years old, for a time. My grandparents replied, saying they agreed. In the spring of 1922, they went to pick her up. My parents enjoyed her company; they liked children and were happy to have a little five-year-old running around the house. My mother kept busy by feeding Marcelle tasty and healthy meals, doing crafts with her in the afternoon and reading to her in the evening. Marcelle filled the void left by Papa's absences and overnight shifts.

An overnight shift for Papa might occur when a freight train slowed to a crawl going over the White Mountains. Sometimes there could even be a layover of eight hours or more.

Marcelle stayed in Concord for four months until it was time for her to start school in September. By then, Maman was four months pregnant, busy crocheting a baby's layette, and gradually assimilating to her surroundings. She started to enjoy independence from her family and was looking forward to a family of her own.

Qui Regarde?
(Who's Peeking?)

Madeleine was born February 7, 1923, in Concord, New Hampshire. Having a baby was a life-changer for Maman. It gave her a purpose every day, and even on those days when Papa was away, my mother was no longer lonely—there was no time to be. Papa once told me he wondered who got more pleasure from rocking their new infant, Maman, or baby? Watching each milestone Madeleine achieved made my mother feel so proud and filled her with joy. She truly loved being a new mother. Madeleine was a healthy little girl with a perpetual grin. She was a pleasant and happy baby.

My mother travelled to Canada when Madeleine was three months old to show her off to her family. Of course, they all thought she was a sweet little thing. Grand'maman Pinard took charge, as my mother knew she would. She held and rocked her, fed her, and gave her baths, which gave Maman a bit of a break. The week went by quickly, and before they knew it, they were back on their way to the States.

As Madeleine got older, six months to a year, she developed a pattern where, according to Papa, she cried wildly in the evening. She also had a habit of sucking her thumb. Therefore, Maman came up with an idea. She bought Madeleine a pair of angora wool mittens. Every night when she had been a 'good girl' during the day (which was every day), Maman would let her wear the mittens to bed. This seemed to comfort Madeleine and she would soon go to sleep. One night when Madeleine was a bit older, she started to scream after being in bed for some time. This was so unusual that both my parents rushed to her room. They couldn't imagine what was wrong with her.

"I was a good girl," Madeleine cried on. Maman and Papa laughed, realizing that my mother had forgotten to put the mittens on. Madeleine was once again happy with her mittens and soon went to sleep.

My mother became ill at ease in their apartment because the landlord, Mr. Blythe, who lived on the second floor, started peeking in the windows at night. By this time, my parents had lived in this apartment for almost two years, so the landlord's sudden behaviour change was puzzling. Although Maman would lower the shades, it still made her uncomfortable. This upset Papa terribly. He threatened to go to the police if he did not stop this outrageous conduct. Mr. Blythe did stop; however, my mother still did not trust him. I'm sure my father felt the same.

Maman once again went to Canada to visit her family when Madeleine was two. When she returned, my father met her at the station and escorted her to a waiting taxi. He had previously given directions to the cabbie to drive them to a new address on Grove Street, a few blocks from their previous apartment. Papa had had enough of Mr. Blythe peeking in the windows, so he recruited his best friend,

Clyde Lambert (a railroad man), to help him move to a new apartment he had rented while my mother was away. Papa rented a horse and cart to move their belongings. Maman was thrilled! My parents and Madeleine lived in the back portion of the house. They were much, much happier living on Grove Street.

Soon, more diapers would be needed ...

Le Début de L'empire des Jupon
(The Start of the Petticoat Empire)

I was born three weeks late, January 4th, 1925, in Manchester, New Hampshire. My parents had spent New Year's weekend with Uncle Charlie (Dad's brother) and his wife, Aunt Irène. They offered to keep Madeleine for a few weeks knowing Maman was due to have the baby very soon. Madeleine stayed behind, and Maman gave birth a few days afterwards.

Madeleine, 2 years old, wearing Papa's Cap, 1925
Courtesy of Sylvie

By the time I was two and a half, my mother gave birth to a third girl, Thérèse. My mother was not to be lonely again with three little girls to look after!

I remember crying loudly one evening as Maman was putting me to bed. It was after supper, still full light outside, and it was a hot day. Maman kept repeating soothing things as she removed my clothes and put on a nightgown, but I cried on.

Finally, she asked with a quizzical look and a puzzled tone in her soft voice,

"Why are you crying so much, Pierrette?"

I didn't know.

"Since you're so tired, I'll sit with you while you fall asleep. It will make you feel better."

She went to her room and brought in a small, armless rocker made of dark wood that had a pale caned seat and back (that I came to know extremely well), and she sat near my bed. I stopped crying because I was comforted by her presence and calming words. This was typical of the loving mother I remember.

Whenever a child began to cry because she had bumped herself, caught a finger somewhere or incurred whatever small injury little children are prone to, a large penny (they were about one inch in diameter) was placed on the bump and a bandage wrapped around to keep the penny in place. I never found out if it worked or was an 'old wives tale.'

Bandages were special at our house. Soft, thin, old white cotton material, torn in strips of varying widths, was boiled and dried in the sun to be sterilized, rolled up, and kept in a wooden box. Maman was creative with bandages and tried to make them look pretty for us; I recall bows and rabbit ears. One time Madeleine insisted on a wide bandage on her upper arm with a mercurochrome cross drawn like the Red Cross (À la Red Cross) because she used to say she was going to be a nurse when she grew up.

Madeleine, approximately 4 years old
Courtesy of Sylvie

When I was hurt, if I saw others were hurt (especially my sisters) or when I heard a sad story, I cried.

"You are a sensitive child my little girl (Tu est une enfant sensible ma petite fille)," Maman would say to me.

But despite the tears, I was a happy and content child who enjoyed playing quiet games alone and doing things by myself. Though I started each morning and afternoon playing with others, I would gradually withdraw to play my own games.

Years later, I used to wonder if there was a correlation between being born late and one's natural speed. I came three weeks late and have always been a slow poke. I was often trailing behind everybody, it seemed. As for my sister, Thérèse, she was the opposite of me. "Nobody will be tripping on her coat tails," Papa used to say laughingly.

Le Manteau de Bonbons
(The Candy Coat)

The thing I enjoyed most when I was young was playing. Maman taught us how to play, suggested games, started the play, then let us continue by ourselves. Her mantras included: 'You don't have to scream to have fun', and, 'you don't have to be loud to enjoy yourself.'

My mother taught us how to make toys. She made all sorts of colourful things with paper. Empty toilet paper rolls had a string run through them; we coloured them in zigzags, held the string, and rolled them around the house. She transformed empty boxes into doll carriages, made paper hats out of bags, newspaper—any paper.

During one of my conversations with Maman as an adult, I asked her why she was so creative with our handmade toys (jouets artisanaux) during the 1920s. She could have afforded to buy the toys at that time because it was before Black Tuesday and the start of the Great Depression. She believed that play was important as it helped develop a healthy brain. It allowed a child to be creative, use their imagination, explore, develop hand-eye coordination, and learn to share and interact. My mother was creative, but her hope was to show us how to be creative too.

Being girls, we naturally had dolls and all the paraphernalia, such as a high chair, bath, clothing, and blankets, most of which were handmade. She bought little five-cent celluloid dolls at Woolworths that were five to six inches tall with painted eyes, eyebrows, mouth, and hair. They were always nude at that price, and I recall scraps of material were turned into clothing for them. Papa blunted the scissors we used to cut the fabric and snipped off the ends with pliers for our safety.

To Maman's way of thinking, kids had to play with balls of every size. She taught us many games for playing ball against a wall that consisted of rhymes which had to be memorized and involved a lot of counting. We also played cards often; Battle of War (Bataille) was one we loved. It taught us to love numbers and to count quickly. It was fun.

Math was one of my favourite subjects in school, and it surely stems from learning to count and associating numbers with fun. There were board games that required a bit of skill, like Tiddlywinks; was one we all liked. No one let us win; we had to do it ourselves, fair and square. The satisfaction was greater when one was the author of one's victories.

When Maman decided to teach Madeleine and me to embroider (Thérèse was still too little), Papa panicked because of the needles.

"We can't raise children in glass houses," Maman told him. "I am teaching them to be careful and responsible."

Papa then went along with it, but only after he verified the ends of those scissors were snipped off. He also made the very tip of the embroidery needles dull. We enjoyed this time with Maman, and it was a great pastime.

An ongoing battle with my parents was eating, an exercise I cared little for. I was never hungry, so Maman had to coax and cajole me. She made a game of it. Mashed potatoes were turned into a house with lines drawn with fork tines.

"Can you eat the chimney? Let's try eating the door. Do you have room for a window or two?"

I remember her cutting up apples. She would take slices and cut them up into kite shapes.

"Want a nice kite?" she would say. So long as I ate, she was happy.

My mother liked to do her shopping alone, and went on the days Papa was home during the morning hours. When she needed something for a specific child, she would take that child along. Before leaving the house, Maman would remind us,

"Shopping is not a time to play. We're on a shopping mission, looking for something specific, and now that you're old enough, I trust you can help me with this task."

This made us feel important, and we did not want to disappoint her.

When it was my turn, I liked walking the whole way on the curbing while keeping my balance. When we got to the store, she would say,

"Touch with your eyes, don't look with your hands."

It was tempting, especially in dime stores. But there was no fooling her because it seemed she had eyes in the back of her head. She always made us bring our doll to keep our hands occupied.

One day, Maman took me with her to buy me a new coat and shoes. She pointed out a few suitable items and let me choose my favourite. I selected a coat I was very fond of and referred to it as my 'candy coat.' It was a caramel-coloured soft material with a narrow, straight-up collar that extended into a necktie-like scarf from the chin to about the waist. One side of the scarf flipped over the other and hid the neck button on the buttonhole. There were white flannel appliqués (the candies) about three inches in diameter which were set in place with red embroidery stitches on each of the patch pockets, and both ends of the scarf. I was given the choice to take it home in the box or wear it, I opted to wear it.

We then went to a shoe store where we found soft leather shoes with a T-strap and small buckle the same colour as the coat, stitched in red. I decided to wear these too. I was elated by the match and the whole outfit as we left the store, but not for long. It was just after noon, and there was a throng on Main Street, likely the lunch crowd. A man stepped on my left foot with all his weight. He put his hand behind my shoulder and said,

"Sorry little girl." I quickly looked down at my shoe and saw a V-shaped scuff big enough that you couldn't miss it.

I looked up at him, saw his gold-rimmed glasses, and noticed he was already returning to his conversation.

"Excuse me, sir, you ruined my shoe."

He looked at my mother and said, "I'm sorry, I didn't see her."

"They were brand new. We just came out of that store," I said.

"Really?" he replied to Maman as if children were incapable of carrying on a conversation.

She did not say a word and allowed me to stand up for myself, which I did. Then she showed him the box that held the shoes I had worn to the store.

"How much were they?" he asked.

Maman told him the price—one dollar, perhaps two. He took some money from his pocket and gave it to her. He went back to his conversation as if nothing had happened. We went and bought another pair. This time I wore my old shoes home, just in case.

The day after we purchased the coat and shoes, Maman gave me a long explanation about how expensive coats were. I was not to sit on the ground with a new coat, wipe my hands on it or push down too hard in the pockets. I totally missed the point of her talk. I thought she was saying that the coat was unaffordable and she had bought it because I loved it so much; therefore, I should be careful so it would last for many years. I got a bright idea and decided I would remedy the situation.

Every February and March, Maman sewed our summer clothes. She made each of us a batch of cotton dresses along with the petticoats and often made a pair of panties to match. She left all the dresses and petticoats unhemmed because February to June is a long stretch in a child's growth pattern. She'd show them to Papa who would ask, "Why are they so long?"

I went upstairs and dragged a chair to the light switch, turned it on, then brought the chair to the closet. I took down a pale blue dress with a print of a square divided into four more squares. I took Maman's scissors from her dresser, folded the dress in two to find the middle front, made a little slit at the bottom (as Maman did for bandages) and pulled until it was torn all the way to the top. The only trouble was tearing through the bias tape at the neck opening, but I gouged my way through with the help of the scissors. I put it on over the dress I was wearing, walked down to the kitchen and held my belly in very tight while I crossed one side over the other. Maman saw me and with a surprised look on her face said,

"Pierrot, what have you done?"

"Look Maman, you can return the candy coat. I made one for myself, and when I hold my breath in real tight, it crosses over."

She walked to the coat closet by the front door, took out the new coat and sat on a kitchen chair.

"Come here," she told me as she parted the coat's lining from the top layer. "Feel the thickness of the material."

I did.

"You see, there's a lining to make it thicker. It keeps you warm. The coat has long sleeves to keep your arms warm. It's not because it crosses over that makes it a coat; it's because it's a different piece of clothes made of thicker material. Try it on. You'll see."

It is difficult to convey how stupid I felt. I looked down at the cut-up dress and being sensitive as I was, I started to cry.

"Don't cry; I can repair it easily. Come."

She started looking through her sewing box and took out a piece of light blue rickrack, sat at her sewing machine, made a seam down the middle of the dress, then sewed the rickrack on top of the seam. Crisis averted.

Her patience always amazed me.

I recall her diligence when teaching Madeleine and me how to tell time by moving the hands on a noisy Big Ben kitchen clock. That too was turned into a fun game for us. After teaching and making us practice on the Big Ben clock, she cut out a clock face out of cardboard. She made two different clock hands that were white, one being shorter. She would make up sentences that included a specific time which we had to place properly. Madeleine would look away when it was my turn and vice versa. Thérèse would take a turn and although she was not expected to get it correct due to her age, there was one time when she surprised us all and, just by fluke, got it right!

Papa, who did not hear an alarm easily, had one wake him up which was always set to 5:00 a.m. By now I knew what 5:00 a.m. looked like, so when I happened to be awake at that time, I would yell,

"Allô! (Hello!)" out of my bedroom window and get an answer.

"What's your name?" I'd respond.

Not only did this wake Papa up, but possibly some of the neighbours too.

"Why do you yell like that so early in the morning?" he asked me one day.

"Because I want to wake you up, and I say hello to my friend at the same time. I stick my head out the window and she talks back to me."

"It's not your friend talking to you Pierrette, it's the echo of your own voice," he said.

He explained the echo effect to me, but I didn't believe him.

She answered me!

Between the alarm clock, Maman, and me yelling out the window at five in the morning, Papa was seldom late for work.

My father's job always seemed to go well and was somewhat uneventful, which was a good thing. Up to now he had always enjoyed his job, but this one particular Sunday in November of 1928, he had no idea what the next day would bring; it was impossible to predict his fate.

Un Appel Aux Prêtres
(A Calling for Priests)

November 19, 1928, is a day our family never forgot! Papa's workday started peacefully but was soon to change. He was on duty on a passenger train passing through Lowell, Massachusetts, at one o'clock in the afternoon.

Suddenly, he got this sick feeling in the pit of his stomach as he heard the sound of screeching breaks. Next came a horrific crash! Papa was immediately thrown around in the car of the train. All he could hear was an unbelievable piercing sound of metal on metal. When it finally stopped, there was an eerie silence following the crash; it was as if time stood still for a moment, he told Maman. His first thought was, *I'm alive; I can't believe I survived!*

Train Wreck, November 19, 1928
Courtesy of the Boston Public Library,
Leslie Jones Collection

He wanted to get up and help other injured passengers but couldn't; it was too painful. He did not know what he hit as he was thrown around. He just knew he was hurt. Besides being badly bruised, my father's right leg folded under him, breaking in several places.

He later told my mother that numerous railroad men came rushing from every direction to the overturned cars. He could hear people crying and screaming as passengers were frantic to get out. Papa heard someone say in a panicked voice,

"It's going to burst into flames!"

As he lay there, he prayed it didn't.

He found out from a co-worker a few days later that between thesteam escaping, the dust flying, and the heavy fog, searching for people still on board was much more difficult. Papa was unsure how long he lay on the floor of the train. He was lying in an awkward and uncomfortable position, his body pushed up against a seat. Suddenly he heard someone say, "Are you OK?"

Train Wreck, November 19, 1928
Courtesy of the Boston Public Library,
Leslie Jones Collection

He opened his eyes and realized it was a priest accompanied by a firefighter. They told my father help was on the way, and a few minutes later two ambulance attendants arrived. They laid my father down on a wooden slab, placed straps around him and the board, and removed him from the train to a waiting ambulance. A doctor on site quickly checked Papa and gave a thumbs up to the ambulance attendants to take him to the hospital.

My father got the inside scoop about the accident from people he knew and what little of it he remembered. Survivors, most of whom suffered severe injuries, were also rushed to nearby hospitals by ambulance. Because there were many injured passengers, some onlookers on the scene even took their own vehicles to transport some of the wounded to hospitals.

Papa's leg was X-rayed and placed in a cast that covered a good part of his leg. In those days, blood transfusions were direct. If it was a match, the transfusion was given person-to-person because blood banks were not yet in existence. Papa gave blood while side by side with the recipient.

Train Wreck, November 19, 1928
Courtesy of the Boston Public Library,
Leslie Jones Collection

My father arrived home by taxi the day following the crash. He was using crutches. When Maman saw him, leg in a cast and face so bruised, she passed out on the living room floor. Not yet having mastered the art of maneuvering on crutches, Papa told Madeleine to get a towel and a bowl of cold water from the kitchen. Because he was not able to bend over, he made his way to the sofa, stretched his leg across it, and there he had access to Maman's forehead. My mother came to after several minutes. They teased each other over this for a long time.

"If only you had warned me, Philippe, I wouldn't have been so shocked."

My dad always carried his prayer beads in his back pocket; they had broken into many pieces in the crash. The next day, Maman placed all the parts in their proper order and reassembled them with needle-nose pliers.

"It's a fun puzzle," I said.

Maman looked at me, hesitated, and finally said,

"Not if you saw your daddy's buttock. The grains left a navy-blue imprint there. He is very sore," she said.

I had to take her word for it, though I wondered what it looked like.

Maman sat the three of us down and explained that Papa's leg was broken, told us what a cast was for, said he had a lot of bruises on his body, and that we would have to try and play quietly.

"It's very important to do what I'm asking of you because your father needs lots of rest to heal and regain his strength. The more he rests, the sooner he will feel better."

My dad slept a lot during his first couple of weeks at home. Maman would occasionally say,

"Not so loud, Papa is sleeping," or "Shhhh."

Although my father never saw the accident scene on the day of, he and some of his co-workers sat down together and discussed the incident a couple of weeks later. They told him approximately twenty people were injured, and one man died in hospital several hours after the crash. Tragically his injuries were so severe, they were unable to save him. He sadly left behind a wife and two children.

The trains involved in the collision at the Lowell Yards that day were the *Ambassador* going northbound and the southbound *Express 1.01*. The northbound train sideswiped the other, overturning the smoking car, baggage car, and coach car of the *Express 1.01*. Papa remembered the heavy fog that loomed over the yards that day and believed it to be a factor. His co-workers told him there had been ambulances, fire trucks, police, doctors, and priests called to the scene immediately following the crash. He and his friends wondered if one of the trains did not see the other crossing over to their track due to the heavy fog or possibly did not see a flashing red light.

Papa stayed home for several weeks afterward. He played with us and read a lot. He slowly became restless being out of work and without the use of his bicycle. Once he felt better and had mastered the crutches, he would walk down to the railroad station's engine house to talk with his co-workers almost daily.

Papa's leg eventually healed, and he returned to work. I always thought; *he must really have loved his job to return to it after such an ordeal.*

My father was a very lucky man—he survived the crash! Married with three young children and a young man himself, both he and Maman counted their Blessings.

On S'amuse Avec Papa
(Having Fun With Papa)

My father was always part of the fun on weekends. Where Maman was inventive and artistic, Papa was informative. He would sit one of us on his bicycle handlebars or the long uncomfortable bar between the handlebars and the seat and off we'd go to see something new.

I liked it when he took me down country roads. We could see farmers at work in the fields, children playing, and on sunny days we'd see women hanging clothes on their clothesline. Dogs would run around in the fields all the while staying close to their masters. On occasion Papa would stop to chat with a farmer he knew. I usually played with their dog while my father visited. Papa would later explain what chores the farmers were doing in the fields and what equipment they were using.

In the fall and winter, I recall nuts being opened for us with a nutcracker. We were like birds waiting with open mouths for the next nut.

"It's my turn!"

"No, it's my turn!"

"I'm going as fast as I can," he'd say.

"You're not putting any fun into it," Maman said to him once.

"Okay, you do it then."

"I'm better with a hammer and a breadboard," she remarked.

Smash! Down came the hammer on the nut.

"Ah, you girls will have to dig the pieces out."

She smashed more pieces and left it to us to find every last piece of nut meat. From then on, our father became the expert 'nut crasher' in our house.

Papa and I had a trick we performed together on the front porch. I would put on soft slippers and run towards him. He would bend on one knee and I would put one foot on his knee and the other on his shoulder. I would then put my first foot on his other shoulder while he grabbed my hands and stood up slowly. Once he was standing, he would let go of my hands. We walked around the porch, me with my hands touching the ceiling. Eventually I grew too tall for the 'porch walk'.

In the evenings when my father was not too tired, he read stories to us in English, something Maman could not do because of her difficulties with pronunciation. He usually sat in the large living room rocking chair with one of us on each arm and read. Sometimes he sang to us. He especially liked to sing songs from the Theodore Botrel's songbook. He had a good singing voice. My favourites were the ones where he substituted our names with the ones from the song. Being in his arms was warming and gave us a sense of security. We felt he was big and strong; he was our protector.

One evening, Papa came home excited to tell Maman that the circus was passing through Concord, on their way to Boston, Massachusetts. The circus was to stopover for a day to unload the animals and walk them around on Main Street for exercise, including elephants. Our parents decided this was a must-see. We brought small collapsible seats in the shape of an X to sit on for the parade as my parents stood behind us. Other than cats, dogs, horses, and cows, we had never seen any other animals up close. We were so excited. The elephants walked by in order of size with the trunk of one holding the tail of the other in a line. We couldn't believe the size of an elephant! We were totally impressed with the elephants, it was all we talked about that night, and the next day, and the day after that.

Years later when we were teenagers, the topic of elephants came up at the supper table. Madeleine had read an article that said female elephants carry their babies for almost two years before giving birth. She said it takes a baby elephant at least a year to figure out the many uses of its trunk. Some ethologists view elephants as one of the most intelligent animals in the world. They show behaviours such as learning, grief, play, compassion, co-operation, memory, and communication. They are also known to have a strong awareness of family environments and relationships. She said they can only be separated by capture or death. Thérèse and I were fascinated with this information just as we were with the elephants when they passed through Concord, NH, all those years before. As for my parents, they were most impressed with Madeleine's elephant knowledge!

Les Poupées Aussi Peuvent Voyager
(Dolls, Too, Can Travel)

We had the amazing opportunity to travel quite a bit because my father had rail passes. We all went on short trips, most often to the beach at Portsmouth. We went to Manchester a few times and to Boston once. The major travelling was with Maman to visit her family. Whenever my mother would begin to talk of Canada, she would look at a large oval picture of my grandparents which hung on a wall near the coat closet. I was too young to know what 'Canada' was and could not visualize it. I thought it was something behind that wall.

I was unaware of preparations for the trips. Papa would take us to the train station in Sainte-Monique, kiss us all many times, wish us 'Bon Voyage', and put us on board! Off we'd go, the three of us girls each carrying our doll and Maman carrying a small satchel and a large leather suitcase which Papa had bought. My mother said it was heavy when it was empty, so when it was full, she could not lift it. She always had to get help because she only weighed about 105 pounds. Several other cases had to be checked through also.

Railway Station, Sainte Monique de Nicolet, QC, about 1910
Stanley G. Triggs
Courtesy of the McCord Museum MP-0000.1096.7, Montreal, QC

We were never without our doll because Maman felt if one of us became separated from her or somehow felt frightened at some happening, holding on to a familiar object would make us feel secure. It also provided us with something to play with. She made us care for our dolls and we had to make sure they had the right clothing for the weather. We always kissed them goodnight and held them as we went to sleep.

"Where's your doll?" Maman asked frequently.

We sat in a double seat with two of us facing the two others. I recall it was rather boring, however, Maman brought an attractive lunch. Delicate sandwiches, celery, radishes, cucumber slices, and cookies for dessert. Madeleine travelled to the water cooler often because she was the self-appointed water carrier for the family. We were constantly told to speak softly to avoid disturbing other passengers.

We all wanted a window seat, of course. When the crowd thinned, Maman would let us sit alone (but always in her line of sight) by a window with our doll.

"Watch for a river or lake. When you see one, come and tell me," she'd say.

My mom's plan was that watching the land go by would put us to sleep, which it always did at some point. It was a long trip, close to ten hours.

When we arrived at Windsor Station in Montreal, Maman would hold Thérèse by the hand and Madeleine held mine while we waited for a Red Cap to round up our luggage and flag down a taxi.

Windsor Station, Montreal, QC, 1889
Associated Screen News Ltd.
Courtesy of the McCord Museum VIEW-1947.1, Montreal, QC

We visited Aunt Cécile, Papa's sister, whenever passing through Montreal. She lived in a new building on Papineau

Street called, Le Pont Neuf. Anytime we arrived at her apartment and she was not home, the concierge would let us in. Aunt Cécile was a nurse and a supervisor of operating rooms at Hôpital Notre-Dame. Her apartment was across the road from the park and hospital. My Aunt and Mother slept in her bedroom, usually talking half the night having long, jovial conversations. Madeleine, Thérèse, and I slept in the living room on the pull-out couch, falling asleep to the sound of streetcars going by. I remember the sound so vividly.

Aunt Cécile married Albert later in life and continued to live there until she died. Although they loved children, they never had any.

The next day we trekked back to Windsor Station to board the train for Sainte-Monique station where we were met by horse and carriage, a ride that always fascinated me. Someone was generally on the large columned veranda at my grandparents' house waiting to greet us.

"How tall you've grown," they'd notice. "Children can grow a lot in a year," Maman would respond.

Six people lived in my grandparents' home at the time: my grandparents, my godmother, Aunt Marie-Anne (who was five years older than my mother), Marcelle (a teenager by now) and two nannies, one for cooking and one for house cleaning. It's a good thing it was a big house.

The two large bedrooms on the first floor were the guest room and my grandparents' bedroom which had, in addition to a regular double bed, a large lounge recliner bed with a built-in riser which was used as a chaise lounge. There was a total of seven bedrooms. Maman slept in the guest room on the main floor, and we all slept upstairs.

We were each assigned our rooms; Marcelle, Aunt Marie-Anne, the nannies who shared a bedroom, Thérèse and I in one, and Madeleine in the other. The upstairs was split in two distinct areas. The front section of the upstairs was usually for girls and the back section for boys. Many houses were built that way at the time, and I gather this was so the girls who wore complicated underwear, stays, corsets, petticoats, and garters could feel free to walk around without scandalizing their brothers. They had to fetch a pitcher of water daily to wash with (baths were a Saturday affair), so this arrangement made them feel more comfortable.

There was a total of sixteen rooms in my grandparents' house. The back stairway had a narrow gallery surrounded by a banister with doors (under the stairway) all around. All these doors opened to shelving for storage. One contained towel's, one sheets, one for miscellaneous items, and one had toys of every kind, all in their original boxes and in good condition. They were Maman and her siblings' toys, and we were welcome to play with them, which we did.

There was what we called 'our secret hiding place' in my grandparents' house. What my sisters and I thought was so unique, secretive, and fun was a second stairway on the other side of the house where one of the bathrooms was. What made it special was that to get to the stairway, one had to access it through the bathroom! There was a door on the back wall of the bathroom, and when you opened it, VOILÀ—there it was—a hidden staircase! We were so amazed by this. Any time we had to go upstairs, we always went through the bathroom and the 'secret door' because it was exciting to us.

Usually on the first morning after our arrival we would go and see Grand'papa in the store. We liked spending time there and my grandfather did not mind so long as we were polite and well behaved. My sister's and my absolute favourites were the candy jar and the cookie barrel that sat on the large U-shaped counter near the back of the store. Grand'maman baked the cookies and always made sure the small cookie barrel was full. They were delicious. We always kept an eye on the candy jar too, which we loved. Cookies and candies, and lots of them; what more could a little girl *ever* wish for, I thought?

Grand'papa was a severe looking man; he was tall and wore a white beard and gold-rim bifocals. His voice was naturally loud and projected far, like a microphone so to speak. He intimidated me though I admired him because he took the time to truly listen to a child. He asked a question and always seemed interested in the answer. One day he said to me,

"That box of candies I gave you girls the other day, is it empty yet?"

"No, there's still some left in it."

"Go and get it."

I thought he was going to take it back, but he walked me to the candy counter instead.

"Tell me the kind you like best," he said.

I pointed, and he filled it to the brim. It was always left at Maman's discretion when we could eat them.

One time he called me in the store and introduced me to a candy salesman. He asked me if I would be interested in tasting the candy for him. *Would I?* For sure, it was every child's dream! I tasted and gave my opinions. They were all good in varying degrees. However, the salesman handed me a pink marshmallow candy, and I popped it in my mouth. I couldn't believe candy could taste bad, but this one did, and my expression likely changed.

"Is it good?" Grand'papa asked. "I want the truth now; I don't want to sell bad candy to my customers."

"It tastes like soap," I blurted out.

I was attentively and respectfully thanked for my services and felt valued as a, 'Candy Judge'.

My grandparents served food to children in granite plates that were metal with a thick coating of enamel (much to my discontent) so we wouldn't break any dishes. It made me feel like an 'ungrownup'. They came in primary colours with a white pattern and with flat-bottomed cups to match. I did not care much for the food, but it was difficult to refuse as Grand'maman would want to know why I didn't want it. One time I made eye contact with my mother signaling that I didn't want to eat what I was served. She acted as if she was not in a position to come to my rescue.

Beef soup was made from scratch almost every day. Potatoes, meat, and vegetables for the main course was always followed by an abundance of homemade pies and cakes for dessert. There was also plenty of fresh milk. My Uncle Antonius, who lived a couple of streets over, came to milk my grandparents' cow, Mathilde, for them daily. The milk was poured hot from the pail into large, shallow bowls that were placed in the dairy room, a small addition off the end of the back veranda. It was vine covered to shade it from the sun, and there were blocks of ice covered with sawdust underneath it. The room was about 7" x 9" with three tiers of shelves all around. The bowls of milk were placed there and covered with cheesecloth. Meat, pies, cakes, butter, cream, and the like were also stored there.

One favourite dessert of several family members, especially Maman, was to take a slice of bread, spear a fork into the thickness of the bread and quickly put it on top of a bowl of milk, removing it as fast as possible. Thick cream, akin to 'double cream' in England, remained on the bread, and we added strawberry preserves, maple syrup, maple sugar, brown sugar or some other sweet. It was a popular dessert in the Pinard household.

There were two homeless families who lived in Sainte-Monique. They were the Morency's and the Trudel's, and both had several children. One family lived in an abandoned house and the other in the rectory's barn. These families had no means of support.

My grandparents helped feed these two families daily with the dinner leftovers. The food was placed in blue or red five-pound honey cans with handles, making it easy to carry. One or two of the Trudel children arrived barefoot through the dining room door after dinner to pick up their cans of food and to return the one from the previous day. They made their way to the kitchen and stood at the door waiting to be handed their food and any special warming instructions. They left again silently through the dining room. Then the other family representatives arrived, and the ritual was repeated.

"Would you like to pick some fresh vegetables from the garden?" Grand'papa asked on occasion.

"No," one of the children would quietly reply.

My grandparents would go to the garden later, fill hand baskets with tomatoes, carrots, cucumbers and the like and leave them by the door to be picked up after supper. When these were handed to the children, they took them gladly. The handbaskets always came back empty.

Occasionally, my grandfather asked the men from either family to unload wagons of merchandise or shovel snow, and they obliged. The odd time someone might say,
"We ought to stop feeding them. Maybe they would decide to go to work full-time, make a decent income and be able to look after their families."

"Why should the children go hungry and suffer?" Grand'papa would respond.

One sometimes hears the expression 'the town character'. Small towns proportionally do not have more people with unique traits, rather it is simply that their uniqueness stands out more in a small village than in a large city.

One such person in the village of Sainte-Monique was a lady named, Jacqueline Paladine. Many people wondered whether it was a made-up surname, mostly because it rhymed. Penniless and homeless, Jacqueline arrived in town one day and decided that Sainte-Monique was where she wanted to live. She was as thin as could be and wore clothes that were a few sizes too large. She had a small roll of personal possessions and offered help in the kitchen for free to whoever needed help at the time. Her favourite chores were washing dishes and floors, but her very favourite was scouring pots and pans. She scrubbed them to a shine with steel wool. She had a voracious appetite, and food sufficed for payment. She refused to use a bed, instead preferring to sleep on a rug.

Whenever there was a new baby or a sick person or a wedding in preparation, Jacqueline was sure to arrive. The village residents always made her feel welcome.

"Madame Fortin had her baby during the night," someone would say in the store, then add, "Jacqueline arrived at seven this morning."

She worked furiously. If she was asked to do something differently, she complied. If no one required her services, she went to the homes of the elderly or the rectory and did a good house cleaning for them.

Jacqueline liked my father. Shortly after we arrived in town, she would come over whenever Papa was sitting on the front porch.

"Would you give me a little white nickel if I sing for you?" she'd ask shyly, knowing he would say yes.

Jacqueline had a nice singing voice. She would sing a song or two, and Papa would give her a nickel. This coin, exactly half the size of a dime, was made of silver rather than nickel. They were not too common, and my father collected them for her benefit. Eventually they disappeared from use.

That summer in July, we celebrated my sister Thérèse's birthday with a cake on the porch of my grandparents' house. Jacqueline came and so did my grand'papa Vincent. By this time, he had moved back to Saint-Célestin from the States. We did not often see Grand'papa Vincent, so it was sort of a big deal that he was there. Uncle Antonius (Maman's brother) and his daughter, Suzanne, were also there. For some reason, Suzanne told me that Grand'papa Vincent was her grandfather too. I tried explaining that he was not, so she finally asked him.

"I am the grandfather of all little children (Moi je suis le grand-père de tous les petits enfants)," he said.

Jacqueline heard him say that, and it put a smile on her face. *Maybe she never knew her own grandfather,* I wondered.

I was not at all impressed with my grandfathers' logic in this instance because I felt cheated out of my exclusive right to my grandpa. But I always liked Suzanne, she was nice, and I also loved the fact that she looked so much like my mother. She always did.

Shortly after Thérèse's birthday party, Marcelle mentioned that Jacqueline likely never had a birthday party and that we should have one for her. Marcelle did most of the planning and made the cake. We all wrapped a trinket of some kind as a present. The piece de resistance was a 4" x 20" corset box stuffed with candy of all sorts. Jacqueline was so surprised. She was elated and laughing as she hid her almost toothless smile behind her hand. Jacqueline stood out from other people and was different, but she certainly knew how to thank people and show appreciation in her own way.

When Jacqueline became elderly and too frail to work, she was placed in the nursing home in Nicolet, against her will. She stopped eating. A nun made a list of all the people she lived with over the years, and from then on, her food came to her from 'the Pinard family' or 'the Boivin family'. That food she ate.

No one in the village ever knew Jacqueline's age, her story, or where she came from. People guessed she was likely in her late forties when she chose Sainte-Monique as her home. Villagers wondered if she had ever been severely abused when she was younger. Jacqueline stayed around for about thirty years before going to the home in Nicolet. Everyone in Sainte-Monique had always treated Jacqueline with much kindness, so Sainte-Monique had been a good choice for Jacqueline after all.

The greatest fun of the summer at my grandparents was when we played hide-and-seek with Uncle Antonius doing the hiding. I remember when he hid Thérèse in a large open drawer in the back of the store. To our surprise, she fell asleep and had to be awakened for supper. We couldn't believe it! I once hid in a tree on the rectory lawn across from the store. I had a marvelous view. I told my uncle and he hid us in high enough places where he knew we would have a good view from then on. We played for hours.

The month came to an end all too soon. We had to pack up, take a final carriage ride to the station, board the train to Montreal, see Aunt Cécile, then take the train back to Concord, all the while hugging our dolls. We highly anticipated seeing Papa with his warm smiles, hugs and always a kiss on the forehead. Soon, we all settled down to life on a smaller scale.

These trips were, of course, exhausting for Maman with three children in tow. One year as she was preparing to go to Canada with all of us, Uncle Henri came by. He had a new car and suggested that she go with him.

"I'll help you with the children," he said.

She accepted. Papa thought it was great that his brother would drive us door-to-door and help along the way. It turned out not to be such a good plan after all because priests are not used to being around excited, restless, crying children.

At one point when all were tired, they decided to stop at a restaurant. Again, not a great plan. Uncle Henri took off his roman collar and said,

"This way they won't know I'm a priest and I can help you with the kids."

Maman and Papa were always so easy going with us at the table, but Uncle Henri played the role of the stern father, which did not go over too well. We had fairly good table manners and knew how to eat properly, but we were not angels. We dropped things, knocked things over, sat in awkward positions because the table was too high and the dishes and silver too large. Could have been any number of reasons. Madeleine suddenly got tired of being bossed around by my uncle.

"You're not my father!" she announced loudly for all to hear. "He's a Catholic priest, you know," she said to the waitress loudly and with a smile.

Uncle Henri and Maman, red as beets and uncomfortable at the stares, were relieved to see the meal finally come to an end. He never offered his services again; we returned by train.

Ma Soeur, Madeleine
(My Sister, Madeleine)

The first time Maman sent me and Madeleine on an errand together was very early in the morning. Shortly after seven.

"Would you girls go to the A&P and get me a can of Bokar coffee? We don't have enough for breakfast. You know where the store is."

She gave us money, told us how much change we would be given, gave us a kiss, and sent us on our way. We had to turn left out of the yard, walk past the Gardner house to the corner, turn left again to the end of that block where Fyfield's ice cream parlor and the A&P were. We returned home shortly with the coffee, very proud of having gone shopping by ourselves.

After that, we were considered old enough to go on errands. On occasion, when I got a bit older, I would go to Fyfield's to get a pint of ice cream for dessert. One time I lost my half-dollar on my way there. I was looking for it in the grass when, James, who lived down the road from us and who I cared little for came by on his bike.

"What are you looking for?"

"I lost fifty cents," I answered naïvely.

Pretty soon he found it, flipped it in the air, laughed and said,

"See ya." I returned home in tears.

Maman sent Madeleine with another half-dollar. She was much wiser than I was, but not only because she was two years older. I think it was part of her character to be self-sufficient; she radiated confidence and was sure of herself in a quiet way. She was my heroine. I wanted to go where she went and do what she did most of the time. Madeleine always took good care of me.

I remember the time when Madeleine and I went to Fyfield's together for an ice cream cone. We came out of the store, and while I was taking the first lick, the ice cream fell off. She interrupted my tears before they got started.

"Take mine," she offered.

I did, and she started nibbling at my empty cone.

"Wait for me here. I'll be right back."

She came out with a grin on her face, licking a new cone.

She explained, seeing the surprised look on my face.

"I told the man he gave my little sister an ice cream cone but didn't push down on it, so the ice cream fell off at the first lick. I said I traded with her but I thought he should give me another scoop and push down on it this time."

From then on, we always finished our ice cream orders by saying, "And push down on it please."

Another time that Madeleine displayed magnanimity was when I had a loose tooth and Maman suggested she could pull it with a pair of pliers. She promised not to hurt me, said I could put the money the dentist would have charged in my piggy bank and that it would be balloons for everyone. I went along with the plan. Out came the tooth painlessly, as promised. Balloons suddenly materialized from one of Maman's caches. She blew them up, tied a string on them and off we went. I walked too close to the rose bush and—Bang!—Tears!

"Here, have mine. It was your tooth," said Madeleine.

Off she went with my busted balloon, sucking on a piece of it to make a smaller balloon which she twisted tightly. She proudly showed it to me, her slightly buck teeth shining through her grin.

One night during the summer, I woke up sitting on the edge of the double bed I shared with Madeleine. I had wet the edge of the bed, dreaming I was in the bathroom. As usual, I began to cry softly. This had never happened. I had trained very young and it had never been a problem before.

"Madeleine, I wet the bed," I cried.

"Don't wake Maman, I'll take care of this."

After closing the door, Madeleine turned on the light and pulled the bedspread, blanket, and top-sheet off. She removed the wet bottom sheet, sponged the mattress, and placed a bath towel over the wet spot. She put on a clean sheet, made the bed, turned off the light and walked in the dark to the hallway off the kitchen to dispose of the sheet in the washing machine.

"I'll sleep on my side, you can sleep in the middle," she said.

Madeleine solved many problems for me when I was young, especially during this period. She was only about seven, but she had a sense of understanding far beyond her years. In any situation that was even remotely akin to nursing, she jumped in and performed admirably.

Mr. Chapelle, a well-known contractor, was a very wealthy man of French-Canadian descent in Concord, NH. Madame Chapelle was a tall, slender woman with mostly silver hair and a healthy complexion with very rosy, red cheeks. They lived next door to us. Their two sons were in their early twenties and their two daughters in their mid-teens. Adrien, the oldest son, had a car, which was rare then. One fall day, Adrien asked my mother if she wanted to go for a drive.

"Can I bring the children?" Maman asked.

"Yes, of course," he said. "So long as they don't eat or drink in my car."

We had never been in a car before, so this was a big deal! It was a big black Ford with leather seats that started with a crank in the front. The windshield opened from the bottom to let air in. It started to rain, so we had to put down the side curtains which had been rolled up and tied with a short piece of braid, a knot and bow, so that when you pulled on one end of the braid the curtain came rolling down.

"I'll do it," I said, beating Madeleine to it.

We were extremely impressed by both the ride *and* the curtains.

The back door to our house opened onto a woodshed. To the immediate right was a stairway up to the attic under which was another stairway down to a small, black, dark basement. The basement floor was of beaten earth, and there were cords of finely chopped wood for the kitchen stove in there. One evening, Maman was sitting alone in the kitchen reading. Suddenly, there was a loud noise as if someone was running up to the attic. Then there was a louder noise that sounded like someone running down the steps. Maman froze, her heart pounding. *Was someone in the basement,* she wondered. The kitchen door was not locked. Maman was paralyzed with fear, too scared to get up and lock the door. Then it started again. The noise level was increasing, and she knew she had to do something.

She crept to the Chapelle's door and explained the situation. Adrien and his brother, Étienne, came over and sat at the table and talked with Maman. She felt safer with them there. They listened, but nothing happened, so they decided to keep quiet and wait. Madeleine startled my mother as she walked into the kitchen to get a glass of water.

"Why are you all sitting here not talking?" my sister asked as she joined them.

Maman was afraid the boys would think it was a made-up story as they could hear nothing, but it wasn't going to be a long wait. Madeleine suggested they wait by the basement door so if they heard something they could open the door quickly and surprise the culprit. Shortly, the noise started again. Étienne was nearest to the door so he opened it suddenly. What he saw was not a person, but squirrels—several of them scurrying around with nuts and pears in their mouths. There was a pear tree and a walnut tree in the backyard, and these unwanted guests were doing their winter shopping while one of us had left the outside shed door open.

Bière et Liqueurs
(Beer and Liquor)

Prohibition was at its height in the 1920s when there was a nationwide ban on the sale of alcoholic beverages in the United States. The 18th Amendment of the U.S. Constitution officially went into effect with the passage of the Volstead Act on January 17,1920, when prohibition was enforced. It was against the law for businesses to produce, sell, transport, or import alcohol.

This ban is what prompted new establishments known as *speakeasies*. A distinctive characteristic of a speakeasy was its anonymity. These were illegal saloons/bars that sold alcohol without a license. The name speakeasy referred to speak softly or whisper about these establishments so as not to alert neighbours or the authorities. To allow entry into a speakeasy, many used passwords, secret hand-shakes, and hidden doors to avoid suspicion. A patron had to 'speak easy' through the small opening of the establishment's door to gain entry. These codes, so to speak, were given to select regular customers of the establishment. For newcomers, these secret codes were passed on by word of mouth. Even the locations of speakeasies were kept secret. In one way, it made them more intriguing and appealing to customers. The illegal import and illicit sale of alcohol, known as bootlegging, lasted throughout the decade of prohibition.

Some common denominators to speakeasies in the later years of prohibition were: alcohol, gambling, women, entertainment/music, and, of course, secrecy. Because there were plenty of these popular establishments, it made them one of the biggest businesses during that era. Some proprietors even had drop shelves, secret cabinets installed, camouflaged doors, or false walls built where they stashed the alcohol to cover up the real intent of their business in case of a raid.

In 1932 Franklin D. Roosevelt ran for president against Herbert Hoover. Because repealing prohibition was part of Roosevelt's campaign, it was most likely a factor that helped him win the election in November of that year. Speakeasies operated for thirteen years, then started to disappear when prohibition ended on December 5th, 1933.

During prohibition, however, it was not illegal to have an alcoholic drink in one's abode. That meant those who had liquor stockpiled before the ban came into effect were free to consume it in the privacy of their home.

Most men, however, were not convinced prohibition was such a great idea, so they schemed to find ways of getting beer and liquor. Papa was no exception. He and Maman made root beer (which Thérèse always called 'roof beet') and bottled it with an elaborate device of nickel pipes and other items, which seemed complicated and time-consuming. We thought the elaborate gear was just for root beer, but they also made regular beer, which I found out many years later. It had to be hidden in the basement.

There was a crawl space under the kitchen's extension which was unpaved, cold and accessed by a door in the basement wall at the basement window level. It was bigger than the window and just big enough for Papa to fit through. Whenever he went into the crawl space, he used a flashlight so he could see everything. He would line up the bottles, including the beer, against the far wall so they were out of sight. One would have to put their head all the way into the crawl space to see them.

When Papa's friends stopped by, he would sometimes offer them a drink. My father was not a big drinker, but he did like to have it available for visitors. On hot summer days, he might sit on the front porch with one of his buddies from work. They would have a chat while enjoying a beer or two together.

People did almost anything for a bottle of liquor in those days. I remember my father telling us the story of the paymaster at the Boston and Maine Railroad. He required a copy of Papa's birth certificate for the personnel office. My father kept forgetting to get it whenever he went to Canada, so he kept telling the paymaster,

"Next time I go to Canada."

When he finally remembered, he figured he would bring the paymaster a 40 oz. bottle of good rye whiskey to make up for the long delay. When he went to see the paymaster, he put the bottle (in a brown paper bag twisted around the neck) on the corner of the desk away from both of them. He apologized for being so late in producing his certificate to which the paymaster said he was just glad to finally have it and would put it in his file. Papa glanced at the bottle, thanked him, and left leaving the bottle behind without officially offering it. My father never looked back to see if the paymaster took the bottle, however, Papa wondered if he did accept it, and how long it took to uncork it!

Une Voix Feutrée
(A Muffled Voice)

Maman made a lot of hoopla over holidays, Christmas, and birthdays. Ah, Christmas. That was the happiest day of the year. We didn't receive mounds of presents, but the finesses and thoughtfulness that went into the preparation made it such an impactful day.

Every Christmas Eve Day, Papa would go into the bush and cut down a tree for Christmas. One year, he arrived home with his friend, Adam, from work, with the tree on the roof of Adam's Chevy. I remember our excitement as we saw them pulling into the driveway.

Maman had taken out the decorations during the day. After an early supper we decorated the tree in the living room near the stairway. Maman and we three kids made lots of the ornaments out of festively-coloured paper maché—Santa's, elves, Christmas bells, and snowflakes are some I recall. We also had glittering garland. The children did all the decorating by putting the ornaments and garland on the tree. Of necessity, these were along the bottom of the tree and along the side near the stairs which we used as a ladder. When finished the decorating, Maman gave us our Christmas present from her, always a pair of new stockings. We hung one for Santa and went to bed, although too excited to sleep in anticipation of his arrival. During the night, my parents came to wake us up, still in their nightclothes. Whispering, they said,

"I think Santa Claus just left. We heard the door close."

We tiptoed down the stairs in our nightgowns, with Maman in tow. We were guided by the light of the upstairs hallway. Papa waited at the top of the stairs until we reached the last step. As if on cue he happily said,

"Merry Christmas girls! (Joyeux Noël les filles!)" and with that turned the lights on to reveal the beautiful tree we had decorated and all the presents.

In the enthusiasm of the moment, we were not aware that even more decorations were added to the tree by expert hands (ornaments of glass balls with Santa faces and Maman's homemade baskets).

My mother made a four-section hanging basket from construction paper for each of us every Christmas. Our name was written on the outside. Each contained a treat of sorts, Christmas type candy. The presents were all at the foot of the tree, and the last ones were our 'piece de resistance'. Three boxes dominated the pile, and each contained a new doll—a big one, a medium one and a small one to match our sizes. There were smaller presents hidden here and there in the tree as well, some of which were identical except for the colour. Madeleine had red, I had blue and Thérèse had green, always. These were the colours Maman chose for us. We were permitted to eat some candy and peanuts while we unwrapped, and our parents allowed us to stay up and play with our new toys for a little while before we all went back to bed.

The next morning, we were up early, eager to play with our new toys. Unfortunately for us, extra trains were running for passengers during holidays, so Papa was often at work on Christmas Day. Maman made it festive just the same. Decorations were everywhere, and she made food look very attractive—especially for the children.

Every year, for example, there was a Christmas log (Bûche de Noël) made with chocolate frosting which was sculpted to look like bark. She would lightly dust it with powered sugar to represent snow for the finishing touch. Maman also made fudge (sucre à la crème) and candy canes, the latter of which were made from white pull candy. She saved a part of her mixture and added red or green colouring. Before pulling it, she would put a drop or two of wintergreen or peppermint in her hands, which flavoured the candy. She would pull until it was white as snow, then cut it in long pieces, shape the top of the cane and dribble the red or green clear candy she had previously prepared. My favourites were the green ones. She made some of these in sticks and placed them in glass jars on the top shelf in a kitchen cabinet along with other such homemade delicacies.

This Christmas my mother suddenly remembered a present she had forgotten to place near the tree. A baby carriage had arrived from my grandparents as a present for the three of us, several weeks before. She had hidden it in the coat closet, between the tree and the front door. Maman, not wanting to blow 'Santa's cover', used her resourcefulness.

"We should make a baby carriage so that you can each give your dolls a nice ride. Now let me see what we could do. How about a box and a string?"

She fetched a ball of string and the kitchen scissors.

"I think I have a large cardboard box at the very back of the coat closet," she announced as she headed for the closet and removed overshoes and rubbers.

Suddenly we heard a muffled,

"My goodness! (Mon Dieu!)" from the back of the closet.

She extricated herself from behind the clothing and out came the carriage.

"What is this? A beautiful surprise from Santa. Isn't *he* the tricky one?"

"Why did he do that?" we asked.

"Because Santa likes to make Christmas special for good little children."

'Santa' did indeed make the day special for us.

La Bulle Éclate
(The Bubble Bursts)

It was an ideal life for us in Concord. We were happy, well cared for and well dressed. My family was well off and, above all, we had loving and attentive parents. All our needs were met.

It was September 1929, and I was almost five. Madeleine had abandoned me to start school. I felt alone for a while, but then I developed a closer relationship with Thérèse, who was two and a half by then.

CRASH went the stock market! Life was never to be the same. During the summer of 1929, the United States started to show a mild decline in its economy. Investors became nervous, and on October 24, 1929 (black Thursday), it was the biggest sell-off of shares in the history of the United States. The market crashed five days later, on October 29 (black Tuesday) when on that day alone, some sixteen million shares were traded on the New York Stock Exchange. Billions were lost, wiping out thousands of investors. Hence, the beginning of the Great Depression.

It started in the United States; however, it affected every sector of the economy and most countries around the world. Millions of shares became worthless. Everyone felt its impact and panicked. Consumer consumption and investments dropped drastically. As a result, employment and industrial output were on a downslide, causing companies to lay off countless numbers of employees. People were stuck with debts they could not repay. Other people, fearing they would lose all their savings (including Papa), chose to withdraw all they had from the banks, and all at once. Banks did not have enough cash to go around forcing them to liquidate assets at below-market prices. The Great Depression is known to be the longest, most severe, and most widespread depression of the twentieth century. It is remarkable how drastically and quickly the global economy can weaken. Greed, fear, and panic are emotions that sometimes factor in the fluctuation and uncertainty of the stock market. The crash of 1929, some believe, was in fact due primarily to fear and panic, causing total havoc and disarray. The Great Depression changed life as we knew it.

Word of the crash spread quickly. Papa was at work and as soon as he heard, he contacted Maman in a panic.

"Eva Rose, you have to go to the bank right away. Take the kids with you and remove all our money from the account. If you don't go now, we could lose it all."

Maman got us ready and we left immediately. Unfortunately, it was already too late. The money in the passbook savings was worthless, they lost it all. The only thing Madeleine remembered of that day was the mass number of people lined up to the street, waiting to enter the bank. Because my parents did not want to discuss finances in front of us, they would send us out to play to be out of earshot. They talked together for hours, it seemed. Often the small top sideboard drawer opened and out came the bank books. I knew they were there with our birth certificates and the moneybox. The large black account book in which my mother kept track of all expenses and revenues surfaced frequently. My father started staying home more because there was less work at the railroad.

Like almost all the young men of his age, he had gotten into the stock market. Not only had he invested a sizeable portion of their savings, but he had also bought on margin, meaning he borrowed money from the bank to buy securities with the intent of paying them back from the stock revenue. He did this without telling Mother. She was very cautious and had warned him not to do so, but he had kept his purchases secret, thinking he was going to make a killing. Financially, it wiped him out. What little money they had left in other investments, they settled with the bank (which had largely overextended itself) for half of one percent.

Mother's savings were worthless except that she had invested $2000 given to her by her father as a wedding present in General Electric and another blue chip. GE often gave special dividends in the form of shares in a new, small aviation company called Sperry Corporation (later Sperry Rand), and she kept this stock intact. Although now worth very little, she decided against selling in hopes the market would go back up some day. Since she had stock certification to prove ownership, she was able to do so. However, those like my father who had bought and sold almost daily only had the brokers' slips of paper. These were worthless as the brokers with whom Papa invested, were broke.

Children are aware when the tempo changes in a home. We asked questions and were given truthful though limited answers. I did not understand the lack of money. They had not spent it, and the passbooks were still in the drawer in their usual place.

Because of the sporadic work, Papa's salary dropped drastically. He was home a lot, so there was time aplenty to worry and ponder. There was less hugging between my parents. There was no belligerence, but they were cooler towards each other. We would catch Maman crying sometimes. In retrospect, I think my mother felt betrayed by the margin purchases, and my father felt guilty and gullible.

The motto which people lived by in the 1930s was; wear homemade clothes, hand-me-downs, use and reuse, stretch your food budget, no throw-aways, and do without non-essential things. It became the way of life for almost everyone, including us. Women became more innovative in their kitchens, and planting large fruit and vegetable gardens became a common practice; anything that could be homegrown, was. Any used piece of material that could be reused and made into a new piece of clothing, was. Of necessity, people made things out of practically nothing, and to waste was unheard of. The empty flour cotton sacks that Grand'papa had in the store never went to waste either. They were reused by Maman and made into aprons, dish cloths, and clothes for our dolls. Women started making their children's clothes out of this cotton material. When manufacturing companies became aware of this, they decided to help the families and began printing the sacks in a wide variety of colourful and beautiful patterns, which the women appreciated. When these patterns came out, the women started making dresses for themselves too. Maman would save the sacks, clean them, dry them on the clothesline, and give them to the women she knew would use them for clothing. These flour cotton sacks became so prevalent during the Great Depression that for those struggling, it allowed them to update their wardrobes.

Not only did my mother sew most of our casual clothes, school uniforms, Sunday dresses and doll clothes, my parents never let food spoil. For example, what was a bacon and egg breakfast one day became bacon roll-ups the following day. Left over meat became a sheppard's pie for another day. Creamed chicken became chicken on biscuits. Banana breads were made of ripe bananas and applesauce or apple pudding from ripe apples. Food never went to waste.

Families and neighbours were supportive of each other by way of sharing food, used clothing, fabrics, tools, and the like. People chit-chatted over the fences or across their clotheslines about ways to be resourceful. When something needed repair, they would get together amongst friends and neighbors and help each other, loaning their tools if one was without.

Whenever we were visiting Sainte-Monique, one outing that was enjoyable for Maman and Aunt Marie-Anne during this time were the church potlucks. It was a wonderful way for them to socialize, have fun, share food, and recipes. This was something Maman always looked forward to. Sometimes they even came back with leftovers!

The Great Depression was not the only privation of the 1930s. Another devastating situation of the '30s was the Dust Bowl. Dust storms caused extensive damage to the American and Canadian prairies. This catastrophe was due to farming practices and severe drought. Their failure to apply dryland farming methods caused the loss of the thin layer of topsoil that would have allowed grasses to root and retain their moisture. Unanchored soil turned to huge clouds of dust, blackening the skies during some of these severe storms. The choking swells of dust were referred to as 'black blizzards' or 'black rollers' as they travelled cross-country.

The Dust Bowl intensified the hardships of the Great Depression and the economy in the affected areas. In 1934, twelve million pounds of dust were deposited during a two-day dust storm alone. It made breathing difficult, and people developed dust colds and sore throats as a result. Although the Dust Bowl came in three waves, it lasted for about a decade. The worst dust storm known in history was on April 14, 1935. Referred to as the Black Sunday Dust Storm, it swept the Great Plains from Canada to Texas. It was so severe that people said day seemed to turn into night. During that winter, red snow fell on New England. Thousands of people had to abandon their homesteads; they were left homeless, hungry, and jobless.

Although the Dust Bowl did not affect my family, I do remember my parents discussing the storms and I was old enough to know it was a terrible thing.

Because work had dwindled so much, Papa was struggling to support the family during these times, so he decided to write to a first cousin, Xavier Dubois. He was assistant general manager of Massey-Harris (later known as Massey Ferguson), a company that manufactured agricultural machinery in Montreal. He had frequently offered Dad a job since he had difficulty finding bilingual employees. Xavier replied saying that though business was still good in Canada, the bottom could drop out there too. He could hire Dad on a trial basis for six months.

The day my father left we were all glum. It was early May. We had dinner and bedtime came.

"I want Papa to sing songs to me," Thérèse said in a determined voice.

"Papa won't be home for a long time," Maman replied. "I will sing you some songs."

And she did. Still Thérèse would not go to bed. Nothing could be said or done to convince her.

"I'm going to wait for him."

"Well, my little Théréson, you can wait. We are all going to bed," she said, winking at Madeleine and me.

Understanding her dilemma, we went upstairs even though it was not yet our bedtime. Maman turned off the lights. Suddenly Thérèse started to cry:

"I'm scared in the dark all by myself!"

She cried on.

"It's not nice of Papa to go away."

Maman brought her upstairs, and Thérèse finally settled down.

After sixteen years on the Boston and Maine Railroad, my father went to Montreal somewhat unsure of himself. Selling was easy in a store when people came to you. For a shy person, approaching total strangers was difficult. However, his selling background and the fact that he was bilingual made him attractive to Massey-Harris. Shortly after arriving he was told by the company; he would need a car. My mother gave him the money from her savings, which brought her account down considerably. Six hundred dollars for a new 1930 Chevrolet.

They wrote to each other frequently, but Maman was clearly lonely. She had never been without him in the United States. It was fortunate that she spoke some English by then, and she read it well because she had translated all the issues of the *Saturday Evening Post* for years. However, not having an adult to converse with enhanced her loneliness.

Mrs. Vaillancourt, who lived down the street from us, heard about my mother. She was also French, and she started coming over to talk with Maman. It turned out she had two teenage daughters, and they all liked to play cards. They started to come over often, so at least now my mother could speak her native language.

Quand on Veut, on Peut
(Where There's a Will, There's a Way)

Not long after the close of the school year at the end of June, we once again left Concord to spend the summer at my grandparents' home. Papa was stationed in Joliet, near Trois-Rivières, Quebec, which was about an hour away and meant he could come see us in Sainte-Monique.

Papa was living in a boarding house. He was being trained by a Mr. Marchal who was teaching him all about modern farm implements, selling tactics and company policies. Part of Papa's job was collecting overdue payments from farmers.

My father was a very sound sleeper, and there was the odd time when he would not hear the alarm. The first time he slept in, he rushed out the door, forgetting to shave. He told Maman he was so embarrassed to have to knock on people's doors looking like that, he was going to make sure that never happen again. He bought a straight razor, which he kept rolled in a towel in the trunk of his car. On the days he forgot to shave, he would look for a brook, a stream, or a creek. Once he spotted water, he'd park the car and with razor and towel in hand, he would carefully wind his way down a small embankment to shave.

Our stay in Sainte-Monique was not very different than other summer vacations had been, though we stayed longer this time. The Morency's and the Trudel's continued to pick up their daily food, that had not changed. All the vegetables Grand'maman cooked in the summer came from their garden. My grandparents' vegetable garden was not only beautiful, but it was also enormous. It was meticulously arranged in plots divided by low alleys. There was a flower garden near the back porch, a bocage at the back of the garden, and a barn just beyond for their cow, Mathilde.

Aunt Marie-Anne took me to church every day to say her 'way of the cross'. While I was not happy to have to go with her, I passed the time by listening to the clock tick. I had never heard a clock tick so loudly. I did enjoy the fact that the church was cool and smelled of flowers.

It was customary at my grandparents' house to wait for the church bell to ring the Angelus at noon and at six o'clock. At the first strokes, everyone stood behind their chairs, and Grand'papa intoned Angelus Domini Clamiavit Maria (The Angel of the Lord declared onto Mary). He said one portion and all the others replied, back and forth, till the long prayer was said. One day as Grand'papa was ending the prayer, he said,

"Amen ... THE CROWS! (LES CORNEILLES!)"

A horde of crows was covering his corn stalks. He grabbed a dish towel and ran out the back door with others in pursuit. We frightened the crows away. He finished his meal, constantly turning sideways to check for return thieves. After dinner, the children all went out and helped him make a scarecrow. Where there's a will, there's a way!

Ça C'est de la Science
(Now *This* is Science)

We returned to Concord at the end of summer. I started school—French in the morning, English in the afternoon—at a parochial school taught by nuns in a mainly French parish. I enjoyed it, but I was disappointed that Madeleine was not in my room.

My classmate, Olivia Nilsson, invited me to her birthday party. In our house we spoke French and outside we spoke English, but in Olivia's house we spoke Swedish. What little I knew, Olivia taught me.

"Hej Mrs. Nilsson, är Olivia hemma? (Hello Mrs. Nilsson, is Olivia home?)" or "*Nej tack, jag är inte hungrig* (No thank you, I'm not hungry)."

Unfortunately, I could not go to Olivia's party because I was sick with a cold. My tears added to my discomfort, but Maman did not want me to give my cold to other children, so I had to stay home. Mrs. Nilsson sent a tray of sweets and treats for me. There was one item on the tray that I had never seen before. A 'man' made of individually cellophane wrapped orange candies about eight inches tall. I was so impressed by this candy man that I wanted Papa to see it. I felt he too had never seen a man made of candy before. I felt so proud to have something so unique.

"But Papa is not here," Maman said, as if I did not know.

I missed him so much.

"I'll save it until he comes back so I can show him," I said, hoping it would be a matter of days.

Maman put my candy man on the top shelf in the kitchen cabinet. The Vaillancourt's came by unannounced one evening, and they played Whist, a card game. When they stopped, Maman expressed her regrets that she had nothing to offer them for a snack.

"We have some candy," Madeleine volunteered.

"Madeleine, you know we don't have any candy," said Maman reproachfully. She had been made to sound like a liar.

"Oh yes we do. Do you want me to show it to you?"

"Yes!" said Maman incredulously.

Madeleine went to the kitchen, climbed on a chair and onto the kitchen counter, and went digging in the high cupboard. I suddenly understood what she meant, and I shuddered. I looked up to Madeleine so much, how could she do this to me?

"That's mine! I'm saving it for Papa," I said.

She jumped down, ignored me as she marched to the living room and plopped it on the card table with a sense of satisfaction that she was right.

"Here!"

"That's Pierrette's. Oh well, you don't mind sharing it with our guests, do you Pierrette?"

I was sensitive enough to realize that she was in a jam, which left me in a position where I couldn't protest. I kept silent.

"Get me a bowl and knife, Madeleine, would you please," said Maman as she was put on the spot.

Maman took the knife by the blade, and without unwrapping the candy, began hitting the candy man with the handle. It was as if my bones were being crushed. I turned around, climbed the stairs to my room and buried my head in my pillow. I cried. This was unforgiveable! Orange was my favourite colour, I loved anything that tasted of orange, and, above all, I really wanted my father to see it.

The minute the Vaillancourt's left and Maman knew they were out of ear shot, she said to my sister,

"Madeleine how could you? You knew perfectly well that your sister was saving her candy man to show your father when he comes home." She was talking loudly; I could hear her.

"The next time I say we don't have any to guests in our home you are not to say differently, ever! I want you to go upstairs and apologize to Pierrette right now."

Madeleine did. Although I accepted her apology, I certainly didn't feel it. When she went back downstairs, Maman came up to talk to me.

"I'm very sorry, Pierrette; Madeleine should not have done that. I do know, however, that if you tell Papa about your candy man, he will love to hear all about it."

That made me feel a bit better, but the wound took a long time to heal.

It was a beautiful, colorful New England fall. We took walks around the square in the evening as the sun was setting. One balmy evening when it was dark, we went for a walk with the Vaillancourt's, two by two down the sidewalk. I was with Thérèse. She asked me what the stars in the sky were. I gave her a very good explanation, or so I thought.

"The sky is a huge blue tablecloth, but it's old with lots and lots of holes in it. At night when they turn the lights on in heaven, you can see the light shine through the holes."

Now, *this* ... is science!

On December 12 when I came home from school, there was a truck in front of our house. As I turned to walk towards our door, to my great surprise, there was Papa carrying one end of the living room sofa with another man. He said a brisk hello. We were moving to Canada! Madeleine ran back to school to get our sweaters which all the children kept at school in case the winter turned cold.

We said our goodbyes to our friends, Maman wrote down their addresses and we left late at night the following day in the 1930 Chevy with the moving truck following us.

We were moving to the unknown.

La Curiosité Peut Être Choquante
(Curiosity Can be Shocking)

We crawled into Sainte-Anne-de-Bellevue, Quebec, near dawn in a snowstorm. Visibility was about ten feet. The headlights shone on the flakes in a pretty but dizzying fashion. There were fifteen inches of snow on the ground, at least half of it new. We were not dressed for the bitter cold nor did we have boots, so we had to be carried into our empty, cold duplex one by one. My parents started fires in the stove and in a small upright furnace. This house had been unheated for some days and began the long process of warming up. Having to keep the front door open while the furniture and the boxes were moved in didn't help, but we huddled upstairs in an empty room to be out of the draft.

It was not a cheery welcome for Maman. There was much work on the horizon (unpacking, cleaning, settling us all in), and she had to deal with us three cranky children who had slept some but had not been to bed all night. We were trembling from the cold and keenly felt the insecurity of being uprooted and the strangeness of our new locale.

"Put your hands on your cup, it will warm them. When your hands are warm you get warm all over," she said, attempting to cheer us (and likely herself too).

Hot chocolate never tasted so good!

The truck was empty, the driver paid and our move to Sainte-Anne finally came to a close. We all crowded into the kitchen, which offered a semblance of heat. A laundry basket full of food for the family sat on the kitchen counter. It was what we would eat until my parents went grocery shopping for the first time. In those days, stores selling groceries were open from 7:00 a.m. until 6:00 p.m., except on Fridays and Saturdays when they were open until 9:00 p.m.

Sainte-Anne-de-Bellevue was a pretty town located in southwestern Quebec. My parents said its population was approximately 1500 when we moved there in December of 1930. They used to say that between its beautiful waterways, canal, and main street stores, it was a quaint and picturesque town. Its uniqueness made it picture-postcard, one could say.

Hockey legend Alfred 'Pit' Lépine, who played for the Montreal Canadiens, was a native of Sainte-Anne-de-Bellevue. He joined the team in the 1925-26 season and remained with them for the next thirteen seasons. During his hockey career, Lépine and the Canadiens won two Stanley Cup championships, in 1930 and 1931.

I was sitting with Papa before supper one night when I told him about Olivia Nilsson's birthday party. I explained how I couldn't go to the party because I was sick and told him how Mrs. Nilsson had brought the candy man for me.

"I was saving it for when you came back," I told him. "It was Madeleine's fault; she gave it away. I've never seen anything like it and I just really wanted you to see it too. It was made with orange candy, my favourite!"

I went on to tell him how tall it was, the cellophane she used and how it was made to look just like a candy man.

"Pierrette, you did such a great job of describing it to me that I can picture it in my mind," he said. "So you see, I don't even have to see your candy man because I can imagine it already."

That made me feel better and helped heal the candy man wound a little faster. As an adult, the thought crossed my mind that my mother had likely told my father all about it to give him a heads up.

A week later, on December 20th, Grand'papa Vincent died. Maman decided that only Papa and I should go to his funeral in Saint-Célestin since he was my godfather. We would pick up Aunt Cécile in Montreal on our way. I went to bed early since we had to leave when it was still dark. I woke to sunshine. The temperature had fallen to -17 celsius (1.4 fahrenheit), and since I had had pneumonia at age four, Maman explained that it was foolhardy for me to go. I consoled myself quite rapidly. It was a long drive and it was an insightful decision since on their return, a windy snowstorm developed that filled the roads with high drifts. The car had to be pulled out of a snowbank twice. Horses and sleighs mainly used country roads, and a plowing system had not yet been initiated. Farmers welcomed the snowdrifts; they charged two dollars to have their horse extricate a car from a snowbank.

Papa returned Christmas Eve. He had been named the only heir, for which he inherited his father's muskrat-lined black dress coat and $120 in debts (for a horse), which my father paid within a few months.

Christmas was jolly despite Grand'papa Vincent's passing. Although I'm sure my father was grieving, he put on a jovial demeanour for our benefit. From what I remember, my sisters and I had a good Christmas that year.

My sixth birthday, January 4, was celebrated on Epiphany, or Three King's Day, (Jour des Trois Rois) as we called it, which was a Sunday. From this time on, our birthdays were always celebrated on the Sunday nearest to our birthday so Papa could share in the festivities. My Aunt Cécile came. I recall a fine dinner in the dining room that ended with a King's Day Cake (Gâteau des Rois) which, according to tradition, has a pea and a bean inserted in the cake. No one knew where the pea or the bean was, or so we thought. Whoever lucked out and had the bean in their piece of cake was king for the day, and whoever was served the piece containing the pea was queen for the day. There was no cheating. It was coincidental, I'm sure, that my father (the only male) was lucky enough to get the king-making bean. And on this particular Sunday, I just so happened to be the queen. Maman could be tricky when need be. The privilege of such royal rank was a special paper crown artistically made by Maman and dispensation from wiping the dishes.

As I grew older, my curiosities changed. One of my less bright experiments was trying to figure out how electrical outlets were made and what made them work. Kneeling on a kitchen chair, I kept plugging and unplugging the toaster. Plugged in, it worked. What made it work? I was determined to find out. I took the kitchen scissors, opened them, and stuck a blade in the outlet as Maman was walking into the kitchen. I saw a ball of light as I was thrown off the chair. My back bottom teeth suddenly hurt as if a major drilling project were in progress! The scissor blade had separated in two and both flew in opposite directions.

"Oh my goodness, Pierrette! What *are* you doing? (Ah mon Dieu, Pierrette! Mais qu'est-ce que tu *fais*?)"

Once I was over the shock of being shocked, Maman sat me down and explained the serious dangers of playing with electricity. She made me promise I would never attempt anything of that sort again. It was a promise that was not hard to keep because it scared me way more than it shocked me, if that's even possible. Not an event I was soon to forget. I took electricity at face value that day and from then on, it was a mystery not to be explored too deeply.

The winter months in Sainte-Anne-de-Bellevue were long and cold for most of us, but perhaps not Madeleine. She had a chinchilla-type coat, a thick woolen material (perhaps boiled wool), with a surface similar to goosebumps. The coat was in a claret red. I would watch my sister enthusiastically play in the snow in her red coat. No matter how cold it was, there she was on top of a pile of snow, enjoying herself; she was tough. Unlike Madeleine, I remained inside most of the time, fearing the cold. I was sickly that winter. We all had the measles and chicken pox. Thérèse added whooping cough and croup to her list and I added ear infections. Maman settled for morning sickness—she was expecting another baby!

My mother always kept little piles of cardboard squares about 3" x 5" made from cereal boxes and such. They were handy for emergency pick-ups such as food dropped on the floor and messes of all sorts. In Sainte-Anne, the bathroom was on the second floor at the opposite end of where the stairway landing was. If Maman became ill in the kitchen, she had to run through the dining room, up one flight of stairs, then down the hall past two bedrooms to reach the bathroom. She was asthmatic and did not run fast. Often, she did not make it on time. I recall Madeleine so vividly saying,

"I'll get it Maman."

And she'd arrived with little cardboard squares and a wet cloth. Maman never asked. Madeleine was not a goody-two-shoes but rather a take-charge nurse, a trait that seemed to be in her blood from the time she was young.

One day I caught Papa sneaking up the stairs. He had entered through the front door and closed only the outside door. He had a large box that appeared to be wallpapered in white with small blue flowers. Maman was at my heals.

"Oh! I bought a new suit," he informed Maman.

"That's fine," she replied. "Come to the kitchen, Pierrot."

I followed without question.

On February 7th it was Madeleine's eighth birthday, and out came the mysterious 'suit box'. It contained a set of dishes for eight, all white with a wide royal blue border. The dinner plates were the size of adult bread and butter plates. There were soup bowls, a sugar bowl, a creamer, a teapot and, of course, cups and saucers. It was an impressive little set of dishes. I asked Papa why he had lied to my mother and said it was a suit. He explained that Maman had known he had gone out to buy a birthday present and she understood what he meant. He had called it a suit so I would not know what it was.

"Surprises must be kept secret. It's not a lie, just delayed truth," he said, since I would know in a few days what the box really contained.

From the time we went to school, we had to go to Vespers on Sunday afternoons to listen to Latin being sung in Gregorian chant and to the priest singing a lot of Dominis Vobiscum. We didn't like it, but we had no choice. One particular Sunday, Madeleine told Maman and Papa that many kids from her class were going skating on the river instead of going to Vespers and she had decided to go with them. My parents vetoed her decision.

"You're going to church," they both insisted.

So, she did. On her way back from church, Madeleine stopped at the river's edge to see her friends. There was a crowd of people standing by the river. There were rumors of a drowning.

One of Madeleine's classmates fell through the ice and by the time she was found, it was too late. Madeleine had to go to the funeral with her class later that week. My sister had not been necessarily close to this girl, but she had been her classmate. Madeleine was very much affected by this drowning, as were other students. My parents did not let the occasion go by without talking of the importance of being obedient and of not going where they forbid us to go. It was serious stuff.

Massey-Harris decided to cut back most of its blockmen, reducing its entire force to six for the whole province of Quebec. They kept the six bilingual men because the districts were now so large that no area was entirely French or entirely English. Papa was given block No. 2, a very large district in square miles that had forty-two agencies to supervise. He was paid $120 per month, six cents per mile and a per diem with specific maximum amounts for breakfast, lunch, dinner, and hotel rooms. However, the company requested he relocate to the district's centre, which meant we were on the road again!

Une Nouvelle Gouvernante
(A New Governess)

On April 27, 1931, we moved to Waterloo, in the Eastern Townships. This was an area east of Montreal that reached from the border of the United States to the edge of New Brunswick and about fifty miles north of Montreal inland from the St. Lawrence River. It is an area similar in topography to the northern New England states.

Foster Street, looking south, Waterloo, QC, about 1910
Stanley G. Triggs
Courtesy of the McCord Museum MP-0000.1040.4, Montreal, QC

Waterloo, a half-English, half-French-speaking town was a long, narrow settlement two streets wide. Main and Court streets were approximately three miles long and there were side streets to the right and left. The railroad track ran the full length of the town. As I remember, the mayor was French-speaking for one term, and English speaking the next term.

Our place was on Court Street in the block next to the courthouse. It was the second and top floor of a large turreted house. There was a long flight of steps on the outside, and a long veranda opened off the kitchen door at the far end. We had a double living room and a turret, which Papa used as his office. My parents' bedroom was at the far end of the hallway, and the dining room was closer to the front of the house. Two steps from the dining room were the kitchen, bathroom, children's bedrooms, and a long back hallway leading to steps down to the back porch. Just off this porch was a large shed for storage of wood, coal, and miscellaneous other stuff.

Sébastien LaRoche, a short and feisty man, and his wife, a stout, well-dressed woman, were the owners and lived downstairs. They had six children. Their daughter, Annette, the oldest, and their five sons: Justin, Oscar, Guy, Samuel, and the baby, Léo. They also had a live-in nanny, Miss Dupré.

After the third week following our move to Waterloo, we went to the Catholic church for the first time. We put on our Sunday dresses, petticoats, and dress-up shoes, piled into dad's 1930 Chevy and off to church we went. It was a big, beautiful church made of grey stone, and upon entering we were mesmerized by its size and beauty. Just before Mass was to begin, the priest called 'the Vincent family' to the front of the church. *Oh no*, I thought. I was nervous and did not want to go up there, but Madeleine kept nudging me saying I had to, so I gave in. It did not seem to bother Thérèse at all. Even Maman who was pregnant made her way to the front.

Catholic Church, Waterloo, QC, about 1910
Stanley G. Triggs
Courtesy of the McCord Museum MP-0000.1041.13, Montreal, QC

The priest quickly made me feel comfortable by whispering in my ear, "Don't worry, I will do all the talking, and it will take just a few minutes (Inquiète toi pas, c'est seulement moi qui vais parler, et ça va prende que quelques minutes.)" He must have noticed how nervous I was. He introduced us to the congregation, and once we were back in our seats, Mass began.

Many of the congregates stood around to talk after church. The priest and several other families came to talk with us. Despite being newcomers, we returned home feeling most welcomed by the parishioners. We later became members of the congregation and attended that church for as long as we lived in Waterloo.

At home we played with the LaRoche boys a lot, but Annette never played outside. Even at school she was standoffish, so we thought maybe she was shy. She was very much into playing the piano, and we had the impression that Annette was made to feel special because she was the only girl in the family.

Mr. LaRoche was a bank manager, and Mrs. LaRoche stayed home to care for the children. She suffered from diabetes and seemed to have a short fuse. I think the boys were more than she could handle.

"I will tell your father!" she yelled incessantly.

Raising six children could not be easy, even *with* a nanny.

Both Mr. and Mrs. LaRoche were pleasant and friendly to my parents however. On Saturday evenings they often played cards together: upstairs one week, downstairs the next.

Because we were new in town, lived in a choice apartment, had a car (a necessity for Papa's work) and a phone, people thought we had money. We were referred to as 'les Americains'. Only salesmen, well-to-do people, and professionals had cars and phones. And so it was possibly because of this myth that we were treated well by tradesmen and store owners.

One grocery store, Jolin's, raffled a five-pound can of Vi-Tone (similar to Quix) every week. They'd put the names of all those who bought over a certain amount in a jar and draw a name at closing on Saturday nights. We won the second week we lived in Waterloo. I was elated that we had won this huge can of a beverage that I loved. Not long afterwards, a man came to our door selling chances on tickets to win a week's worth of groceries. The tickets were ten cents each or twenty-five cents for three. I was sure we would win, and insisted Maman buy some, but she was reluctant. This left me puzzled because we had won such a marvelous treat the first time we bought groceries at Jolin's. She explained that we were buying a slender chance, not a sure thing, but I would not be convinced. To prove her point, she offered to buy a chance or give me the dime. I went for the chance. Madeleine and Thérèse were each given a dime; I got nothing because I won nothing.

"How come we won the Vi-Tone the second week we were in town?" I asked.

"Because we are new in town. This man wants our business, so he arranges to make us the winners. Perhaps he reached into the jar but was concealing a piece of paper with our name on it."

"That's cheating."

"In one sense, yes. But it's his merchandise he's giving away, and he is free to give it to the person he feels will give him business. This affords him the chance to call on us to deliver a 'gift' and see what our house looks like. It may also make us feel obligated to buy from him."

That was a rude awakening for a six-year-old. Maman did not want us to be naïve or to believe in too many myths.

We went to public school for six weeks because we did not have uniforms for private school. Besides, the school had its full complement for the year. Madeleine and I were in French classes because there was no English instruction. It was Madeleine's third school that academic year and my second.

Since Maman was not feeling well because of her pregnancy that summer, Papa hired a live-in nanny by the name of Mademoiselle Bissonnette (Miss Bissonnette). She was a tall, thin woman of thirty-five with no sense of humour. She was rigid and hard working. Going salaries for live-in nannies were $2.50 per week plus room and board. Maman was increasingly sick throughout the summer, her legs kept swelling and her stomach got bigger. She was often in her robe, a pink silky material with a deeper shade of grosgrain ribbon around the edges. It was quite ample, naturally, with three quarter sleeves. It was a hot summer, and she frequently wore her hair in a knot on the very top of her head. She was huge, but she looked beautiful, especially in that dreamy pink robe.

She sewed at her machine a lot, making school uniforms, or 'black convent dresses' as we called them. We were starting at a private convent in September where the students wore uniforms. They were complicated with all sorts of regulations, little pleats in the top portion and a high collar with a hemstitched band sewn by hand. The skirt consisted of a series of pleats with a slit between pleats on the right side. This accessed a type of sac (besace), which was like a money belt. It was a square pouch with a slit that lined up with the slit in the skirt on a belt that had a buttonhole at one end and a button at the other. One kept a handkerchief, small comb, nail file, and whatever young girls considered a necessity at that age in one's besace. It always seemed to weigh a ton. Maman made nightdresses, slips, petticoats, underwear, fall skirts and piles of small handkerchiefs.

The heat stayed in the high nineties. When Papa was near enough in his territory, he came home midweek and took us swimming in Lake Waterloo.

Another refreshing day was when we met Felix Arsenault, the gentleman who lived across the street. He had a very large yard which backed up to the railroad track. It was fenced off from the street by a white picket fence and a lovely lawn. He had no children to wear it down. It had a large, scalloped band of a wide variety of flowers around the perimeter, and a gardener came weekly to weed and mow the lawn. Mr. Arsenault was obviously aware that I spoke English. I was watching him methodically watering his lawn one day when he said, "Go ask your mother if you can put your bathing suit on and I will cool you down with water."

"Can I bring the others?"

He didn't know how many others I meant, and I broadcasted the news. All the kids from our yard went over, and Mr. Arsenault gave us a good hosing down. Occasionally, on extremely hot days, we would show up at his house in our bathing suits to be hosed down. He did not seem to mind.

What intrigued me about Felix Arsenault was his car. Most cars at the time were black or navy blue and very square-ish. Mr. Arsenault's car was maroon and seemed to have a hardware store full of chrome. It had beige upholstery and a convertible with a rumble seat. Nevertheless, the fascinating part for a child was a little square door in the side of the car that opened to let his dog into the rumble seat area. I got close to the car one day and saw two steps inside the small door. Up came the dog, sitting himself king-like on the seat. When the car drove away, the dog watched the world go by, hair tussled by the wind, with an expression of deep satisfaction on his face.

Given the number of people in the house and the fact that we were all milk drinkers (except Maman who drank only tea and morning coffee), we consumed several quarts of milk daily. Part of Papa's job was to collect overdue payments on farm implements, but if payments were overly delinquent, he had to arrange for an attorney to repossess the machinery involved. There was a farmer by the name of Mr. Durand who had not paid for months on a hay mower. Since the man lived only a mile or so out of town, Papa went to warn him that he had been instructed to repossess his mower. Mr. Durand explained that he had twelve children to feed and could not squeeze out even a dollar a month because he would not make ends meet.

"If you take my mower away, I will lose my hay crop, then I cannot feed my cows. My main income is my milk runs, so I will lose my farm," he said.

"I take about eight quarts of milk weekly, and we need eggs too. How about supplying us with milk and eggs? At the end of the month, leave me a bill, and I'll pay that amount to Massey-Harris on your mower and send you a receipt," Papa bartered.

So, we drank Mr. Durand's mower, and after that we drank hay rakes and ensilage machines. The wood we heated with was paid for on a similar basis. Papa kept a list of nearby farmers who had cash flow problems and arranged many of these deals. These farmers remained lifelong Massey-Harris customers.

August 21st was Maman's birthday and it was coming up. We had no money since we had no allowance, so we generally gave her holy pictures for her birthday. They were the ones she had previously given us. We would erase 'de Maman Eva Rose' written in pencil and write in our birthday wishes. This particular year, Madeleine asked Papa for one dollar to buy a present for Maman. She bought a box of chocolates at the drug store. She asked Papa if she could have the change from the dollar to buy a few treats that she shared with Thérèse and me.

This would be our first present to Maman, so it called for a special presentation. We dressed Thérèse up in white, gauzy material we found in a trunk in the shed and hid her in the coal section. Madeleine was to send her a signal of when to come out and bring the present with her, via the nanny. Madeleine and I sat in the living room with Maman having warned her that something special was afoot, and we waited and waited and waited. We told Maman that Thérèse was in the kitchen with the nanny, but then we heard Thérèse howl! She arrived in the living room having been rescued by Miss Bissonnette. Apparently, we had forgotten to show her how the barn-door-like opening worked! She had been sitting down there crying and wiping her tears with coal-dusted hands. What a picture she made: dress with black patches on white, face blackened, crying, holding Maman's present in her coal-covered hands, inconsolable.

"What have they done to my little Thérèson?" Maman asked.

We explained as Maman consoled her, then went to clean her up. We waited until Thérèse had settled down and then Madeleine who had wiped the present clean, fetched the box of chocolates. We waited, fidgeting for Maman to undo the large red ribbon on top. We were eager to share her present, which she did in time. The chocolates were whitish and stale as they were bought in early August in the days before air conditioning from a store that sold little by way of candy. They had likely been sitting there for a year. Maman was kind, though, thanked us for our thoughtfulness and told us how she would cherish the box. It would be fair to say that our mother never forgot our first true present to her! She held on to that box for years.

There was a guard-rail made of square uprights at regular intervals from each other all around the veranda of the house where we lived. One day I had the bright idea to put my knee between two uprights and my arms on the railing while I talked with someone in the yard below for a long time. When I tried to leave, my knee had swollen and I could not move it out; it was stuck! I panicked and screamed for help. Maman came and tried ice from the icebox, chopping it in little pieces and holding it on my knee in a facecloth. The swelling remained.

"No problem," she said. "Just stay here, I'll make a phone call and I'll be right back."

As if I can go anywhere! I thought.

When she came back, she said, "Mr. Paquet will come right over and he'll take care of it."

Not long after, the man who had added a glass case in our dining room and a large linen closet in the bathroom drove up and emerged from his car with a saw! *Oh No! A saw and my leg!* I panicked! He walked up the steps, and I started to scream, trembling like a leaf.

"Please, please I don't want my leg cut off!"

Maman approached me but I pushed her away. *Why would she allow something like this? It made no sense!* I could visualize the blood dripping all the way down to the LaRoche's porch downstairs. I could feel the pain already. She sent Mr. Paquet, his gold tooth, and his saw into the kitchen to calm me down. She explained that it was the upright that was going to be sawed off, not my leg. She went into the house and asked Mr. Paquet to be very careful and unthreatening and to stop if I requested it.

He was very nice and consoling, but I didn't trust him. All I could see was his saw. Finally, I had to give in. I had no choice! *I'll have to live the rest of my life on the veranda in between these two uprights if I don't let him cut it off,* I thought. I asked him to go slowly and not to cut my leg. He reassured me and with that, started up his electric handsaw. What a horrible sound it made! I closed my eyes and Maman held my hand. He finally sawed through the upright and it gave way—and none too soon! I carefully moved backwards with a huge sigh of relief, and Mr. Paquet nailed the upright back into place. Maman offered him some money, which he refused. My leg was saved and I was happy.

Although I was still young, I was learning life lessons slowly and beginning to feel a little bit like a grown-up at six years old. I now understood I shouldn't be so eager to buy a raffle ticket when given the opportunity, and I knew that when you put someone in a room you should make sure they know how to get out before you leave. I also realized that squeezing my body into tight places causes swelling! Besides learning from my parents, my sister, Madeleine, helped me all the time too. She always seemed to have the answers, and what I saw as a crisis was always calmly resolved by her. She taught me many things just by way of example. I was growing up, a little…

School was soon to begin, but having my sister by my side was comforting and I worried a whole lot less. I was looking forward to it.

La Nature se Transforme en Technicolor
(Nature Turns to Technicolor)

Since I was her godchild, my aunt Marie-Anne sent me a special present. It was a brown, thick cowhide school bag with my initials printed in gold. I was six, and this was the first time I had a personal possession with my initials on it. I often confused the word 'initials' with 'essentials' and kept telling people about my school bag with my essentials on it.

Beautiful September came along and we climbed up the hill to go to the Maplewood Convent, our new school. Madeleine was in second grade. I had to start over because I spent under three months at school in New Hampshire and only six weeks in public school in French. They taught in both French or English at this school, and I was to study in French.

Maplewood Convent, Waterloo, QC, about 1910
Stanley G. Triggs
Courtesy of the McCord Museum MP-0000.1040.7, Montreal, QC

"I can't go to French school," I complained. "I have to be able to speak the language of the country."

"Canada is your country now," Papa said.

"You said I could choose when I grow up, and I want to be an American."

I often opened the small top left drawer of the buffet in the dining room and looked at my birth certificate. That was my proof. My parents discussed it amongst themselves. They leaned towards French, but I was convincing. They decided that since we only spoke French in the house, I could benefit by learning a second language.

"If you're sure that's what you want to do, then we'll put you in English classes," Papa said.

So, I went into the English program. Madeleine and I were called 'day scholars', which meant that we did not live at the convent as most students did. My parents, however, had arranged for us to be boarding scholars later if necessary. Hence, Maman's sewing binge. She completed all the clothes the school required for us.

To enter the Maplewood Convent we passed under an arched wrought iron entrance with its two wide swinging doors that were locked at night. The doors were between stone pillars. On top of each stone pillar was a round, opaque light fixture. These doors opened onto a paved driveway which was lined with trees, including a huge oak tree (the school's emblem). On the right facing the main school entrance was a large, round basin in the centre of which were dragon heads with water cascading from their mouths into the basin; it was an impressive cast iron fountain. Receded at the left of the main entrance was a grotto with running water, and a statue of the Virgin Mary. At the bottom of the rock formation was a statue of a kneeling Bernadette Soubirous holding a candle. There were trees all around, and it was a natural setting. Hidden behind and partially under a rock near Bernadette was a grate to catch the running water which made its way through an underground pipe and ran into a large artificial pond about one hundred feet lower on a different level. The pond was stocked with small fish, frogs, and ducks. This school itself was a beautiful mansion built at the top of a hill covered in maple trees in Waterloo, Quebec. Personally, I thought it looked more like a castle.

Statue of the Virgin Mary at the Maplewood
Convent, Waterloo, Quebec
Courtesy of Sylvie

The mansion had been built at the request of Senator Asa Belknap Foster in the last quarter of the nineteenth century. He moved from the States in the mid-1860s into what was the largest and most magnificent residence in Waterloo, and he named it, The Maplewood. He was known as the King of Canadian Railways and became Waterloo's first mayor in 1867. He had grandiose dreams and tastes. The talk amongst the students at the convent was that when he built the Maplewood, he ordered fourteen—or maybe even sixteen—marble fireplaces in different colours from Italy, crystal chandeliers from Belgium, and countless other exotic materials. The senator, however, ran out of money, and the rumour was that he was being hounded by his creditors. By the mid-1870s, Foster was in significant financial trouble, and we heard he declared bankruptcy in 1877. On November 1st, 1877, Foster passed away from heart problems. He left behind children, only one living at home at the time, and a wife.

Maplewood Convent, Waterloo, QC, about 1910
Stanley G. Triggs
Courtesy of the McCord Museum MP-0000.1041.15, Montreal, QC

His widow, Elizabeth Fish, born in Hatley, Quebec, inherited the mansion. She was left with debts and, as the saying goes, a white elephant. Apparently, she did not want to sell it for a song because she still had a son to look after, feed and support, so she advertised it for a moderate price and other considerations. In 1882, she sold it to the Sisters of the Holy Names of Jesus and Mary, of Montreal, for an undisclosed amount. The whispers amongst the girls were that Mrs. Foster got to keep one room and a connecting bathroom in the mansion reserved for herself for as long as she lived. In addition, she was to receive tuition for her son at a university of his choice. She lived her days at the Maplewood as a 'grande dame'. Another of Mrs. Foster's requests was that her husband's picture remains hung in the building. The image was a lifelike black pen drawing. Madeleine, Thérèse, and I passed by it daily for years.

The sisters who purchased the mansion converted it into a convent where they offered English and French education for girls. They kept the Maplewood Convent running until the 1960s.

Today, The Maplewood Convent has been restored and is now the beautiful *Manoir Maplewood*. It is said to be a wonderful place to stay in one of the most beautiful regions of Quebec.

Over the decades, there were several notable people who made Waterloo their place of residence. John R. Booth, born in Waterloo, later became known as The Lumber King of Canada and was one of the wealthiest men in Canada during the 1800s. Lucas Huntington, a member of Parliament and a resident of Waterloo, revealed certain details in a speech in Parliament that came to be known as, The Pacific Scandal. This caused the first Prime Minister of Canada, Sir John A. MacDonald, to resign, but then he was back in power five years later. Another was James Davidson, who made Waterloo his summer residence in the 1880s. His father, Thomas Davidson, was the founder of Thos Davidson Manufacturing Company Ltd., a producer of enameled tinware. They were successful and had offices across Canada and around the world.

For us, school began in glorious surroundings. Although we were being taught in English, the language spoken to and from school was always French. My mother was getting bigger and bigger, but still, she insisted on helping us with our reading and spelling every afternoon after school. For me math was a breeze, maybe from playing number games at home.

I was in a room with around twenty-five other students from prep course through to third grade. I did not care for my teacher, as I felt she had no sense of humour and no understanding of children. After three o'clock she taught seniors, which she liked, but she seemed to have no use for children. She was my teacher for four long years before I graduated to teachers I liked. When Thérèse was old enough, she also joined us at The Maplewood Convent.

A less pleasant experience with a student one day was when a girl tried to steal from me. Bernadette, who sat next to me, had my only pencil. When I told the teacher and she asked Bernadette about it, Bernadette denied everything.

"It's a red pencil and my name is printed in gold on it. My father had it made for me at the Toronto Fair," I argued.

"Her name is written on it because I was thinking of her when I had it printed, so I gave her name by mistake," Bernadette sheepishly and maliciously countered.

The teacher said Bernadette could keep the pencil since it was hers. It was a blow to me that an adult could be so patently unfair. When Sister Lavigne found me crying, she said,

"Now why are you crying? For a five-cent pencil? You need to grow up; you're not a baby anymore."

"I'm not crying for the five cents; I'm crying because it's just not fair. My father had it made special for me."

When I told Maman, she saw my point of view. I had been cheated.

"Go next door and speak to Mrs. McGregor. Defend your rights," she said.

The McGregor's lived a couple of houses down from us, beside a lot of empty land. It was as large, if not larger, than the house we lived in. Mr. McGregor was the Imperial Oil dealer for most of the Eastern Townships at the time, and he owned a fleet of oil trucks. They were well off but not pretentious.

They wanted children but could not have them, so they fostered Bernadette. She came from Montreal because her father had set fire to his business when he was in financial straits. A wall of the building collapsed, killing a firefighter. He was wanted for murder and it was believed he had fled the country, leaving his wife, Bernadette, and a younger girl to fend for themselves. The mother went mad and the children were placed in foster homes. Perhaps this is why the nun had let her have my pencil. Though living in a rich home, Bernadette was deprived of her parents and her sister. She was Jewish, lived with a Protestant family and went to a Catholic school, all of which must have been disorienting for a child.

I walked up the steps and rang the doorbell. Mrs. McGregor answered and asked me to come in. I declined and explained what I wanted. She was gone for some time and returned with my pencil and a candy bar—a whole bar! At our house we shared a candy bar or two, but we never had whole candy bars.

"No thank you," I replied to her offer as I reached for my pencil. "I just want what's mine."

I felt Mrs. McGregor was attempting to buy me, but my mother explained that the candy was likely offered as a form of apology. She added that I had been right in maintaining my independence. A couple of years later Bernadette moved away.

Nature turned to Technicolor in Waterloo. The leaves were falling, and the locals made fires using maple leaves, which gave a pleasant aroma. There was always a wooden barrel of McIntosh apples in our hallway off the kitchen, and we had a big, red, juicy McIntosh each day after school.

Although school was occupying my thoughts and probably Madeleine's too, my parents' focus was on something altogether different. My mother was due to soon have her baby.

Surprise, surprise!

Un Accouchement Difficile
(A Difficult Delivery)

Quite early on a rainy Saturday morning, October 17, 1931, to be exact, Maman told the three of us that we had been invited for special treats and dinner by the spinsters, the Misses Fontaine, (les Demoiselles Fontaine), who were two elderly retired nannies that lived on the top floor of the big house next to ours. They were the owners and had little money but lived reasonably well (from what I saw) on the rent from the first floor. I had spoken to them briefly a time or two but felt ill at ease with them. Maman insisted we all go despite our protests.

Papa had not come home on Friday evening. He often worked into Saturday, or if he was far away, he'd drive part-way until he got sleepy, then stay at a hotel and come home Saturday.

My sisters and I reluctantly went to les Demoiselles Fontaine. They served us lunch and put pepper on my food, which I had never seen before.

"Why do you put dust on the food? Maman doesn't do that," I said.

They explained pepper to me.

After lunch, I was bored and tried to leave, but the deadbolts were locked. At about three o'clock, there was a knock on the door and Mr. LaRoche said that he had come to get us. As we crossed his lawn, he announced,

"Your mother had twin girls today."

"I don't believe you," I said.

When we walked into the house, we saw one baby in a small crib in the living room and the other in a large cane basket (our clean clothes basket) on a sofa beside the crib. One had dark hair, the other a blondish fuzz. Miss Bissonnette, the nanny, and Mrs. Delisle, a midwife, would not let us see Maman.

My father arrived at about five o'clock. He went to see the babies, looked excited, happy, and proud, then disappeared to spend some time with my mother. Next, he went to his office and called my grandparents. I remember overhearing part of the call.

"We have some news. (On a du nouveau). No, it's not a boy. No, it's not a girl. It's ... two girls!"

Next, he called his brother-in-law, Onil (Maman's older brother) and Aunt Germaine (his sister) who told him they would come over the following afternoon.

We mostly hung around the babies that Saturday evening until our bedtime. We watched them sleep, we watched Papa hold them, and we watched Miss Bissonnette feed them. Papa was up and down like a yo-yo; he kept running upstairs to see how Maman was doing, then back down to the babies. He gave us a talk about how to behave around newborn babies. We were strictly forbidden to pick them up.

"They're too little yet," he said, "but in time you'll all be able to hold them. Your mother and I will let you know when we think it's OK."

If we touched the babies, we had to wash our hands with soap first, we were not to handle any of the babies' milk and we had to try to speak softly when around them.

"So you don't wake them up," Papa said.

He had quite the list of rules, and we all understood the importance of what he was telling us. Thérèse needed more reminders, though, because she was only four at the time.

We asked my father if we could see Maman. He said, "Not tonight, your mother is very tired and needs her rest, maybe tomorrow," which left me feeling sad.

On Sunday afternoon there was a quiet knock at our front door. It was Aunt Germaine and Uncle Onil. They had previously been asked to be the godparents of the expected child. They had had twins themselves not all that long before, but, sadly, the babies died at birth. Nevertheless, they still wanted to be godparents.

My aunt and uncle stayed downstairs with all of us for a little while, then went upstairs for a short visit with Maman. Afterwards, my father asked us to stay in the living room while the adults had a hushed conversation in the kitchen. They must have been discussing Maman's condition, their concerns and what they could do to help her. My mother was so weak she could barely get out of bed. For her to see her babies, Papa had to bring them upstairs and ever so gently lay them on the bed by her side. Because of her frail condition, Papa decided to delay the baptismal celebration for two weeks, thinking it would give my mother time to rest and that she likely would feel much better by then. My aunt and uncle also thought that was a good plan.

Although my siblings and I were much too young to understand the state our mother was in, it must have been difficult for her to hear her little babies cry and not be able to do a thing about it. She didn't have the strength and she was too sick to see them unless my father took them to her.

We never got to see our mother until Sunday evening. She was, if possible, whiter than the proverbial sheet and her voice was almost inaudible. A buzzer had been rigged up so she could call for help when needed. The babies were doing well; Maman was not.

Our mother had hemorrhaged almost to death during the delivery and became very weak. Papa asked us all to keep very quiet for her sake. He spent a lot of time with her and helped with the babies. Miss Bissonnette was upset that she had been hired to take care of one baby, not two. In addition, Maman was more work than anticipated.

By the time my mother had gone into labour, Dr. Remy, whom she had seen regularly during her pregnancy, was out in the countryside delivering twins. There was no phone at that home, so there was no way to contact him. Mrs. Remy suggested that Maman call the English doctor, but he was unavailable as well. Maman then called Dr. Cohen, the Jewish doctor, and Mrs. Cohen gave the same response as the others. In desperation, my mother called Mrs. Remy back who said she would send a very capable midwife (sage femme), named Mrs. Delisle, and her son, a first-year medical student. When they arrived, it was clear that the midwife knew her business, but the son had never seen a live birth before. After the first baby was born, the midwife took the baby to the bathroom to clean and wrap her in a blanket. Maman told Mr. Delisle that she was still in labour, but he insisted these were afterbirth pains.

"This is my fourth delivery and I know what labour pains are," she told him.

He was embarrassed at her insistence and at being alone with a woman in such a state of undress, I imagine. He took a bar of soap, went to a bowl of fresh water, washed his hands thoroughly and reached for a clean towel from a pile on the dresser. He went to the coat tree in the hall directly across from (vis-à-vis) Maman's bedroom door, put on his jacket and raincoat, ignored her request for further help, assured her she would be all right and left.

The second baby came but in breech position. Maman reached with much difficulty for the baby. She made sure the baby was breathing and placed her carefully between herself and a pillow she had laid lengthwise close to her. Maman looked at the clock, recording the time of birth in her mind (11:20 a.m.). Louise, the first baby, was born at 11 a.m.

When Mrs. Delisle entered the bedroom to show Maman her new baby, she was not prepared for what she saw. She found my mother lying sideways on the bed, bleeding badly. She screamed for the nanny to call the doctor. Mrs. Delisle packed her with clean cloths in an attempt to stem the flow of blood. Miss Bissonnette called for the various doctors but none were back. Maman had always delivered under anesthetic in a hospital with doctors and nurses around, so this was a big shock to her system. The doctor finally arrived later that evening and told my father she was very weak. He suggested a few things to do to help her regain her strength as she had lost a lot of blood.

We went to school as usual on Monday, and Miss Bissonnette took care of the twins. Papa went to work but only in the immediate vicinity, and he came home every night. Maman was getting weaker and suffering from dizziness, so Dr. Remy stopped by daily to check on her.

During the week after the twins were born, Papa did not want to sleep in the same bed with Maman when he was home. He felt she was too ill, I'm sure. Madeleine and I shared a double bed in the back bedroom and Papa resorted to sleeping sideways on the foot of our bed, frequently not even undressing. Miss Bissonnette and the babies slept on the sofa-bed in the living room, and Thérèse slept on a cot in the dining room.

Me and Madeleine could hear Papa sob sometimes during the night and felt helpless to make things better. He was aware of how much Maman was declining. He was not yet thirty-four, had a wife whom he'd loved from childhood that was near death, five children from eight on down, a nanny who was threatening to quit, not much money (medical insurance had not yet come into existence) and he desperately needed to keep his job. The most crucial time of the year was coming up where he had to take inventory and collect all outstanding monies due before November 30th.

On the Sunday of the baptism, my aunt and uncle arrived in their small green Ford around one in the afternoon. Two of their children were in the rumble seat and one was in the front with them. The baptism was set for three o'clock. Maman was still not well enough to attend, so my father hired Mrs. Delisle to stay with her while they were at church. Mrs. Delisle not only accepted but also refused to take any money; she was happy to help.

My aunt and uncle were godparents of one child. Their oldest daughter, Marie, aged fifteen, and their son, Henri-Paul, aged thirteen, were godparents of the other twin. The carriers (porteuses) were Madeleine, then eight, and Françoise, my aunt and uncle's youngest daughter, aged eleven. The baptismal procession was made up of very young people.

October 16 is the Feast Day of Sainte Marie-Marguerite d'Youville. She founded the Order of Sisters of Charity of Montreal, also known as the Grey Nuns of Montreal, in 1737. Marie-Marguerite was the first Canadian-born saint. In 1959, she was beatified (one step before sainthood) by Pope John XXIII. Thirty-one years later, in 1990, she was canonized by Pope John Paul II and has since been recognized as Sainte Marie-Marguerite d'Youville.

Having only been prepared for boys' names and because the twins were born on October 17th, one day following Feast Day, Maman decided on Marie for the oldest and Marguerite for the younger. Papa did not like those names because he thought it was frequently slurred and came out as "Magritte," like the painter. With Maman's approval, he changed the names to ones they both liked. The oldest by twenty minutes was baptized as Louise Rose Marie, and the younger baby as Marthe Eva Marie. They would be known as Louise and Marthe. The name Marie was always added to all girls' names by the church. Because Maman's name was Eva Rose, the twins were named after her. Papa told the bell ringer he would reward him if he rang the bells with more emphasis to announce the birth of twins, and he did it so thoroughly we all thought the bell ringing would never cease.

My father returned home excited. He went straight upstairs to Maman's room and asked,

"Eva Rose, did you hear the church bells ringing? I asked that they ring the bells longer and louder for the babies."

"How could I not hear?" Maman said with a smile.

"We have two beautiful twin girls, you and me," he said smiling back at her.

Papa had had a case of soda delivered to our house earlier that week. My uncle gave all the children twenty-five cents. Usually no one could pry a penny out of me, but I blew the whole quarter on sugared coconut and shared it with the others. That night, we had a good supper prepared by Miss Bissonnette and then the company left.

We kept mixing up the twins, but my father differentiated them by the distinctive pattern of their cries. Finally, a pink ribbon was tied to Louise's wrist and a blue one to Marthe's.

Two and a half weeks after the twins were born, Dr. Remy told Papa that my mother's condition was declining even more and she should be taken to a hospital. It was decided she would be taken to Sherbrooke Hospital. She would have gone there and had a doctor present had she not delivered two weeks early. My parents discussed the situation after Dr. Remy left that day. A small suitcase had already been packed in preparation for the delivery trip to the hospital.

The following morning, Papa warmed up the car, and Maman was wrapped up in a sheet and blanket. My father laid her down on the back seat of the car and covered her with more blankets. She had lost so much blood that she was freezing. At the last moment, Papa insisted I go along so he could have someone in the car to return with to keep him awake. All this was taking its toll on him too, so I went on the forty-mile trip to Sherbrooke. The road was not paved, and it took more than two hours to get there.

Maman was taken from the backseat of the car by hospital staff and admitted to the hospital. It was so difficult to watch my mother, whom I loved so much, be carried out and taken away like that. I cried as I wondered when I would see her again. Papa tried to reassure me, but it didn't help much at the time. I was filled with fear of the unknown.

I had an aunt and uncle who lived in Sherbrooke, and they came to pick me up. We had supper, but Papa was not there because he had stayed with my mom at the hospital. He came back late, looking haggard, and ate a bite. We left in the pouring rain. The unpaved road was a muddy soup, and Dad drove with one wheel on the shoulder and the other in the wheel ruts. Headlights were not very strong in those days, and the rain made visibility even worse.

Meeting another car presented a problem. Both cars approached each other gingerly, one driver standing on his mudguard, yelling, "Does it look wide enough for me to continue?"

"No, but I saw a place that is wider about twenty feet back. I'll back up."

"All right, I'm far enough back. Make sure you drive on the shoulder though."

Slowly the car came forward. Windows were down on the drivers' side, and the consultation continued until the cars had passed each other.

"Good night!"

"Thank you and good night," Papa would say.

We proceeded at a crawl, and at every car we met outside a village, the same scene was repeated. The ditches were steep, and the hills from Sherbrooke to Magog had not yet been graded. A driver had to keep one's speed to at least twenty miles per hour to make it to the top in second gear. Papa was also sleepy.

"Pierrette, talk to me. That's why I brought you. I have to stay awake."

I didn't know what to talk about and I hadn't yet become the talkative person I came to be, so I resorted to asking the most complicated questions that came to mind, questions requiring long answers. I also talked some despite my own sleepiness. We arrived home after midnight, more than four hours after my regular bedtime; however, they let me sleep in the next morning. My father must have told Miss Bissonnette not to wake me.

Papa called my grandparents and advised them of Maman's plight. He asked if they would take one twin for a while to keep Miss Bissonnette from quitting. Aunt Marie-Anne, who lived with my grandparents, arrived a day or two later. Papa drove her back to Sainte-Monique with little baby Marthe.

The unknown ... I was so scared that my mother might never be coming back. I worried about my new baby sister too. When was *she* coming back? For a short period of time, I would quietly cry myself to sleep. Every night

Madeleine would console and reassure me that our mother and Marthe would indeed be returning home.

"Maman just has to get better first, we have to be patient," she would tell me.

But what if Madeleine is wrong? I couldn't help but wonder ...

La Vie Sans Maman et un Bébé
(Life Without Maman and a Baby)

Miss Bissonnette moved Madeleine and Thérèse into the big leather sofa-bed in the living room proper, she gave me the cot in the dining room, and she took the back bedroom for herself and Louise. She loved Louise, was nice to Thérèse, did not like me and disliked Madeleine, who acted as if it were immaterial to her whether she was liked or not.

I had always slept in the same room as Madeleine, my protector, role model and helper, so I was afraid to sleep in a room by myself. The absence of a parent in the house added to my insecurity. I stayed awake for hours in the dark waiting for noises, and I heard them like shots and would sit bolt upright. After a few days, I realized that the noises that sounded like shots were created by the wood in the stove and furnace exploding. There was also the cracking of clapboard and the breaking of nail heads from the cold. I felt alone and afraid. Much to my relief, within six months Miss Bissonnette once again switched me and Thérèse so I was back to sharing the bedroom with Madeleine. I don't think Thérèse ever minded being by herself.

Life without Maman was dull; no affection, no caring, no treats, no positive attention, no laughing, no ombudsman, no teaching, no goodnight kiss, and no Papa most of the time. But there was lots of yelling and kneeling in corners. Lunch food was presented in an unappetizing manner with an eat it and be quiet attitude. Those were aplenty.

We escaped to school but had no one to come home to. There was no one to greet us with a glass of milk and cookies, no one to help with reading and spelling. Miss Bissonnette knew no English except for the phrase, 'I no speak English.'

One of the worst aspects was we had to wear boy's long underwear to school in the winter. I don't know if that was Papa's idea or Miss Bissonnette's. They were one-piece affairs made of small cotton knit with a three-button flap for bathroom use. The cuffs at the wrist and ankles were very narrow ribbing, and because they were washed in water that was too hot, they soon stretched. I could not put my stockings over this long underwear without huge lumps. The only way to do a presentable job was to hold out the loose portion of the cuff at a right angle to the leg with the right hand, place the left index finger on the leg to hold the ribbing, fold over the extra ribbing flat on the leg, keep it tight in that spot with one hand and pull the stocking over it. But at that stage, one was fresh out of hands. It was doable for someone with large hands maybe, but it was too much for a sleepy child of six or seven in a cold room. I cried, missed some school because Miss Bissonnette would not help me or arrived very late when she finally figured out that helping was the only way to get rid of me. Madeleine sometimes helped me, but most of the time she was told that I had to learn to do it on my own. If Maman were there, she would have helped me or shown me a useful trick. I hated to dress for winter for a long time, and I'm sure it dates back to the 1931-32 winters and those awful, long boy's underwear.

1931 was the first winter I went to school, and it was the first winter I had to deal with snow in such enormous quantities and with such intense cold. Life settled into dullness. Papa came home for a while every weekend to do the major marketing, especially the meat, to pay the nanny, leave her money for necessities during the week and to open his piles of mail. He seldom laughed, and he always seemed distracted.

All Papa said about Maman was that she was very sick. One time, he took me to Sherbrooke to a doctor's office in the hospital, and a sample of my blood was taken. It was thought that since I looked so much like Maman, my blood might match hers and they could take small amounts of it periodically. It did not match. Apparently, they never did find a match. Later, Papa mentioned that Maman was so sick that she was transferred to a Montreal hospital.

Only when I was eighteen did I find out the rest of the story. Maman had been transferred to Hôpital Saint-Jean-de-Dieu in Montreal because she was in a very deep depression and nothing seemed to pull her out of it. Because Maman was in hospital for so long (almost a year), kids would say to me,

"Your mother's crazy."

"So is yours!" I would answer.

Kids can be so cruel. I did not know my mother was suffering from depression, nor would I have understood it because I was too young. All we knew was what Papa was telling us. Maman was very sick. I loved my mother so much that being told she was crazy made no sense. As an adult I was able to confirm that she was not crazy, as the kids would say, but she was however, severely depressed.

Apparently, Papa argued, begged, and pleaded with Saint-Jean-de-Dieu doctors and management to have my mother placed in a semi-private room rather than by herself. He felt the distraction would do wonders for her. However, they kept her in a private room where only medical personnel had access. Papa's chief argument (he told me years later) was, how does one who is sane but depressed get better when they are by themselves day in and day out? How do they emerge from the depth of a depression by being alone all the time? Papa also asked the hospital to let him hire two special nurses, which they agreed to. One started at seven in the morning, and the other stayed until eleven at night. Papa gave them money to buy special foods that could not be obtained in the regular kitchen.

The cost of the room was $5 per day, which was $150 per month. Papa made $120 per month plus his expenses. Additionally, he paid the nurses and the food. Many family members, aunts, uncles, cousins, and Grand'papa Pinard thought he was crazy to throw so much money away. The family was scandalized. Papa tried to borrow from Maman's father (Grand'papa Pinard), but he refused and told my dad to accept his fate. He figured this was as good as she was going to be and that he should bring her home rather than spend more money he did not have. Some relatives came to see my mother, but their attitude and talking as if Maman was not there upset her. Papa requested that a sign be placed on her door that the only visitors allowed were to be himself and Aunt Cécile, his sister. She was a nurse and supported Papa's decision; she said it made sense. At least there was one person in his corner.

Papa got behind in his bills with the hospital and the doctors but not the nurses or the nanny. He began charging groceries and everything he could. He explained to the nuns that he could not pay our entire tuition but would eventually catch up.

Christmas 1931 without Maman was not bad. We went to my grandparents' in Sainte-Monique for a week and brought Louise along. We were so excited to finally see the twins together and my father thoroughly enjoyed having this time with Marthe.

At my grandparents' house, Christmas was treated as a religious holiday. My grandfather always kept the store open until one o'clock on Christmas Eve, "For any last-minute shoppers" he used to say. There was an elaborate midnight Mass followed by a Christmas Eve dinner (Réveillon), which was a dinner that lasted for hours. Réveillon was a traditional meal of tourtière (pork pies), meatballs, vegetables, potatoes, fancy sandwiches, finger foods, Christmas aspic, cakes, pies, fudge, and a Christmas Log (Bûche de Noël). Incedentally, my aunt Marie-Anne made the best fudge (sucre à la crème) in the village. It felt good to laugh again. It seemed like we hadn't laughed ever since my mother had gotten sick.

There were no presents and no Christmas tree at my grandparents'. However, on New Year's Day they exchanged presents much like my family did at Christmas. The children received presents from the Child Jesus rather than Santa, and Grand'papa's gift to everyone was always money. He always gave $50 to Maman, $25 to Papa and $5 to the children. That year I gave my money to Grand'papa and asked him to open a savings account for me. He did, gave me my first passbook and from then on, I always brought my money to him and he entered it into my passbook. My passbook was a special sheet with my name on it in a large ledger book. He added six percent interest per year.

It turns out that the real reason we went to Sainte-Monique that year was because the nanny wanted a week's vacation to visit her family. She deserved it. Life was bleak for her too, and she had very little time off. So our visit was good for us and for Miss Bissonnette.

When we returned to Waterloo after the holidays, Santa had come by in our absence and filled the tree we had trimmed before going away. Papa had left gifts which he and Aunt Cécile had shopped for and which Miss Bissonnette had placed at the foot of the tree after we left. When the holidays were over, Madeleine told me I was old enough to know there was no Santa Claus. She explained it logically, so I believed her.

When my seventh birthday came on January 4th, Madeleine dressed me up in my snow gear and pulled me along on our sleigh as a birthday present. We went up to the convent to slide down the hill near the entrance and down past the duck pond. It was a long, steep hill that flattened before another hill and another flat all the way down the railroad track fence. At the end of an hour my feet were cold so Madeleine walked me back home, took her sled and was gone for the rest of the afternoon. She always loved the outdoors.

Our nanny often managed to find some real or imagined offense on Madeleine's part to deprive her of dinner, especially on Saturdays for some reason.

"You can do without dinner today," was standard.

I felt sorry for Madeleine and told her so.

"Don't worry, I always ask someone for a peanut butter sandwich later. They understand," she said.

Madeleine never got punished when Papa was home, and she never told my father about how she was treated. She instinctively knew he had enough problems without her adding to them. She fended well for herself and was a good mother substitute for me and Thérèse.

Only two other persons were nice to me besides Madeleine and Thérèse. One was a senior student whose last name was Villeneuve. She was assigned to me during the winter months, and when it was raining, she would make sure I was well-dressed before I left school. The hook for my outerwear was directly below hers, and we shared a small cubby hole at floor level for our overshoes and rubbers. She was pleasant and took good care of me.

The other person was one we called 'the pretty girl' ('la belle fille'). She had to be at work at 8:30 a.m., and we had to be at school at the same time. She didn't work every day, so we never knew when we would see her, but we watched.

"Here comes the pretty girl," we'd say as we rushed to put our coats on.

She was tall, slender, and long-legged. Her pace was hard to keep up with, and we had to trot here and there.

But she was sweet to us, greeted us in a friendly manner and always wished us a good day at school.

We looked forward to Saturdays. Madeleine and I often stayed in bed late on Saturday morning if the sun was shining. The blinds were closed on the two windows that faced us. The windows faced east so that the sun made the blinds very light except for the shadows of the leaves of several trees in the yard. There was just enough distance between the trees that their shadows were barely separate. We saw these as caricatures of people, and each of us represented one side. We made up stories and short movies with dialogue about these people. On very windy days, we saw battles with infernal equipment, and other times they were cowboys. In retrospect, I marvel at the thought that we were perhaps inventing the concept of television.

One Saturday in the dead of winter, Papa arrived around one in the afternoon. He was sitting in his little turret office going over his mail while I was playing in the living room. Thérèse came in and said to him, "Papa, we don't have any lice in our hair you know."

Miss Bissonnette had told us all, "Don't tell your father you have lice or I'll lose my job."

Papa looked up and caught me giving Thérèse the signal to shush. He looked incredulous for a moment, shot up out of his chair and walked out the front door. I saw him walking down the street and turning the first corner. He returned about two hours later with his hair cut shorter than I had ever seen it before. He was carrying a bag of medications and white fine-tooth combs. He tied a large bath towel around his middle, motioned me to the bathroom, put some kind of a grey cream in my hair, had me sit for something like a half hour, then shampooed my hair in the bathroom sink. After untangling my hair, he combed it with the fine-tooth comb and told me to let it dry. He then tackled Thérèse, then Madeleine.

We all went through a second round Saturday evening, and no one went to church on Sunday. We had several repeat sessions. On Sunday, Papa called the Sister Superior and asked for a 7:00 p.m. appointment. He told her and a cohort what had happened and asked that they make an announcement to check everyone, both day scholars and boarders. He treated this as an illness. Papa called Massey-Harris on Monday morning to say he was cancelling his appointments for part of the week because of the children's illness, and he stayed with the shampooings until we were clear. Papa certainly had a well-developed sense of responsibility. He did not rely on the nanny to take care of this problem. He did it himself to be sure it was truly resolved and did not recur. Miss Bissonnette did not lose her job.

The hairstyle for little girls suddenly changed around this time. Instead of wearing bangs, girls were letting their hair grow, parting it on the side and wearing a bow. We asked Papa to let our hair grow, but he said Maman might not recognize us when she came home if we had different hairstyles.

On April Fool's Day (Poison D'Avril), April 1st, Papa was home. It was a French tradition where one would play a prank on someone that day. The most common prank was to make paper fish and attach them to the unsuspecting person, in this case, our papa. We would attach the fish to his back by taping them to his shirt. On this day our dad was sitting at the kitchen table reading the newspaper, leaving himself open for us to plaster paper fish all over his back. After a while he got up, acting as if he had no idea his back was covered, and theatrically announced he was going to the store. It was a coldish day but out he went with no coat on for all to see the fish we put on him. We were jumping with joy thinking we fooled him. He came back with meat, the fish on his back and a special April Fool's treat: three pounds of peanuts in their shells. He never did let on he knew.

On a beautiful spring day in April, we were extremely excited to hear the news that Maman was coming home. She was fragile, weighed about ninety pounds, looked pale, had circles under her eyes, did not smile and mainly stayed in her bedroom. Papa gave us all kinds of orders. Baby Marthe remained at my grandparents as they were unsure of Maman's condition.

"Do not disturb your mother. Be quiet. Be good girls, it's important."

I blew it! During that week it had been the Blessed Sacrament which was on the altar for forty hours and someone had to be in the chapel at all times. At the end of the week there was a special ceremony at seven o'clock so we had to go back up the long hill to school. I did not want to go, but Miss Bissonnette said we had to and she would not let me appeal it to my mother. I was ready to leave but sat in the dining room to present my appeal in case Maman came out of her room. When I heard her in the hallway, I impulsively hid behind the door, and as she went by, I yelled, "Rrrrraaaahhh!" She jumped in fright, looked at me, began to cry and scurried to her bedroom.

Papa came to me the next day and asked why I had done this.

"For fun. We do that at school all the time."

He explained how fragile Maman was. She had just come out of months in a hospital and needed quiet. He called her doctor in Montreal and spoke in whispers and then called my grandparents. Shortly after, he left with Maman. So, to our disappointment, she went to live with her parents, Aunt Marie-Anne, Marcelle, and our baby sister Marthe.

We had only seen Marthe once, at Christmas, but Papa went to visit her frequently when he was in that area. He talked about her often. He would tell us what a happy baby she was and how much she was changing. He always seemed so proud when talking about her, and he did his best to retain a connection between us and baby Marthe. Little baby Louise was becoming increasingly attached to Miss Bissonnette as she was the only mother figure she knew, almost from the day she was born.

We all went to my grandparents' to visit, including Miss Bissonnette, one weekend during that summer. I have a picture of my mother that was taken that weekend. Maman still didn't look well in that photo.

Once again, my mother stayed away for a long time. It was difficult for Madeleine, Thérèse and me to be without our mother for almost a full year. We missed her dearly. Miss Bissonnette was not nearly as nice as Maman was. Our mother always treated us with much kindness and respect. She was a caring mother who had such a gentle way about her. We had always felt safe and well-cared-for by two loving parents.

School, in a sense, was our saviour. At least we did not dwell on the fact that she was sick while we were in school. Homework helped us too. We focused on our work, not Maman. She had left for the hospital in October 1931 and did not return to stay home for good until September 1932, a day we were all looking forward to. Life would return to the way it used to be, at least that's what we hoped for ...

Maman et Bébé Reviennent Pour de Bon
(Maman and Baby Return for Good)

When my mother came back to us in September with Marthe, she looked sooo much better! She had put some weight on, her colour had improved and her spirits seemed up somewhat. She once again took an interest in us. Our wish was coming true!

We all marvelled at the reaction of the twins to one another. They played well together and seemed polite and shy around one another. If something was wrong or one fell or hurt themselves, Marthe would run to Maman for comfort; Louise would run to Miss Bissonnette who had been her caregiver since birth. They had seldom been out of each other's sight. It was understandable that Louise turned to Miss Bissonnette, however, it was hurtful for Maman to watch. She was neither jealous nor resentful, she understood, but it just was not easy to see your child run to someone else for comfort.

The household became a very busy place with two wee toddlers wanting to explore the world. Miss Bissonnette became less and less content with her job, although my mother helped too. There was a lot to do, especially mounds of laundry. The twins' clothes were often changed more than once in a day depending on food spills. Hand-washing diapers for two babies was time-consuming. Miss Bissonnette did not complain too much, but Maman could tell she was not happy and started thinking of replacing her. She kept her eyes and ears open in search of a new nanny.

Life was slowly getting back to normal for us all. Our new normal had suddenly become a 'very busy new normal'. We got to know Marthe, and we loved the twins equally. Louise got to know Maman, and my mother became 'Maman' to her in a fairly short period of time.

Papa took my mother to Montreal with him when he had to go on business, and he took her to nearby customers' farms. Maman would sit and read in the car while he did his business. He enjoyed the togetherness, but he was mostly concerned that she would become depressed again.

One Sunday in October, they left and said they would be back after supper. Along the road they met a couple when the two cars were going to pass each other. This couple just happened to be on their way from Joliette to visit with my parents. Both cars stopped. The couples spoke, my parents turned around and the Beaufort's followed them back to Waterloo. They arrived home and found that Madeleine, Thérèse and I had been locked out of the house. We were without coats and Miss Bissonnette was in the house alone with her boyfriend while the twins were sleeping. It took my parents some time and incessant knocking to have the doors unbolted. They told the boyfriend to leave, and both he and Miss Bissonnette left the house.

Maman and Papa prepared supper for all of us and our visitors. My parents were very upset over this incident but did not discuss it in front of their guests or us. Later that evening when Miss Bissonnette returned, my parents had a talk with her and warned that if this happened again, she would be let go. They felt they should fire her at once, but because she apologized profusely and promised it would never happen again, they decided to give her a second chance … not a good decision.

Not long after, Maman was combing Madeleine's hair when she noticed a scar on the bridge of Madeleine's nose.

"What's this scar?" she asked.

"It's nothing," Madeleine replied.

"It's not nothing, it's a scar. I want to know how it got there."

"I got two candy bars not to tell, so I won't tell you."

"Ooooooh," said Maman angrily as she walked to her bedroom door and locked it.

"Sit down, Mado. We will leave this room when I know what this scar is all about. You can take your time; I have a lot of patience and will wait for as long as it takes."

Madeleine knew my mother was firm enough not to flinch, so she finally admitted that Miss Bissonnette had hit her across the face with Papa's razor strop, and the metal ferrule left a scar after the bleeding stopped.

Maman who was so opposed to hitting children had made this very clear to Miss Bissonnette when she was hired, so she was overwhelmed at the thought that she had hit Madeleine—and in the face of all places. She confronted Miss Bissonnette with her evidence, and she admitted to it. Maman told her to pack her things and that she was leaving, today!

"You will let my husband know where to drop you off as soon as he gets home from work."

Papa drove Miss Bissonnette to her brothers in the country, and we never saw her again.

The thought of being without a nanny worried my father because he felt all the work was too much for my mother, and rightfully so. To his surprise, though, it was no time at all before Maman announced she had hired a new nanny. A neighbour told my mother of a young lady who was looking for housekeeping employment. Because the neighbour knew the young girl and her family, she reassured Maman she was a hard worker, reliable and a kind and honest person. When my mother met with her, she got a good feeling about her. She was hired. In my wildest dreams I could never have guessed who our new nanny was going to be!

Les Chuchotement d'une Corde à Linge
(The Whispers of a Clothesline)

One Monday afternoon, I came home from school shortly after three and walked into the kitchen. I almost lost my breath. Standing there in our kitchen, of all places, was 'the pretty girl' from school!

"Pierrette, this is Elissa LaRoche. She is our new nanny. You can call her Miss LaRoche."

"Allô," she said pleasantly.

She explained to Maman that she would prefer to be called Elissa since the people who lived downstairs were also named LaRoche.

"So, we'll call you Elissa then."

"Pierrot, there's a barrel of McIntosh apples which Papa brought home today. They're in the back hallway. You can have one now."

"Can I have one for Madeleine too?"

"Yes."

I took one for each of us and went outside to eat my apple. I was bursting to share my joy at having Elissa as our new nanny. On an impulse I ran up the hill and waited for Madeleine to come out of school to announce my great news.

"I don't believe you!" she said, taking the apple I offered her.

As we walked home, the joy on her face mirrored what I felt, so she must have believed me.

It was a lovely fall and a good winter. Life was back together again for all of us. The Great Depression was becoming more severe, but children are not so aware of finances. I thought my parents were very open with us on that subject, but in reality, they weren't always.

Elissa was a fairly quiet person and hard-working. The minute we left for school on Monday, she'd start the laundry and had it on the clothesline before we got home for dinner. We had been used to Monday dinners with little piles of wet clothes everywhere in the kitchen and a very cranky Miss Bissonnette. With Elissa we always came home to a clean, orderly house. I really liked her, we all did.

Papa had the day off for some reason on this particular Monday. Between my two sisters, Maman, myself and the nanny, there was an abundance of petticoats in our closets. Papa visited with his brother-in-law, Uncle Onil, in the afternoon and returned shortly before supper. He eventually made his way into the kitchen and when he peered out the window, he saw the backyard and our clothesline. The nanny had hung up the last batch of wash, which consisted of petticoats: Mom's, the children's and her own. Five petticoats all lined up in a row! "What is this," papa chuckled, "the petticoat empire?" From then on, my father jokingly referred to our home as, *The Petticoat Empire (L'empire des Jupons)*, a concept which came from the Vincent clothesline!

In those days, clotheslines seemed to take on a life of their own. Everybody had one and they were installed outside for all to see. To me it was as if clotheslines were magical, whispering secrets, softly blowing in the wind. One day when my mother was hanging clothes out, I said that to her.

"Perhaps," she said with a smile.

Papa used to say,

"You can tell a lot about somebody by their clothesline."

Many people took care hanging out their clothes to make sure they were hung proper and pleasing to the eye. They knew it would probably be seen by neighbours and passersby. If you happened to be a quilter, you were proud to display your quilts on your clothesline. If you hung out the clothes early enough on a sunny day, you could catch the birds singing in the background while the sun warmed your body. It was a wonderful feeling of tranquility and peacefulness. If you hung them out exceptionally early, you might be lucky enough to catch a beautiful sunrise.

Then there were the times when hanging clothes on the line turned into a bit of a social event. If you happened to put your clothes out at the same time as your neighbour, it was an opportunity for a chat and a good time to catch up on neighbourhood news. And, of course, there was always the smell of clean, fresh clothes which you could only get by hanging your clothes in the great outdoors. No matter how you look at it, I always thought there was something special and unique to one's clothesline.

There was one time, however, when our neighbour's clothesline solved a mystery. My parents decided to have cold pork roast for supper one night. It was a medium size, and since Papa and his good appetite were there, it wouldn't last long.

"Pierrot, go to the ice box and bring the roast," said Maman.

I came back empty handed from the long hallway that led to the back porch and said,

"I didn't find it."

"Go back and look harder this time."

I came back with the platter she had described, but it was empty. I placed it on the table.

"Is this the plate you wanted?"

"Well look at that! There's thumb marks on the plate," said Papa. "Someone stole the roast—just grabbed it and left the plate."

After dinner, Elissa went out to the back porch to take some clothes off the line. When she came back in the house, she went to find Maman.

"Madame Vincent, there are several bath towels missing from the clothesline."

The mystery deepened. *The secrets of a clothesline*, I thought. I wanted to help solve this mystery, so the next day I hid in the bushes where I had a view of our clothesline. I saw no one. After a while, Thérèse spotted me.

"Why are you hiding in the bushes?"

"Shhhh," I replied. "Go away. I don't want anybody to see me. I'm surveilling the clothesline, but don't tell anybody."

Thérèse left. I don't know how long I hid there but it seemed like forever. I started to feel cold and claustrophobic, so I decided to give up. I figured my family would soon start to wonder of my whereabouts. *It's time to abandon my detective work*, I concluded.

When Papa told Sébastien LaRoche what had happened, Sébastien said,

"Us too. Our six-month-old's clothes have disappeared from our clothesline."

They did not solve much then, but a few days later we clearly saw men's large footsteps in the snow that led to the side door of the Fontaine's house, the two spinsters. Their tenant had come and helped himself.

Sébastien called Papa.

"Are those your towels on the Fontaine's clothesline? My wife says our baby's clothes are there too."

Maman and Elissa peeked out of the bathroom window and confirmed the towels on their line were ours (they were US bought).

"Let's put our coats and overshoes on and take back what belongs to us."

So they went outside in the bright sunshine, climbed the few steps, took the clothes off the line while the renter was in plain sight in his kitchen and could see them. My mother and Elissa walked back with our property. Mr. LaRoche did the same. No one ever mentioned it again. My parents and the LaRoche's figured he was going to keep the bath towels and sell the baby clothes. This man never stole another thing that we knew of, not from our house anyhow.

My mother did most of the cooking, all the major shopping and all the sewing while taking care of Louise and Marthe. Life was busy. The nanny was responsible for the cleaning, washing the floor, the laundry, dishes and keeping the fires burning. When time allowed, she helped Maman with the twins. There were three children at home to be taken care of while Madeleine and I were at school.

By mid-afternoon, Elissa was finished with work and the children were taking their afternoon nap. This allowed her to frequently have an hour to an hour and a half of downtime.

"Sit," Maman would say when she noticed Elissa trying to create work to keep herself busy.

"I just can't sit there."

"Is there anything you'd like to do? Like embroider perhaps?"

"I like to knit," Elissa announced.

At Maman's suggestion, out came the knitting. After a few days of enjoying her afternoons and evenings knitting, Elissa started having qualms about having free time. She felt she should be working.

"I would be happy to knit for you in the afternoons and for myself in the evenings. It would make me feel better."

"What will you knit for me?"

"Things for the children: mittens, sweaters, tuques, scarves—anything you want. I would just need you to get me some wool."

Maman got wool, and not only did Elissa knit, but she also taught my mother how to knit. They spent part of their afternoons' knitting and talking together. Elissa was such a non-judgmental, easy-going person with an infectious laugh, and she was a great help in Maman's recovery that winter.

Although I've never heard anyone say so, nannies in our house were treated like friends of the family rather than housemaids. They ate at the table with us, although they got up to clear one course and serve the next. After the meal, everyone pitched in to clear the table as everyone had pitched in to set the table. My job was to put bread and butter on the table. Nannies washed the dishes while one or two of the children wiped them dry.

"This way the nanny can have the time to relax in the evening or sometimes go out if she wishes," Maman told us.

We each made our own bed, though the nannies straightened up, dusted, vacuumed, washed windows and so on. We all treated them politely and with respect, which is why my mother could be friends (to a point) with a nanny without it being out of place.

After watching Maman and Elissa knit together for a time, I decided I also wanted to learn how to knit. I liked sitting with them in the afternoons when not in school, listening to their conversations and joining in by asking questions—I was inquisitive. Maman said it would be OK for me to knit, but first she had to go through the safety rules of using knitting needles.

"They are not a toy, you can only use them when you are sitting down, you can't swing them around, and you can not point them at anyone. I'm going to give you a basket and when it's time to put them away, I want you to place them in your basket along with your wool. I don't ever want to see you walking around with knitting needles in your hands. Now, if you don't follow my rules, I will have to take them away from you," she said.

Seemed like a lot of rules to me, but I really wanted to learn so I promised to do as she asked. With the promise to follow her rules, that's when I learned how to knit. I used string I'd saved and knitting needles I borrowed from Elissa.

When Papa saw me with needles, he was taken aback.

"Put those away! I never want to see you use them again. You are going to put your eyes out with those things. Just think if you fell."

"Maman knows I knit," I said.

He turned on his heel and went looking for Maman. He came back and gave me his blessing because he trusted my mother's judgment. I picked up my knitting and kept going. Although I was not yet a grown-up, it made me feel a little like one because I was doing this with my mother and Elissa. I was using a tool that required one to be responsible. It was also an opportunity for me to show my parents that I could, in fact, be responsible.

Le Radio Crosley
(The Crosley Radio)

Christmas was once again around the corner, but first came Immaculate Conception Day on December 8th. I was received into the order of the Child of Jesus Society. All first graders were. The priest said a special prayer over each of us individually and held a medal of the Child Jesus for us to kiss. It was attached to a quarter-inch-wide red satin ribbon which, in turn, was attached to a red moiré ribbon about one inch wide that was placed around our necks. This formed a red V on the front and back of our black school dress, and we wore them for all special events through fifth grade.

The part I anticipated most was not the ribbon or the religious ceremony, it was the impressive banquet that followed. I was not disappointed. It was delicious.

"I went to a special banquet today," I proudly told the family that night.

Christmas 1932 was another lovely holiday punctuated with a few store-bought gifts. We received mainly handmade things: little red cinnamon and white clove fish as well as Maman's traditional four-compartmented hanging decorations which contained special goodies. Children thrive on small surprises as much as costly items because they do not put a price tag in their minds on the gift received.

The LaRoche's downstairs got a Crosley Radio for Christmas, and we were most impressed. Although we had heard of radios, we never knew anybody who owned one. Thérèse and I would lay down with our ear on the living room floor to listen to it. Because we had never seen a radio, we were curious as to what it looked like, so one day we asked the LaRoche kids if they could show it to us. Downstairs we went. We were awe-struck to see how it worked; we had never laid eyes on such a fancy piece of equipment as this before.

Nineteen thirty-three proved to be a warmer winter that was not as cold as others in the past. No long johns this year (I was sooo happy)! Just longer panties with an elastic that went over the stocking top, and heavier petticoats. Maman knew how to keep children warm. For the cold winter days, we had thin mittens covered with large mittens knitted with two strands of wool. They were very narrow at the wrist and had a long, wide cuff that went over our coat-sleeve. It kept the wind and cold out of our sleeves—no cold hands. We had scarves that weren't bulky but warm and stocking caps that went down over our ears and our foreheads. Maman and Elissa made them all.

I always looked forward to snuggling up with Maman during the cold winter months. She used to read in bed at night, sometimes until very late. I think she did not feel brave because she would let one of us sleep with her whenever Papa was not home. We took turns sleeping in her bed. Just having someone with her added a sense of security, but she never admitted her fears to us. For example, whenever there was a thunderstorm, she would raise the blinds to the top of the windows and open drapes and curtains so we could all watch the show together. I was an adult when I found out she was afraid of thunderstorms. I reminded her of watching the show with us.

"That's so I would not pass my fear on to you. I was afraid of the dark, too, but I used to send you upstairs in the dark to fetch a handkerchief I did not really need so you would not be afraid."

Maman vividly remembered one Sunday long ago when she was a teenager seeing a young girl putting up a brave front. My mother was approaching the church and saw this young country girl walking up the steps to the church when she was suddenly unable to advance. Of all things to happen, her red flannel petticoat fell to the ground around her ankles! A number of parishioners saw this too! The girl looked down, saw her petticoat, stepped out of it, picked it up, gave it a quick snap, folded it, rolled it, tucked it under her arm and had the wisdom to walk into the church with her head held high. Maman could only imagine how embarrassed she must have been, but she admired her self-assurance.

"I never forgot that," my mom told us.

I think she shared this story with us to stress the importance of self-confidence and how you can overcome challenges by having a positive mindset, being strong, and feeling secure with your decisions. Maman believed that self-assurance and success go hand in hand.

Dynamique Familiale Mal Interprétée
(Family Dynamics Misunderstood)

Most of the time the atmosphere in our home was lively, loving, and warm. That is not to say that there were not sibling rivalries and pettiness, infractions to the rules, squabbles for the same toy and messes created by children which involved reprimands and punishment. This is where Maman excelled. She was the authority in the house, and when she said, 'No', she never changed her mind. She stood firm.

Routine punishment meant sitting in Maman's rocking chair for a set period of time. One could knit, embroider, read, rock, or sit still, but they could not talk to others. When time was up, an apology to Maman was expected. There were times when two of us would have to sit in rocking chairs. Give Madeleine thirty minutes in a rocking chair? She could sit there for hours absorbed in her book or whatever she was doing. If Maman mentioned her time was up, she'd say,

"It's okay, I'm comfortable; I'm enjoying this book."

For major crimes, we had to go to bed at seven o'clock, which meant no interacting after dinner. Other times Maman would say, "There will be no dessert for you tonight."

Whenever Madeleine, the independent one, was denied dessert, she would say,

"Well, I didn't feel like it tonight anyhow."

If we ate soup, Madeleine would have not one but two bowls knowing there was no dessert for her.

"This is great soup," she'd say.

Then she would eat the main course.

"Ah, this is delicious, I think I'll have some more."

She ate with more relish than usual. Come dessert time, she would say,

"I really don't care what it is tonight. I'm stuffed!"

She would watch us eat our dessert as if she were sick to her stomach. Maman would tell her to stop but Madeleine always tried hard to make it unenjoyable for us whenever she couldn't have any.

The few times my sister had to go to bed at seven, she started yawning at around six, so she had everyone yawning. She would put on her nightgown and robe and yawn some more. By six-thirty she'd announce,

"I just can't stay up anymore. Maman, I will give you a goodnight kiss now; I'm just too sleepy to stay up."

And off to bed she'd go.

Years later, Maman said to me that she never knew if she was punishing her or doing her a favour, so I asked Madeleine one day.

"Were you punished or did you really not care?"

"Yes, for sure I felt punished, I just didn't want the others to know it had an effect on me."

Madeleine was quite a performer.

Maman knew that Papa was in financial difficulty.

"I'll manage," he would say.

However, the next time we went to my grandparents in the spring, Grand'papa Pinard asked my father how he stood financially. My father told him the truth.

"Send me your bills. I'll pay them," Grand'papa said.

Although he did not like to do so, Papa sent him the bills because they were choking the family. He also wanted things to be pleasant for Maman and did not want her to worry. Though he had asked that she not open his mail, she saw the envelopes and knew he was being dunned.

Papa said to me much later that he felt rescued to a degree when Grand'papa paid the mountain of bills, but he found it difficult to feel warmly towards him because when Maman was so sick, he had refused to help when it was so badly needed. Grand'papa later apologized to my father. He had felt that my father was holding on to false hope by keeping her in hospital, especially when he couldn't afford it. Grand'papa did not understand depression and thought it was unreasonable to keep her there as she would never get better, so what was the point of spending all that money he didn't have?

"Just bring her home," he used to tell my father.

Papa never told my mother the cost of her hospitalization.

"We earned it together, we spend it together," he would say.

They never discussed this part of their lives in front of us, and Maman never even mentioned to me that she had been hospitalized. I once read in a magazine that a man had been to jail for something and when he was released, his wife would not take him back.

My father was an honest man who would never get into trouble with the law, but I asked Maman a hypothetical question one day:

"If Papa went to jail, would you take him back when he came out?"

"He has been so good to me, beyond what you can ever understand," she said. "There is nothing I could not forgive him for, unless it was a terrible crime, of course."

And Papa always said, "Your mother is the best person in the world."

I heard him say that hundreds of times, and I'm sure all my sisters would say the same. Between my father's love for her, our love for her, and her faith, my mother was a very lucky woman!

La Saison du Carêmes
(Lenten Season)

During Lenten season it was customary in all the parishes to have a retreat of sorts that lasted for weeks. Missionary priests serviced the parishioners by preaching the sermons for the duration of the retreat.

One week for women, one week for men, one week for children and youth. Although the style of preaching differed from parish to parish, the sermons in our church during Lenten season seemed to be a time where all possible sins were brought to light. The focus was more on what not to do as opposed to positive encouragement. Perhaps it was in the hopes it would lead parishioners to ask for forgiveness or even a lifestyle change for some.

Some of the parishioners were left feeling somewhat belittled and almost guilty by this style of preaching. Life was difficult for most during the Great Depression; they lived payday to payday. They did not have the wherewithal to commit most of the sins that were talked about. Factory hours were from six in the morning to six at night with an hour for lunch, six days per week. There were those who were starving because there was no work or public support of any kind in small towns and villages. There was barely enough money to put food on the tables in many homes, and people used the least heat they could because the money to keep warm and toasty was not there. Many people let their stoves die out at night only to get up in freezing houses in the morning so the wood pile would last through the winter. Children and young people often went to school wearing insufficient clothes to be comfortable. They wore worn-out shoes with cardboard inside to make them last longer. Life was difficult for so many, and Maman felt the church should be offering compassion, reassurance, and hope for this population of hard-working people.

Confession was on Wednesday evenings of each of these retreat weeks. In addition to the regular confessional, collapsible ones were set up in the main aisle. Everyone had to go to confession when it was their retreat week. Women talked about it amongst themselves. Those who had not gone questioned in trepidation. Some who had gone said it felt like the priests were a little bit tough, while others explained their relief by feeling forgiven for whatever sin they had committed.

Collection plates went around every day to pay the visiting missionaries for their service to the parish, but the money donated was probably minimal. The people really had little or no money to give.

Maman dutifully went to sermons several times; however, Papa had asked her not to go to confession, fearing it might upset her.

"We're going to do something different this year," Papa said.

He called a Monastery in Granby, Quebec, twelve miles away, made an appointment with a monk for Saturday afternoon and took my mom there. My father explained

Maman's medical history to him and said more children was out of the question. He understood. Every couple of months thereafter, my parents went to confession together at the Granby Monastery.

We loved Easter when we were young because we didn't have to wear rubbers to church with our new Easter outfits and we received nice Easter eggs. Hunts were not customary throughout my childhood, and Maman sent out a warning this particular year.

"Don't expect too much for Easter because there's not much money these days."

Before she went to bed every night, Maman set the table for breakfast, but on Easter morning she had turned our cereal bowls upside down. Of course, we peeked. Under each bowl was a paper egg Maman had made. Her drawing style was easy to recognize—lots of colourful and detailed flowers, very embellished. Another warning now came from Madeleine.

"Don't look disappointed. Say how pretty the eggs are. Don't complain. If they don't have the money, they can't buy the eggs."

Of course, we were disappointed. We went to Mass, came home, and sat down to breakfast. No one was in a hurry to turn over her bowl. Thérèse finally did and—miracle of miracles—the eggs had turned to chocolate with sugar flowers of many colours. In fact, all the eggs had turned to chocolate. We were not made to admit we had peaked; our faces surely gave us away.

In April, Maman was once again at the sewing machine preparing summer dresses. She took me to the store to pick material and to look at patterns. She let me choose things, but she guided my taste.

"This print might be a bit too large; don't you think?"

"I'm wondering if this pattern might be too complicated?"

"Oh yes, that's a lovely small print and a very pretty colour. Or a nice solid colour would be pretty too, but you choose the material you would like."

We bought thread and other notions. She made chambray dresses in pale green and medium blue for the twins, and both sets were embroidered. The green one had yellow cats chasing a ball of gold wool just above the hem. The blue dress had a white peter pan collar with gold cording ending in a tassel down the front. Five girls' times several dresses each to wash and iron each week was a lot of laundry.

While Maman paid for her clothes from her private revenue, she knew it was important for Papa to dress well so he looked successful and prosperous. Customers would have more confidence in a well-dressed man and the merchandise he sold, so the clothing budget was used almost exclusively for him. To do this, she had to recycle Papa's clothes. He wore white or light blue shirts with a fine print, and the collars eventually wore out. She did a fine job of removing shirt collars and sewing the undercollar on top. Once the collars were worn out completely, she would cut the shirt into squares and transform them into handkerchiefs. When the seats and the knees of Papa's pants showed wear, Maman would cut off the legs which were very wide during the thirties, take them apart, clean the material, press it, and make pleated skirts. These skirts were warm and comfortable and easy to hang up. If she had enough material, she was able to make a small beret to match on occasion. In our kitchen there was a built-in cabinet on the wall which held the fold-down ironing board. I never knew if my father built that or if it was already there when we moved in, but it was where Maman did her ironing and the board was out of the way when not in use.

The thick overcoats men wore in those days were solid colours on the top, however, the underside of the material had a small plaid pattern. Maman took the worn coats apart, cleaned and pressed the pieces and made a coat, plaid side out, for one of us out of those portions of the material which had remained unworn. I know I had two such winter coats before I was fourteen.

By the time fall was approaching, Maman would pack away our spring and summer clothes in trunks we had in our bedrooms, as we might still fit into them the following year. Whatever did not fit anymore were either kept for the twins or donated to our church for families in need. Once everything packed away, out came our fall and winter clothes. We settled in for winter to arrive, which was just around the bend.

Captivé par la Messe de Minuit
(Captivated with Midnight Mass)

For Christmas 1933, Papa and Maman decided we should go to my grandparents' for the holidays. We left in the early afternoon on December 23rd for the seventy-five-mile ride. Heaters in cars were not what they are today, and not much heat travelled to the back seat. Before we left, Maman heated four bricks for hours in the oven and then placed them on the floor in the back of the car. We were warmly dressed and had a car blanket and Papa's raccoon coat to keep us warm. Maman was in the front seat wearing her black Persian lamb coat, and Papa wore the muskrat-lined coat he had inherited from his father.

All went well until the car broke down. Papa tried and tried again, but it would not start. We were on a narrow country road that was further narrowed by high snowbanks on each side. Papa pushed the car to the side of the road to allow oncoming cars to pass. He was afraid the radiator would freeze, so he placed the raccoon coat over the hood of the car and left on foot wearing his muskrat-lined coat. As he passed each farmhouse, he looked for telephone lines going to the houses. He saw only one. He went along a long driveway, knocked at the door, identified himself as

Vincent from Massey-Harris, explained the situation and asked to use the phone. The woman said no! Papa thought perhaps she was alone and was too fearful to open the door. My father understood because there were so many needy people walking from town to town who were looking for food, a bed or anything people could spare.

Two hours or so after he left, Papa and a mechanic arrived in a truck. The mechanic could not find the trouble, so he towed us about four miles to his garage; not the most reassuring position for those in the car. It was a long, cold, bumpy ride. We were all wondering how long it would be before we would be on our way to my grandparents'. The mechanic looked at the car's insides and could not find the problem, so he raised the car to the garage's ceiling on the hoist. Nothing. There was no public transportation to Sainte-Monique or Waterloo from Acton Vale or Roxton Pond (I'm not sure what town we were in), but the mechanic had a friend who had a horse and buggy so he suggested we call him. When he arrived, we all climbed in and off we went. We eventually arrived in Sainte-Monique after a two-hour ride. It was cold, but we were happy to be there.

At almost nine years old, Maman felt I was old enough to go to midnight Mass. Getting up at eleven at night out of a dead sleep was not easy. It was bitterly cold outside, but at least the church was directly across the street. High Mass started and a priest, accompanied by several altar boys, brought out the statue of the Child Jesus and placed it in a large manger (crèche) where all the other personages were waiting. The pastor was in the loft playing the violin—he was very good—along with the organist and the choir.

After the Child was placed in the manger, a large group of boys aged about six to twelve entered. They were dressed in sheepskin and holding tall staffs. They marched slowly around the church, singing in the high-pitched voices of youth, and looking for the Child to adore.

When the service was over, Maman made us wait for people to leave, then said,

"Let's go see the Messiah (Allons voir le Messie.)"

I thought it was all so impressive. It was a fine service; I was captivated by the midnight Mass. It was the one I most enjoyed of all those I'd been to.

As we entered the house after the church service, we couldn't help but notice the aromas of Christmas cooking and the woodstove burning.

"Go put your coats up in your bedrooms, children (Allez mettre vos manteaux en haut dans vos chambres, les enfants.)"

We chose to go upstairs through the 'secret door' like always, as Grand'maman knew we would. We were so surprised when we opened the secret door. On the stairs were thirteen small gift-wrapped boxes all the way up the steps, one for each child. Each box had our name on it with the message: Joyeux Noël de Tante Marie-Anne (Merry Christmas from Aunt Marie-Anne). We excitedly showed our parents when we went into the dining room. They acted as though they were as surprised as we were and told us to go ahead and open them. They were beautiful hand-sewn Christmas ornaments made by my aunt. They had our first initial on the reverse side. Mine was a gingerbread man, Thérèse got a candy cane with a bow on it, Marthe got a stocking with cuff, Louise a present with bow, and

Madeleine's was a Santa. Because Marthe and Madeleine had the same initial, my aunt put 'M E' on Marthe's as her middle name was Eva. Other ornaments I remember were a bell, a star, a church, an angel, and a tree. Each one of us hugged our aunt, thanking her. Every Christmas after that we always hung our special ornament on our own Christmas trees.

While we were at midnight Mass, the nannies had set all the food out on the extended dining room table. They put a gorgeous flower arrangement in the centre of the table and a candle burned at each end. Christmas music was softly playing in the background. My grandparents, Aunt Marie-Anne, Marcelle, the seven of us, Uncle Antonius, his second wife Margueritte, the four children from his first marriage, Uncle Onil, his wife and their three children—twenty-two in all sat down; ready for the Réveillon to begin. We were thankful for large rooms and plenty of them.

Our meal was the traditional tourtière, meatballs, vegetables, homemade bread, potatoes, and desserts of all kinds. There was always plenty of leftovers for Christmas day. Between the sweet smells of Christmas, the table setting and the food, I was in heaven. The laughter and chatter filled the room, and we were surrounded by people we loved and who loved us. It was a Christmas to remember, a memory etched in our minds.

The weather turned bitterly cold on December 26th. The pipes froze several times, and the uncles and Papa worked with torches to thaw them out in the morning. Since the house was made of clapboard, there was always the danger of fire, so the children were kept well out of the way.

Uncle Onil and his brood left shortly after Christmas since he had to go to work. We were to stay on through New Year's Day and return by train since the car was still in whatever town we had left it in before Christmas. The weather became increasingly cold.

On January 3rd, we got up in the middle of the night, got dressed, had a warm breakfast, and were loaded into two sleighs to go the four miles to the station to catch the seven o'clock train. We arrived in good time—with Papa this was a must—and waited outside in -33°F temperatures while farmers arrived with many tall metal milk cans. Finally, the station master let us in the station. We waited with many others. At nine o'clock it was announced that the train was not coming because it was stuck somewhere, so we rented two sleighs and returned to my grandparents'. We had always been most welcome at my grandparents' home until this time. Aunt Marie-Anne opened the door and looked at us with an air of discouragement.

"I've just changed all the beds," she said almost in tears.

My parents understood. The nannies were normally the ones to change the beds but Maman figured that Marie-Anne was helping them out. It was a lot of work to entertain the seven of us over a week-long stay.

Maman and Papa took the clean sheets off, folded them and put the less fresh ones back on the bed to reduce my aunt's workload. They would have preferred the clean sheets, however, my mother always preached 'Peace in the family'.

Sometime after lunch, Thérèse was alone in the kitchen and we heard a loud crash. We all ran to see what happened. A heavy, grey, wooden picture frame of the Holy Family beside the door that led to the store had fallen and crashed on the back of a chair on its way to the floor.

"What did you do to the picture?" Aunt Marie-Anne asked with frustration in her voice.

"I was just looking at it and it fell," Thérèse explained.

No one seemed to believe poor little Thérèse other than my parents, and she maintained throughout her life that she was just looking at it when it fell. Recently, we had a mirror that fell in one of our bathrooms because the heavy string had simply worn out; no one was even looking at the mirror when it fell. It made me think of Thérèse and the Holy Family picture.

On January 4th, my birthday, we got up around 4:30 a.m., had a silent breakfast, piled into the two same sleighs, and trekked to the train station where we waited until nine o'clock once again.

"At least they were polite enough not to say, don't come back this time," Maman said laughingly to Papa.

It was sotto voce, but I heard.

A friend drove Papa to Acton Vale to pick up his car a few days after we got home. This was a good thing because he was going to need it for the house hunting that was just around the corner.

Au Revoir Monsieur et Madame Laroche
(Goodbye Mr. and Mrs. Laroche)

Elissa had had a boyfriend for a long time before she came to work for us. At first, he came to pick her up and they went for walks, but eventually Maman told her if she wanted to receive him at the house, she could. He sat in the living room with her on Sunday afternoons. He was pressing to get married, so, sadly, Elissa left us and was replaced by her first cousin, Juliette Desjardins. We really missed Elissa and her quiet and loving ways, her quiet laugh, and her lively grey eyes. Juliette was as hard working, but not so quiet. She was vivacious and had an infectious laugh—everything was funny to her. She was twenty-three, flushed, a bit overweight, busty and had curly black hair.

In mid-March, Elissa's sister Lucie, who worked as a nanny for Dr. Richelieu, a dentist, called and asked Juliette to meet her at the dentist's home after supper. Lucie said it was very important.

"I had better go," Juliette said to Maman. "She has never called me like this before. It must be urgent."

She returned clearly shaken.

"I'll tell you about it later," she said, which meant after the children are in bed.

Apparently, Mrs. LaRoche had gone to the Richelieu's home in the afternoon to play bridge. She had laughingly said that they had decided to get rid of us as tenants because they had found a couple with only two daughters, so it would be much quieter. Mrs. LaRoche added that she was tired of hearing me jump the two steps between the dining room and the kitchen. Maman frequently told me not to do that, but I forgot just as frequently. Mrs. Richelieu asked what my parents' reaction had been, but Mrs. LaRoche said they would wait until the last minute to tell us. Perhaps they had regretted lowering our rent to $18 from $23 a month when Papa's salary was lowered from $120 to $90. Such was the economic squeeze of the times. Mrs. Richelieu felt it was unfair not to let people with five children know as far ahead of time as possible and asked Lucie to call Juliette and forewarn my parents.

Papa and Maman began looking for a large, well-kept apartment in earnest but were unable to find one. Maman decided to sell her General Electric and another stock which she had held on to for years and to invest that money in a house, so they began a house search. A short time later they bought a house from Benoit Joubert, which was always known to us as, at the Joubert's (chez les Joubert). The asking price was $1800, my parents offered $1700 and they settled on $1750. It was probably worth a lot more, but those were the prices amid the Depression. They bought it for a song, as the saying goes. My parents could not pay it in full however, so part of the payment was a loan from the bank.

With five children, a nanny and my parents, we had aplenty to move. A couple of Papa's friends who had trucks offered to help which was a tremendous help to my father. It was May 1934, and the weather was not cold.

What we called 'our new abode' in Waterloo was a farmhouse with a lot of property. It had a covered, closed-in porch at the front that was almost the full length of the house. We walked in through the vestibule. There was a place for our boots, shoes, and a rack to hang our coats. Maman put a chest there for all our mittens, scarves, and hats. To the right of the vestibule, you entered a small parlour that Papa claimed for his office. There was a dining room and kitchen on the other end of the house. Beside the kitchen was a pantry and a storage room, and down the hall was the master bedroom which Maman and Papa took. One feature my parents were impressed with was that a second small bathroom had been added beside the storage room. There was no bathtub in this one, only in the bathroom upstairs. With eight of us living in the house, the second bathroom was extremely convenient. There were three bedrooms upstairs, the main bathroom and a linen closet. Madeleine had one bedroom, Thérèse and I another, and Louise and Marthe were in the same bedroom with Juliette.

We had a very large yard and lots of room to play. Our closest neighbour to us were the Savoie's. They had three children—two girls and a boy who were approximately the same ages as we were. Amongst other games, we used to like to play tag and hide-and-seek outside. We had a big old oak tree in our backyard as well. Sometimes I would climb the old tree and hide in there. Thérèse followed me a lot when playing hide-and-seek, and she would hide behind the tree while I was up, in the tree. They would find Thérèse first, then me. Part of the fun was climbing the tree. Uncle Antonius had taught me to hide in high places to have a good view of everybody and everything, and I never forgot that.

Madeleine would play hide-and-seek with us, but on other nice summer days she would sometimes wander off to the old oak tree by herself with a book. She liked munching on a nice juicy apple as she read. Maman always knew when it must be a good book because she would sit out there for hours. My sister always did love the outdoors.

Maman and Papa became friends with Mr. and Mrs. Savoie, and they would come over on Saturday nights to play a few games of cards. Juliette would prepare snack foods in the afternoon, which we were not allowed to eat as they had to be saved for the company. Although we were not involved in the adult card games, we enjoyed the snacks. Juliette always made enough for everybody.

There were four rocking chairs in our house, and my favourite was Maman's bedroom rocker because it was small and comfortable. It was the chair she used to rock babies in, to create a bond with them, to make them feel her presence and her warmth. There was the huge leather rocker with wide, flat oak arms in the living room which my father used to rock us in while singing songs to us. The third chair was a large, cumbersome chair that was best suited for the porch. The slats in the seats were bothersome, and the parts which made up the back were too far apart to be comfortable. The fourth chair, and my second favourite, was a smallish criss-crossed caned chair that was painted in whatever colour spring had inspired Maman that year. The front legs protruded slightly above the seat, and Maman had made a cushion for it that had a story of its own.

When my parents married, Papa had an old sweater which he loved dearly because his mother had knitted it for him. Since his mother had died, the sweater had become irreplaceable but tattered beyond use. Under the circumstances, Maman did not have the heart to throw it away, so she cut it in pieces and stuffed it in a pretty cushion she made. She never said a word about it and hoped Papa had forgotten.

"Whatever happened to that sweater of mine that was in rags?" he asked one day. "The one my mother made for me."

Long silence.

Maman whispered, "You're sitting on it."

Recycling, regardless of the item, was never taken for granted during the Great Depression. In this case, it was a sentimental item that she did not take for granted either. She knew it meant a lot to my father and would never disrespect his emotions. To Maman's contentment, my dad did not have a rebuttal. At least the sweater was still around, albeit in a second incarnation.

La Vie sur la Ferme, 1934
(Life on the Farm, 1934)

My father chose to keep his job at Massey-Harris. Although he now owned a farm, this kind of life was new to him. He liked working for Massey-Harris and thought if he ever tired of farm life, at least he would still have a job.

He hired four men to work the farm, and they were more than happy to take the job as they did not want to be sent to war, should another war breakout. Working on a farm meant one could be exempt from going to war as the job was considered essential because of the food chain.

Papa decided to purchase four workhorses, half breads or grade horses as they were called, for working the fields. There was already a stable on the property for the horses, and he also purchased a buggy as an extra means of transportation.

My father was not only very protective of his daughters, wife, and nanny, he was also protective of his animals. Maman said he gave the employees a warning.

"If any one of you ever lay a hand on any of the females in this house, you'll immediately be jobless. You'll have to deal with me first, then the police, and I'll press charges.

As for my animals, if anybody hits one, you'll be fired on the spot."

Papa never had an issue with any of them.

My sisters and I liked feeding the horses McIntosh apples, which they never refused. Although all the four horses were tame, one was more domesticated than the others; my twin sisters would say he was a horse with a wonderful disposition. He was calm, patient, intelligent, trusting and forgiving; Papa used to say. If possible, this one seemed to have inherited a quality of trying to please. The twins were around him a lot as they had not begun school yet. My parents let Louise and Marthe choose a name for him, so 'Ti-Lou' it was. Ti-Lou was a catchy name in French which translates to Little Lou in English. Lou can be a boy's name and Lou-Lou can be the short form for Louise, my sister's name (Marthe called her twin sister Lou-Lou her whole life). Both girls became really attached to this horse.

We not only had horses on the farm, but we also raised chickens and had a cow, Bessy. Many chores had to be done in a day: tend to the large vegetable garden, collect wood for the woodstove, milk Bessy (two or three times a day), feed the animals, haul water, clean the chicken coop, collect the eggs, and harness the horses for working the fields.

While Maman and Juliette were busy doing the house chores, the hired help manned the farm, Marthe and Louise played (as little children do) and Papa was gone to work. Madeleine, Thérèse and I either played outside, read, knit, or did crafts and helped with some of the farm chores in between. We wanted to learn how to milk Bessy, but Papa would not allow it for fear we would get hurt. Life on the farm proved to be a busy time for everyone.

My father grew crops and the horses were used to pull the plows, and harvest the crops. Papa managed to maintain the farm and feed his family between his job at Massey-Harris and selling the crops, eggs, milk, and maple syrup.

There was a small mountain close to our house that we called 'the pretty mountain' (la belle montagne). On summer weekends, Papa would sometimes take us to the top. Juliette would pack us a picnic lunch, and my dad would carry the basket up the mountain. My mother was not able to come because of her asthma; the climb and walk was too much for her. She also had the twins to look after. It took us about twenty minutes to make it to the top, and the view was breathtaking! We could see the village and Waterloo Lake, which was surrounded by other small mountains and trees. Sometimes we'd be lucky enough to see a train arriving in the village. Papa would open the picnic basket knowing we were eager to see what Juliette had packed for us. We were never disappointed; she made sure to pack foods she knew we liked. After lunch we would sit for a little before trekking down the mountain again. We enjoyed the splendid view and listening to Papa's stories. He would talk about things like the village, the mountain, the farm, our animals, and the lake. He had a knack for adding humour to his anecdotes. Having time with Papa was always fun.

My father and his brother Charlie were the clowns in their family. They were both very funny people and made us laugh a lot. Papa was a good storyteller, and he had plenty of stories to tell. His sense of humour brightened our day and made us feel good. He seemed to find humour in a lot of things. He was an intelligent man but also quick and witty. We loved spending time with him, so to go to 'la belle montagne' with Papa was a big deal for us.

Most kids have a hobby they enjoy doing. At a fairly young age, Madeleine took a liking to drawing and was good at it. Because she loved the outdoors, she would take her pencil and pad to the old oak tree when the weather was nice. My mother would make a big tadoo over her drawings because they were good but also to give her motivation to draw more.

"It's a way to express your thoughts, your visions, and a wonderful pastime for you (C'est une façon d'exprimer tes pensées, tes visions et un merveilleux passe-temps pour toi,)" she would say to Madeleine.

Country winter scene by Madeleine (Vincent) Libotte, 1938

I am not sure what my sister did with most of her drawings, but I do remember seeing a few hung on the walls of her own home when she was older.

Louise was also artistic and took up drawing when she was around ten years old. Many years later, she had not lost the love of drawing because she once again took up drawing and painting once she retired. She was very good at it too and Louise's artworks were beautiful. In fact, they were displayed in different art exhibitions throughout Montreal.

Maman always set aside about an our in the afternoons every day to do her devotionals and recite the Rosary. In the evenings my parents liked to read. My mother liked to read books of religious content while my father liked psychology and chemistry books. Once the sun had gone down and dusk turned to darkness, Maman would turn on the lights as we settled in until bedtime. Madeleine would draw, I would knit and Thérèse and the twins would play with their dolls. Sometimes we would break out into song. Except for Papa, none of us had a good singing voice, but we all sang anyway. Even Juliette would often join in. She couldn't sing either, but when we all sang in harmony, it sounded pretty good. Strength in numbers …

One warm and balmy summer's night just after supper, Papa said to us, "Come on girls, let's go for a walk." It was the weekend.

Madeleine was at a friend's house, but Thérèse and I were happy to go. We had been walking for ten minutes or so when we spotted a man lying in the ditch! Papa ran over to him. It was old Mr. Gilbert who was known to have a drinking problem. Papa looked at me and said, "Hurry, go get help! Knock on Mr. Pascal's door and explain what happened. Tell him I need help."

The Pascal's lived close to where we were. I must have looked a little shocked because Papa said,

"Go right away, Pierrette (Vas-y tout de suite, Pierrette.)"

I ran up Mr. Pascal's long driveway, knocked and he answered. I told him what happened.

"I'll be right back!" he yelled to his wife, and asked his son André to come with us.

At the ditch, Papa asked Mr. Pascal and his son if they would stay with me, Thérèse and Mr. Gilbert.

"I won't be long. I'm just going to get my truck" (an old Chevy pickup truck for farm use). "Stay with Mr. Pascal and André, girls."

With that, he was gone but returned in no time. My father, Mr. Pascal and his son got Mr. Gilbert up and put him in Papa's truck.

"He's dead weight," I heard my father say.

Papa told Mr. Pascal he was going to drive Mr. Gilbert to our farmhouse.

"You can come with me because I'll need help to get him out of the truck. André, if you could walk my girls back to our place that would be appreciated."

Old Mr. Gilbert lived alone and my father did not want to leave him in such a state. On our walk home, André asked us lots of questions: how many in our family, how long had we lived there, did we have any animals, where did we go to school, etc.

When we arrived home, we saw Mr. Pascal standing outside with Papa waiting for us.

"Where's Mr. Gilbert?" I asked.

Papa told us he was resting on a lounge chair in the living room. My father thanked Mr. Pascal and his son for their help and they left. We walked into the house and saw poor old Mr. Gilbert sound asleep. When he finally woke up, Maman made him a couple of strong cups of tea. My parents then felt it would be safe to take him back to his house. Later that night, I heard my father say to Maman,

"Poor old Mr. Gilbert. He didn't know if he was on foot, on horseback or on third base."

The following day, my parents sat the three of us down. It was time for another life lesson and an opportunity they were not going to let go by without a discussion. They explained the many vices of alcohol to us in an age-appropriate way.

Mr. Pascal's son, André, was Madeleine's age, however, he and I slowly became good friends following the incident with old Mr. Gilbert. I would invite him over whenever we played hide-and-seek or tag, or we would go for a walk or play cards together. Although he was a boy, Maman allowed it because she knew we were just friends.

We settled into our home quite nicely. Madeleine was now eleven, I was nine, Thérèse was seven, and the twins, three.

This was the summer Maman decided to show us how to sew. We had watched her do it our whole life, but now it was our turn. She figured we were old enough and she made sure to teach us all the art of sewing before we left home. She believed it was a very important skill for us to master. Maman pulled out scraps of materials and remnants and made us take turns at her Singer sewing machine. We practiced a lot and eventually got the hang of it.

"Soon we'll make a pretty dress and you will see that it's not complicated (Bientôt nous allons faire une belle robe et vous aller voir que c'est pas compliqué)," Maman said. Then to Thérèse she said, "You and me are going to make a pretty dress for your doll (Toi et moi, on va faire une belle robe pour ta poupée.)"

So the first pieces Thérèse ever made were of doll clothes that she sewed by hand. Because Madeleine and I were older, we each used the sewing machine to make a dress as our first piece. Maman had enough material for one dress which was of a cotton seersucker that was light and cool to wear in the summer. The other was of a different type of cotton material. The seersucker was striped, light blue and white. Because I really liked the colour and thought it would be just perfect for me, Maman said I could make the dress out of the seersucker material. *Oh thank you so much, Maman*, I thought. I did not want Madeleine to know how truly excited I was, fearing she would plead with my mother for the same material. Hence, I put on a good act and got to keep the seersucker material, and Madeleine made her dress out of cotton using a light yellow and white checkered pattern. It was a simple dress pattern, just straight, no pleats. We decided to add pockets at hip level to my dress to give it a different look than Madeleine's. Because we sewed my dress with the stripe pattern lengthwise, Maman suggested we sew the pockets horizontal to give it a little flair. I thought that was a great idea.

My sister and I wore those dresses to church on some Sundays and felt proud of our accomplishment. We continued to practice over the summer and made a few other items of clothing—petticoats and aprons, I remember. Sewing served me well in my adult life and was something I really enjoyed. I did not have to do it, I just really liked to. I made some nice outfits and dresses for myself throughout the years. Madeleine sewed in her adult years too, and even taught some of her children how to sew. Maman's talent and passion for sewing was passed down the generations. All five of us benefitted from knowing how to sew.

By July 1934, our parents were preparing to register us once again at the Maplewood Convent, however, this time they had a very different plan for us. One we could not have foreseen.

À Notre Grande Surprise
(Much to Our Surprise)

My parents had discussed this subject at length before revealing their plan to us. Once Madeleine, Thérèse and I were presented with this new change, we all talked about it together with my parents for days. They wanted to register us as boarders instead of day scholars at the Maplewood Convent. It would reduce Maman's workload and give her more time to care for and spend with Marthe and Louise instead of looking after five of us. It would also eliminate the walk to and from school every day, which we didn't mind because there were some awfully cold days in the winter. I felt the cold a lot, so I liked the thought of not having to walk in the freezing temperatures. Although a little apprehensive, we finally agreed. Thérèse was very unsure, but because Madeleine and I agreed, she did too. As the eldest, Madeleine confidently said it would be a new and fun experience for us. We already had friends there, she said, but to live there would be something altogether new.

Maman helped us pack our belongings in late August and we moved to the convent a couple of days before school was due to begin. Madeleine was right. We liked boarding school and made some good friends along the way.

Our classrooms consisted of wooden desks with the seats attached. We were all assigned our desks, which faced the chalkboard at the front of the classroom. We had to practice writing every day because it was regarded as important that we have neat, proper, and readable handwriting. We used ink pens that were dipped into inkwells to write. I made drips and spills by using too much ink, but I did master the craft with practice. Reading, writing, science, math, religion, and physical education were subjects I was taught. During warm weather, we went outside for our physical education, which I loved.

The norm for a dormitory was four girls to a room. However, my parents had asked the headmistress that all three of us stay together in the same room. She agreed and it made us feel more secure. Our dormitory had a long table with a bar underneath to hang our towels and facecloths. We had to use our own washbowls, soaps, and towels. The large closet and two small dressers with all our possessions were shared amongst the three of us. We were responsible for making our beds every morning before going for our breakfast.

I always thought that our dining hall looked pretty. There were long tables with chairs on either side. They always used white tablecloths except for on special occasions or holidays when flowers were placed as a centerpiece on each table. The dining hall always looked so clean, and the plates and utensils set in an orderly fashion. Our food was pretty simple, usually meat, a vegetable, potatoes, or rice, and a dessert of some sort. However, two of my favourites were the chili and homemade soups that were served during the winter months.

We missed our parents and the twins, but life at the convent was busy and kept our minds occupied. We returned home four times a year: Christmas holidays which were always joyous, Halloween, some weekends during the maple syrup season, and to spend our summers there.

We did not want to miss Halloween when we were young so we made sure to return home in October for this event. Halloween was fun at our house. Because Maman was a pro at sewing and she had such a vivid imagination, she made all our costumes from scraps of materials she had around the house. Some costumes I remember were ghosts, goblins, witches, and clowns. We would go trick-or-treating with Papa and Elissa while my mother stayed home to pass out candy. Elissa came along mostly to keep an eye on the twins. After Elissa left us, it was Juliette who came with us. We were only permitted to go to homes of people we knew. We used pillowcases to hold our candy (bonbons). Upon returning home, out came the candy as we spilled it on the floor. My parents would go through the candy while my sisters and I were busy exchanging this candy for that one. Even when we got too old for trick-or-treating, we still went home for Halloween because we liked taking the twins out in their costumes.

Each time we did come home, Marthe and Louise were always as happy to see us as we were them. We sure looked forward to those three summer months at home. I also missed André while I was at school, so it was nice to hang out with him once again.

The years went by quickly. Thérèse was nine, I was eleven and Madeleine was thirteen in the summer of 1936. In July, Grand'maman and Grand'papa Pinard phoned my parents with a unique request. They asked if Thérèse could come and live with them for a year.

"We are not young anymore, and we could really use the help. We will enroll Thérèse in the Sainte-Monique School for the start of September," they told my parents.

They were feeling overwhelmed.

"She really likes it in Sainte-Monique with us," said Grand'maman, "And we would love nothing more than to have her company."

Although my grandparents had sold their store several years prior and moved to a smaller house, at age seventy-nine and seventy-seven they knew the help would make life a bit easier for them, not to mention the fact that they would enjoy having Thérèse live with them for a while. Life had been so busy for them and they had been used to being surrounded by lots of people, so when it was just the two of them, they felt lonely at times; it was a big adaptation.

My parents discussed it for several days, and after talking with Thérèse, they agreed. Papa contacted the Maplewood Convent to cancel Thérèse's enrollment for that year. Thérèse said she would miss all of us, but she was also looking forward to life in Sainte-Monique. It was familiar territory, she had friends and relatives there, and she loved my grandparents.

Maman and the five of us girls packed our bags in August and headed for Sainte-Monique. We stayed for a week before saying goodbye to Thérèse. Because we had been at my grandparents' a lot over the years, we had made friends in the village, and we had some of them over to play cards and go for walks during the week.

The time came to say our goodbyes to our sister. That was difficult even though we knew we would see her again at Christmastime and the following summer. Maman especially had her reservations; however, she understood her parents needed help. Despite the separation difficulties, we did manage to say our goodbyes and head back to Waterloo.

De Retour à la Ferme
(Back on the Farm)

Life returned to normal back on the farm. Because we were getting older, Papa gave Madeleine and I permission to get Bessy, our cow, from the barn and take her out to the pasture. He wanted us to do this together until we became comfortable by ourselves. My good friend André came over a lot during the summer months, so whenever he was around, he would come with me to take Bessy back to the barn.

One gloomy evening, however, Bessy had a different idea. Without warning she suddenly stopped, turned around and took off for the pasture. André and I looked at each other, puzzled.

"Stay here, I'll get her," he said.

Bessy was half-walking, half-running towards the fence as if she decided she was leaving or something had caught her curiosity and she wanted to investigate! This was unusual behaviour for her. André walked towards Bessy in a slow and calm way so as not to spook her. He stood behind her and slowly got her walking in the direction of the barn. It took some time, but he finally did get her into the barn, safe and unharmed.

The twins started school in September 1936. Incredibly, their means of transportation every day was Ti-Lou, their favourite horse. This still amazes me: the farm employees trained this horse to learn the two-kilometre route to school! It was a straight line all the way except for one turn into the school. So, Ti-Lou drove my sisters, *on his own*, to and from school every day. He was their driver! He was taught the route, remembered it, and knew the routine. The twins did not even have to hold the reins on Ti-Lou, he just knew! He would often pass cars and other horses along the way but was never bothered by any of them and acted like he didn't have a care in the world. He would continue on his merry way because he had a job to do.

"Hurry girls, Ti-Lou has just arrived (Dépêchez-vous les filles, Ti-Lou vient juste d'arriver)," the teachers would often say at the end of the day.

When approaching home, Ti-Lou would always stop at the mailbox to let the girls off and they would walk up the long driveway as Ti-Lou headed for the stable. One of the workers would detach the buggy and Ti-Lou would either go to the field or simply go to the stable till the next morning. We all considered Ti-Lou to be one very special horse, and especially the twins. Ti-Lou continued to take the girls to and from school throughout their elementary school years.

L to R – Marthe & Louise
Courtesy of Sylvie

We all marvelled at how clever he was. One of Papa's worker once told me that some horses are intelligent, have excellent memories and respond well to consistent routines, hence the school route.

By the time Christmas rolled around we were usually ready for the school break. One day during Christmas break, André came over and we decided to go for a walk on our property. We came upon a small Winterberry Holly tree.

"Oh my gosh, André, look at this beautiful tree! It looks so Christmassy and here we are, just a few days away from Christmas. I wonder if we were meant to find this tree today?" I said with a quizzical look.

It was so pretty with its carmine and deep bright red berries against the freshly-fallen pure-white snow. *Picture perfect*, I thought. André stopped me and said,
"Pierrette, make a wish."
"What?"
He said, "Let's pretend that for each berry on this Holly tree one person's wish comes true. So, pick a berry, close your eyes, make a wish, then throw it as far as you can and I'll do the same."
So that's what we did.
"From now on, any time we spot a Holly tree we'll make sure to carry out our secret wishing pact."
He made me feel like this was an enchanted little tree! I never forgot that. It came to be a game between him and me. There's a saying 'Wish upon a star', but for me and André, our saying was:

To see a Holly Berry tree
Means a wish for you and me ...

Papa had a big surprise for us all this Christmas, 1936: our first radio—a Lee de Forest brand. We were excited beyond belief. After supper, we would gather in the living room and listen to the broadcasts and music.

Maman decided she would like to have us come back home for one weekend at the end of January to celebrate my and Madeleine's birthday. Papa came to pick us up with horse, buggy, blankets, and Ti-Lou at the helm. He knew we liked that and knew we were always excited to see Ti-Lou. That weekend we sat around in the living room after eating a delightful supper and a delicious birthday cake and turned the radio on. This is when we heard about the horrific Ohio River Flood of 1937. Papa brought us back to school Sunday afternoon of that weekend and we arrived at the convent in time for supper.

About two weeks later, we received a letter from Maman giving us an update on the Ohio River flood; this amid the Great Depression. Maman wrote: The damage caused by the flood resulted in property losses of 500 million, and one million people were left homeless. Approximately three hundred and eighty-five people died from this flood. She ended the letter by writing: We must count our blessings that we are safe.

On our property were a good number of sugar maple trees from which Papa produced maple syrup. The sugar bush had a small cabin where he boiled the sap, filtered the syrup, and packaged it. I'm not familiar with the whole process Papa used, but I do know those were some of the steps he took to making the syrup. The hired men tapped the trees in January and collected sap from mid-February until the end of March or beginning of April, depending on the weather. They would go to the tapped trees every day with the horses to collect from the aluminum sap pails and bring them to the cabin where the boiler was.

When it was ready to eat, Papa would come and get us from school on those weekends and take us home so we could enjoy the maple syrup as well. Me and my sisters' favourite was the maple syrup taffy. Even my mother, Papa, Juliette, and the workers liked it. We all did. Papa would pour the boiled syrup on clean pure white snow and say,

"You have to let it cool for a minute."

Once it had hardened a bit, we would pull the maple syrup taffy by twirling our wooden stick. We called it our 'taffy lollipop', which we ate while still a little warm. It was sweet and delicious. For maple syrup lovers like us, having a sugar bush on one's own property was grand. Once the maple syrup season was over, we would not return home until May when school ended.

Much to our excitement, it was time for Thérèse to return home. She told us all about her year with our grandparents and her stay in Sainte-Monique. She had really enjoyed her time and made some new friends at school while there. Thérèse came back in July, which happened to be the same month as her birthday. As a 'welcome home' we threw her a big birthday party with friends, family, handmade gifts, and a delicious cake. It was fun for all.

By the time Madeleine was fifteen and we were back in school, she decided to ask my parents for permission to walk downtown on Saturdays. Mom and Dad went over the safety rules with us and verified with the headmistress (directrice de l'école) at the convent that this would be OK. Before leaving the convent for our Saturday stroll in the village, we had to sign out and let one of the staff members know we were leaving the property. We usually went with our friends from school, Marie-Claire and Josée.

By this time, Maman and Papa had started giving us a small allowance. One of our favourite places to go was the small ice cream parlour on Main Street. They had delicious flavours of all kinds, and it was five cents for a two-scoop cone. When Madeleine ordered she still would say,

"And push down on it please."

Soon, the others did the same. With our cone in hand, we would cross the road to Foster Park, sit on the grass, eat our cone, talk, tell jokes, and laugh.

When the subject of boys we liked came up, we giggled like little girls, probably from shyness or embarrassment or nervousness. In any case, it certainly struck our funny bone! They used to tease me that André was my boyfriend, but I would deny it to the end. We enjoyed browsing through the shops and seeing the new fashions. We would say,

"One day when I get a job, I'm going to buy this dress or this purse or coat," to one another.

L to R – Louise (in front of railing) Pierrette, Thérèse (sitting on railing), Aunt Françoise, Madeleine, Marthe (in front of railing)
Courtesy of Sylvie

Occasionally we would stop into the bakery, which was about four doors down from the ice cream parlour and purchase a baked good for after supper. After hanging out downtown for a few hours we would trek back to the convent, always in time for supper. Our trips downtown were something we looked forward to, and they helped break up our week.

Madeleine's first job, of all places, was at the ice cream parlour! She was sixteen and was hired to work there on Saturdays. She was so excited at the thought of earning an income. She made thirty-three cents an hour and loved her job. When she made ice cream cones for customers, she would always, of course, 'push down on it'. She worked at the ice cream parlour until she graduated from the convent two years later.

My first unofficial job, also at sixteen, was during early summer and fall. I stayed at this job for two years. Papa sold eggs to merchants in the village. During the week, the hired help delivered the eggs, but on Saturday afternoons it was me and André. We used the buggy with Ti-Lou at the helm. It was fun.

My first official job was after I graduated high school. I was hired by The Bank of Montreal as a full-time teller. I would stay at this job for a couple of years until I decided to move back to the United States. My friend, Josée, who also worked at the bank, told me of her plans to move to Trenton, New Jersey. After many long discussions with her, we decided to both move there and share an apartment.

It proved to be most difficult to see André for the last time. Although our relationship was platonic, André was truly my best friend. When the time came to say our goodbyes, I did not know how I would ever get through this. He gave me a kiss on the cheek and held me in his arms. Of course, I cried, a lot! He had been such a good friend to me. He was fun, funny, reliable, kind and just an all-around nice guy. He too, cried. We promised to write each other.

"And don't ever forget Pierrette, whenever you see a Holly Berry tree, always remember to think of me and I'll think of you!" he said as he walked away.

From then on, whenever I happened to see a Holly tree, I would pick a berry, close my eyes, make a wish, and throw it with much enthusiasm ... all while remembering my best friend, André!

When Marthe and Louise started high school, Maman and Papa wanted them to go to English school to learn the language, so they sent them to Montreal West High School in Westmount. They had to travel by train to get there. Coincidentally, Papa's office for Massey-Harris was also located in Westmount. Once a week, Papa would make a trip to the office for his work, and he also went by the same train.

Marthe, High School years
Courtesy of Sylvie

All employees sat at the front of the train and all students at the back, so even though they were on the same train they did not see each other until they got off. Papa always tried to get a window seat because the girls were first to get off and he would wave goodbye to them as the train was leaving.

**Louise, High School years
Courtesy of Sylvie**

Life was changing so much for us. We had less free time and more responsibilities. Our interests were different; we focused more on jobs and the possibilities of furthering our educations. We wondered what adult life would look like and where it would take us. Where would our permanent home be?

Maman used to remind us, "Regardless of where your dreams take you in this world, one thing that will always remain the same is family; we will always be here for one another," she'd say.

We were growing up!

S'épanouir à L'âge Adulte
(Blossoming Into Adulthood)

From the time Madeleine was a little girl she wanted to be a nurse, so it was no surprise when she announced she wanted to go to nursing school after she graduated high school. Because Madeleine had lived the first eight years of her life in the United States, she wanted to go back there for her nursing course, and she chose to study in Jacksonville, Florida. It was a three-year course, and I missed her dearly when she moved away.

Madeleine, in her '20s
Courtesy of Sylvie

I went for a week's visit during her training after I received a letter, saying how much she missed all of us. She had the week off from classes so it was a good time to go. We were thrilled to see each other. We ate in restaurants and shopped a lot, something we both enjoyed doing. One day, we decided to hop on the bus and off we went to Jacksonville Beach and its famous boardwalk. There was carnival life on this boardwalk: a Ferris wheel, merry-go-rounds, carousels, bumper cars, cotton candy, candy apples (my favourite), restaurants, food stands and an impressive, huge wooden roller coaster. Musicians played on the pier. Madeleine and I sat on a bench close by for a while listening to the band as a continuous flow of people walked by us. Madeleine told me the boardwalk and pier were a popular place to be in Jacksonville, especially for the young people. It was a great day.

Madeleine in her '20s
Boardwalk
Courtesy of Sylvie

In the evenings we stayed up late, reminiscing. Even the subject of my 'candy man' of so many years ago came up, but this time we both laughed about it.

"I feel so fortunate to have four terrific sisters," Madeleine told me.

"Me too, Mado," I agreed.

All too soon, the week came to an end and it was time for me to return home.

Florida is where Madeleine met the man who was to become her husband. They got married before moving back to Canada after she graduated. The only family members who were able to attend their wedding in Florida were Maman and myself. Shortly after their return to Canada, Madeleine and her husband moved to Montreal to look for work. However, one day our cousin, Henri-Paul, who lived in Sherbrooke, Quebec, contacted them with information of a job opportunity for Madeleine's husband in Sherbrooke. He applied, got the job, and they moved to Sherbrooke. Madeleine also found employment at the Sherbrooke Hospital, where she worked for many years. This is the same hospital Maman had been at so many years prior. They had three children, and Madeleine took a leave from her job until her children were of school age. My sister and her husband lived in Sherbrooke for the rest of their lives and I have good memories of many visits there. In fact, I had many visits with all my sisters, and they are all good memories.

As for me, after I moved to Trenton, New Jersey; I found employment at yet another bank. André and I continued to write each other as promised, more frequently at first. In one of André's last letters to me he told me he had met someone. We then both decided it would be better to stop writing, although I never forgot what a good friend he had been to me. Him, our wishing tree, our first job together, our relationship (as friends), he had been amazing!

Pierrette, in her '40s
Courtesy of Sylvie

One day as I was cleaning the apartment and listening to the radio, I heard about an English literature convention being held in New York City. I'd always had an interest in writing, so I decided to attend as it was only about an hour's drive. This is where I met my husband to be. He was one of the speakers at this three-day convention, and he greatly impressed me. We struck up a lengthy conversation, and the rest is history, as they say. He returned to St. Louis, as he was a professor of English literature at the University of Missouri, and I went back to Trenton. We stayed in contact and visited each other for the next couple of years until we married. After moving to St. Louis, I also obtained employment at the University of Missouri. We worked there until our retirement. We both shared a love for travel, and we found ample time for many beautiful trips together throughout the years.

When Thérèse finished high school, she too announced she wanted to become a nurse. Uncle Henri (Thérèse's godfather) kindly offered to pay for Thérèse's nursing course. She attended the nursing program at Hôpital Notre-Dame in Montreal where she lived on-site in the nurses' residence until her studies were completed. This was the same hospital where Aunt Cécile worked, which allowed for them to have frequent visits together.

When Thérèse graduated, she was offered employment at a rural hospital of her choice. After visiting several villages, she chose to live in Huntingdon, Quebec, where she worked at the Huntingdon Hospital. She met her husband-to-be when he stopped by to see one of his buddies who was in hospital at the time. During one of his visits, Thérèse asked him if he would help her with an oxygen tank. He did, she thanked him, and he left. Within minutes he returned to ask her out on a date. That night, they went out for dinner and it was the start of their wonderful relationship.

Thérèse in her '20s
Courtesy of Sylvie

He was born and raised in Saint-Anicet, Quebec. He grew up on a farm, and when his father decided to sell, they moved to Huntingdon. He and Thérèse met and married in Huntingdon and continued to live there for the rest of their lives. They, like Madeleine and her husband, also had three children.

After graduation, both Marthe and Louise decided they wanted to become nuns. Louise joined the order at nineteen years old and Marthe at twenty. They both joined the congregation of the Soeurs des Saints Noms de Jesus et de Marie (Sisters of the Holy Names of Jesus and Mary), which is a religious teaching institute for the Christian education for young girls. After their training, they took their temporary vows and later their final vows, which made them ready to live a dedicated religious life.

Marthe eventually moved to Sept-Iles, Quebec, and lived there for many years. By this time, she had studied to become a family counsellor and did this on a full-time basis. She chose to leave the order at age sixty, and later moved back to Montreal.

During the time Louise was a nun, she also studied to become a family counsellor, although she chose to leave the order at age forty when she lived in Montreal. After several years of being on her own, one day a friend of hers introduced her to a man who was a widow with four children. They courted for a year or more, then decided to get married. Louise moved to St. Esprit, Quebec, which is where he had his farm. The youngest of his children was approximately four years old when they married. Louise devoted approximately twenty years of her life to raising his children. Although he passed after a twenty-year marriage,

Louise has always stayed in contact with his kids and still talks to them today. She considers them her children. After her husband passed away, Louise moved back to Montreal.

She and Marthe decided to share an apartment together. Thérèse, who became a widow several years prior, also has an apartment in the same building but on a different floor and lives there part of the time. They have their suppers together every night; they are lucky to have one another.

All of us five girls felt so fortunate that we had such loving, caring, compassionate, intelligent, and understanding parents. Maman and Papa were supportive of each other and to each one of us for the goals and dreams we had. We were so, so lucky! Despite all the hurdles—Maman being sick for a time and the Great Depression—we truly had a wonderful upbringing. We were blessed not only with wonderful parents but wonderful grandparents, aunts, uncles, and cousins alike!

Leurs Dernières Années
(Their Final Years)

Once all five girls left the nest, as they say, Papa and Maman decided to move back to Saint-Célestin, Quebec, where Papa grew up.

**L to R: Sylvie, my cousin & our grandmother,
Eva Rose (Pinard) Vincent – "Maman" in the story
Courtesy of Sylvie**

It was approximately six miles from Sainte-Monique, from Maman's hometown. One of Papa's sisters, Germaine, who was by now a widow, and one of Maman's sisters, Marie-Anne, who remained a spinster, also lived in Saint-Célestin by the time my parents moved there. Françoise, who is Germaine's youngest daughter, lived just around the corner too. Saint-Célestin is a very small village, and all four relatives lived only a street or two from each other. They could easily walk to each other's houses, which they did. Aunt Françoise, who was also a milliner, opened a hat shop in the front of her mother's (Germaine's) house. Françoise's shop remained opened until her retirement.

My parents purchased a quaint little house on Albert Street which was perfect for them. It had two bedrooms and a bathroom upstairs, a kitchen, living room and den on the main floor. There was a clothesline (to be sure) and a huge garden with vegetables of all kinds. Directly across the backyard was a pathway which led to the back door of Aunt Germaine's house. To visit her, they simply walked through the garden and down the short pathway. My parents and aunts enjoyed living in proximity as they could see each other on any given day. My parents remained in Saint-Célestin for the rest of their lives.

L to R – Philippe (Papa in the story),
and his brother, Charlie
Courtesy of Sylvie

Maman became unwell in her early eighties and had to be hospitalized periodically until she passed away at the age of eighty-four. For the last three weeks of her life, she was admitted at the Sherbrooke Hospital. Because Madeleine lived in Sherbrooke, she was able to visit her every day. Me and my other sisters were fortunate enough to also see her before she passed. One night in 1981, my mother passed away peacefully in her sleep. It was a sad day. We all loved Maman so much. She had been an amazing mother!

Prior to her passing, Papa had become sick in 1978. Maman was in hospital at the time; my father was at home alone. One Saturday morning, Louise phoned Papa to see how he was doing, as she often did. She lived an hour and a half from my father then. She noticed that Papa appeared to have difficulty speaking and was slurring his words. Although he tried to reassure her that he was fine, Louise immediately jumped in her car and drove to Saint-Célestin. She found Papa lying in bed and not feeling quite like himself; however, his speech was back to normal. Although it was a Saturday, Louise wanted to contact Papa's doctor, but he insisted he was feeling better. My sister decided she was going to spend a few days with him just to be sure and take him to his doctor for a check-up on Monday. That he agreed to. He spent a good part of that Saturday in bed, so Louise mostly stayed by his bedside. They talked about all kinds of things that day, reminiscing together. The following morning, Papa seemed to be doing well until shortly before noon when he told her he was having chest pains. She immediately called for medical help, but before the attendees arrived, Papa suffered a massive heart attack. He died in his home, in his bed, with his beautiful daughter, Louise, by his side. He was seventy-nine. This was also a very sad day for us. My father was such a wonderful man, an awesome husband, and, unequivocally, a 'super-dad'!

During one of their chats the day before, Louise asked my father,

"Were you happy with Maman?"

"Your mother was the love of my life. From the time I was a teenager, I was enamoured with her, and I knew she was the one for me. We loved each other very much and we had a long and happy marriage. Besides," he said looking at Louise with a smile;

> "She gave me the greatest gift in the world,
> she gave me ... *Five beautiful girls!*

Elle m'a donné le plus beau cadeau au monde, elle m'a donné ...

> *Cinq belles filles!"*

* * *

Evangeline: A Tale of Acadie

Henry Wadsworth Longfellow   1807-1882

Prelude

This is the forest primeval. The murmuring pines and the hemlocks,
Bearded with moss, and in garments green, indistinct in the twilight,
Stand like Druids of eld, with voices sad and prophetic,
Stand like harpers hoar, with beards that rest on their bosoms.
Loud from its rocky caverns, the deep-voiced neighboring ocean
Speaks, and in accents disconsolate answers the wail of the forest.

This is the forest primeval; but where are the hearts that beneath it
Leaped like the roe, when he hears in the woodland the voice of the huntsman
Where is the thatch-roofed village, the home of Acadian farmers,
Men whose lives glided on like rivers that water the woodlands,
Darkened by shadows of earth, but reflecting an image of heaven?
Waste are those pleasant farms, and the farmers forever departed!
Scattered like dust and leaves, when the mighty blasts of October
Seize them, and whirl them aloft, and sprinkle them far o'er the ocean
Naught but tradition remains of the beautiful village of Grand-Pré.

Ye who believe in affection that hopes, and endures, and is patient,
Ye who believe in the beauty and strength of woman's devotion,
List to the mournful tradition still sung by the pines of the forest;
List to a Tale of Love in Acadie, home of the happy.

Part the First

Canto I

In the Acadian land, on the shores of the Basin of Minas,
Distant, secluded, still, the little village of Grand-Pré
Lay in the fruitful valley. Vast meadows stretched to the eastward,
Giving the village its name, and pasture to flocks without number.
Dikes, that the hands of the farmers had raised with labor incessant,
Shut out the turbulent tides; but at stated seasons the flood-gates

Opened, and welcomed the sea to wander at will o'er the meadows.
West and south there were fields of flax, and orchards and cornfields
Spreading afar and unfenced o'er the plain; and away to the northward
Blomidon rose, and the forests old, and aloft on the mountains
Sea-fogs pitched their tents, and mists from the mighty Atlantic
Looked on the happy valley, but ne'er from their station descended
There, in the midst of its farms, reposed the Acadian village.
Strongly built were the houses, with frames of oak and of hemlock,
Such as the peasants of Normandy built in the reign of the Henries.
Thatched were the roofs, with dormer-windows; and gables projecting
Over the basement below protected and shaded the doorway.
There in the tranquil evenings of summer, when brightly the sunset
Lighted the village street and gilded the vanes on the chimneys,
Matrons and maidens sat in snow-white caps and in kirtles
Scarlet and blue and green, with distaffs spinning the golden
Flax for the gossiping looms, whose noisy shuttles within doors
Mingled their sound with the whir of the wheels and the songs of the maidens.
Solemnly down the street came the parish priest, and the children
Paused in their play to kiss the hand he extended to bless them.
Reverend walked he among them; and up rose matrons and maidens,
Hailing his slow approach with words of affectionate welcome.
Then came the laborers home from the field, and serenely the sun sank
Down to his rest, and twilight prevailed. Anon from the belfry
Softly the Angelus sounded, and over the roofs of the village
Columns of pale blue smoke, like clouds of incense ascending,
Rose from a hundred hearths, the homes of peace and contentment.
Thus dwelt together in love these simple Acadian farmers,—
Dwelt in the love of God and of man. Alike were they free from
Fear, that reigns with the tyrant, and envy, the vice of republics.
Neither locks had they to their doors, nor bars to their windows;
But their dwellings were open as day and the hearts of their owners;
There the richest was poor, and the poorest lived in abundance.

Somewhat apart from the village, and nearer the Basin of Minas,
Benedict Bellefontaine, the wealthiest farmer of Grand-Pré,
Dwelt on his goodly acres: and with him, directing his household,
Gentle Evangeline lived, his child, and the pride of the village.
Stalworth and stately in form was the man of seventy winters;

Hearty and hale was he, an oak that is covered with snow-flakes;
White as the snow were his locks, and his cheeks as brown as the oak-leaves.
Fair was she to behold, that maiden of seventeen summers.
Black were her eyes as the berry that grows on the thorn by the wayside,
Black, yet how softly they gleamed beneath the brown shade of her tresses!
Sweet was her breath as the breath of kine that feed in the meadows.
When in the harvest heat she bore to the reapers at noontide
Flagons of home-brewed ale, ah! fair in sooth was the maiden,
Fairer was she when, on Sunday morn, while the bell from its turret
Sprinkled with holy sounds the air, as the priest with his hyssop
Sprinkles the congregation, and scatters blessings upon them,
Down the long street she passed, with her chaplet of beads and her missal,
Wearing her Norman cap and her kirtle of blue, and the ear-rings,
Brought in the olden time from France, and since, as an heirloom,
Handed down from mother to child, through long generations.
But a celestial brightness—a more ethereal beauty—
Shone on her face and encircled her form, when, after confession,
Homeward serenely she walked with God's benediction upon her.
When she had passed, it seemed like the ceasing of exquisite music.

Firmly builded with rafters of oak, the house of the farmer
Stood on the side of a hill commanding the sea; and a shady
Sycamore grew by the door, with a woodbine wreathing around it.
Rudely carved was the porch, with seats beneath; and a footpath
Led through an orchard wide, and disappeared in the meadow.
Under the Sycamore-tree were hives overhung by a penthouse,
Such as the traveller sees in regions remote by the roadside,
Built o'er a box for the poor, or the blessed image of Mary.
Farther down, on the slope of the hill, was the well with its moss-grown
Bucket, fastened with iron, and near it a trough for the horses.
Shielding the house from storms, on the north, were the barns and the farm-yard,
There stood the broad-wheeled wains and the antique ploughs and the harrows;
There were the folds for the sheep; and there, in his feathered seraglio,
Strutted the lordly turkey, and crowed the cock, with the selfsame
Voice that in ages of old had startled the penitent Peter.
Bursting with hay were the barns, themselves a village. In each one
Far o'er the gable projected a roof of thatch; and a staircase,
Under the sheltering eaves, led up to the odorous corn-loft.

There too the dove-cot stood, with its meek and innocent inmates
Murmuring ever of love; while above in the variant breezes
Numberless noisy weathercocks rattled and sang of mutation.

Thus, at peace with God and the world, the farmer of Grand-Pré
Lived on his sunny farm, and Evangeline governed his household.
Many a youth, as he knelt in the church and opened his missal,
Fixed his eyes upon her as the saint of his deepest devotion;
Happy was he who might touch her hand or the hem of her garment!
Many a suitor came to her door, by the darkness befriended,
And, as he knocked and waited to hear the sound of her footsteps,
Knew not which beat the louder, his heart or the knocker of iron;
Or at the joyous feast of the Patron Saint of the village,
Bolder grew, and pressed her hand in the dance as he whispered
Hurried words of love, that seemed a part of the music.
But, among all who came, young Gabriel only was welcome;
Gabriel Lajeunesse, the son of Basil the blacksmith,
Who was a mighty man in the village, and honored of all men;
For, since the birth of time, throughout all ages and nations,
Has the craft of the smith been held in repute by the people.
Basil was Benedict's friend. Their children from earliest childhood
Grew up together as brother and sister; and Father Felician,
Priest and pedagogue both in the village, had taught them their letters
Out of the selfsame book, with the hymns of the church and the plain-song.
But when the hymn was sung, and the daily lesson completed,
Swiftly they hurried away to the forge of Basil the blacksmith.
There at the door they stood, with wondering eyes to behold him
Take in his leathern lap the hoof of the horse as a plaything,
Nailing the shoe in its place; while near him the tire of the cart-wheel
Lay like a fiery snake, coiled round in a circle of cinders.
Oft on autumnal eves, when without in the gathering darkness
Bursting with light seemed the smithy, through every cranny and crevice,
Warm by the forge within they watched the laboring bellows,
And as its panting ceased, and the sparks expired in the ashes,
Merrily laughed, and said they were nuns going into the chapel.
Oft on sledges in winter, as swift as the swoop of the eagle,
Down the hillside hounding, they glided away o'er the meadow.
Oft in the barns they climbed to the populous nests on the rafters,
Seeking with eager eyes that wondrous stone, which the swallow

Brings from the shore of the sea to restore the sight of its fledglings;
Lucky was he who found that stone in the nest of the swallow!
Thus passed a few swift years, and they no longer were children.
He was a valiant youth, and his face, like the face of the morning,
Gladdened the earth with its light, and ripened thought into action.
She was a woman now, with the heart and hopes of a woman.
"Sunshine of Saint Eulalie" was she called; for that was the sunshine
Which, as the farmers believed, would load their orchards with apples
She, too, would bring to her husband's house delight and abundance,
Filling it full of love and the ruddy faces of children.

Canto II

Now had the season returned, when the nights grow colder and longer,
And the retreating sun the sign of the Scorpion enters.
Birds of passage sailed through the leaden air, from the ice-bound,
Desolate northern bays to the shores of tropical islands,
Harvests were gathered in; and wild with the winds of September
Wrestled the trees of the forest, as Jacob of old with the angel.
All the signs foretold a winter long and inclement.
Bees, with prophetic instinct of want, had hoarded their honey
Till the hives overflowed; and the Indian hunters asserted
Cold would the winter be, for thick was the fur of the foxes.
Such was the advent of autumn. Then followed that beautiful season,
Called by the pious Acadian peasants the Summer of All-Saints!
Filled was the air with a dreamy and magical light; and the landscape
Lay as if new-created in all the freshness of childhood.
Peace seemed to reign upon earth, and the restless heart of the ocean
Was for a moment consoled. All sounds were in harmony blended.
Voices of children at play, the crowing of cocks in the farm-yards,
Whir of wings in the drowsy air, and the cooing of pigeons,
All were subdued and low as the murmurs of love, and the great sun
Looked with the eye of love through the golden vapors around him;
While arrayed in its robes of russet and scarlet and yellow,
Bright with the sheen of the dew, each glittering tree of the forest
Flashed like the plane-tree the Persian adorned with mantles and jewels.

Now recommenced the reign of rest and affection and stillness.
Day with its burden and heat had departed, and twilight descending
Brought back the evening star to the sky, and the herds to the homestead.
Pawing the ground they came, and resting their necks on each other,
And with their nostrils distended inhaling the freshness of evening.
Foremost, bearing the bell, Evangeline's beautiful heifer,
Proud of her snow-white hide, and the ribbon that waved from her collar,
Quietly paced and slow, as if conscious of human affection.
Then came the shepherd back with his bleating flocks from the seaside,
Where was their favorite pasture. Behind them followed the watch-dog,
Patient, full of importance, and grand in the pride of his instinct,
Walking from side to side with a lordly air, and superbly
Waving his bushy tail, and urging forward the stragglers;
Regent of flocks was he when the shepherd slept; their protector,
When from the forest at night, through the starry silence, the wolves howled.
Late, with the rising moon, returned the wains from the marshes,
Laden with briny hay, that filled the air with its odor.
Cheerily neighed the steeds, with dew on their manes and their fetlocks,
While aloft on their shoulders the wooden and ponderous saddles,
Painted with brilliant dyes, and adorned with tassels of crimson,
Nodded in bright array, like hollyhocks heavy with blossoms.
Patiently stood the cows meanwhile, and yielded their udders
Unto the milkmaid's hand; whilst loud and in regular cadence
Into the sounding pails the foaming streamlets descended.
Lowing of cattle and peals of laughter were heard in the farm-yard,
Echoed back by the barns. Anon they sank into stillness;
Heavily closed, with a jarring sound, the valves of the barn-doors,
Rattled the wooden bars, and all for a season was silent.

In-doors, warm by the wide-mouthed fireplace, idly the farmer
Sat in his elbow-chair, and watched how the flames and the smoke-wreaths
Struggled together like foes in a burning city. Behind him,
Nodding and mocking along the wall, with gestures fantastic,
Darted his own huge shadow, and vanished away into darkness.
Faces, clumsily carved in oak, on the back of his arm-chair
Laughed in the flickering light, and the pewter plates on the dresser
Caught and reflected the flame, as shields of armies the sunshine.
Fragments of song the old man sang, and carols of Christmas,
Such as at home, in the olden time, his fathers before him

Sang in their Norman orchards and bright Burgundian vineyards.
Close at her father's side was the gentle Evangeline seated,
Spinning flax for the loom, that stood in the corner behind her.
Silent awhile were its treadles, at rest was its diligent shuttle,
While the monotonous drone of the wheel, like the drone of a bagpipe,
Followed the old man's songs and united the fragments together.
As in a church, when the chant of the choir at intervals ceases,
Footfalls are heard in the aisles, or words of the priest at the altar,
So, in each pause of the song, with measured motion the clock clicked.

Thus as they sat, there were footsteps heard, and, suddenly lifted,
Sounded the wooden latch, and the door swung back on its hinges.
Benedict knew by the hob-nailed shoes it was Basil the blacksmith,
And by her beating heart Evangeline knew who was with him.
"Welcome!" the farmer exclaimed, as their footsteps paused on the threshold.
"Welcome, Basil, my friend! Come, take thy place on the settle
Close by the chimney-side, which is always empty without thee;
Take from the shelf overhead thy pipe and the box of tobacco;
Never so much thyself art thou as when through the curling
Smoke of the pipe or the forge thy friendly and jovial face gleams
Round and red as the harvest moon through the mist of the marshes."
Then, with a smile of content, thus answered Basil the blacksmith,
Taking with easy air the accustomed seat by the fireside:—
"Benedict Bellefontaine, thou hast ever thy jest and thy ballad!
Ever in cheerfullest mood art thou, when others are filled with
Gloomy forebodings of ill, and see only ruin before them.
Happy art thou, as if every day thou hadst picked up a horseshoe."
Pausing a moment, to take the pipe that Evangeline brought him,
And with a coal from the embers had lighted, he slowly continued:—
"Four days now are passed since the English ships at their anchors
Ride in the Gaspereau's mouth, with their cannon pointed against us.
What their design may be is unknown; but all are commanded
On the morrow to meet in the church, where his Majesty's mandate
Will be proclaimed as law in the land. Alas! in the mean time
Many surmises of evil alarm the hearts of the people."
Then made answer the farmer:—"Perhaps some friendlier purpose
Brings these ships to our shores. Perhaps the harvests in England
By untimely rains or untimelier heat have been blighted,
And from our bursting barns they would feed their cattle and children."

"Not so thinketh the folk in the village," said, warmly, the blacksmith,
Shaking his head, as in doubt; then, heaving a sigh, he continued:—
"Louisburg is not forgotten, nor Beau Sejour, nor Port Royal.
Many already have fled to the forest, and lurk on its outskirts,
Waiting with anxious hearts the dubious fate of to-morrow.
Arms have been taken from us, and warlike weapons of all kinds;
Nothing is left but the blacksmith's sledge and the scythe of the mower."
Then with a pleasant smile made answer the jovial farmer:—
"Safer are we unarmed, in the midst of our flocks and our cornfields,
Safer within these peaceful dikes, besieged by the ocean,
Than our fathers in forts, besieged by the enemy's cannon.
Fear no evil, my friend, and to-night may no shadow of sorrow
Fall on this house and hearth; for this is the night of the contract.
Built are the house and the barn. The merry lads of the village
Strongly have built them and well; and, breaking the glebe round about them,
Filled the barn with hay, and the house with food for a twelvemonth.
Rene Leblanc will be here anon, with his papers and inkhorn.
Shall we not then be glad, and rejoice in the joy of our children?"
As apart by the window she stood, with her hand in her lover's,
Blushing Evangeline heard the words that her father had spoken,
And, as they died on his lips, the worthy notary entered.

Canto III

Bent like a laboring oar, that toils in the surf of the ocean,
Bent, but not broken, by age was the form of the notary public;
Shocks of yellow hair, like the silken floss of the maize, hung
Over his shoulders; his forehead was high; and glasses with horn bows
Sat astride on his nose, with a look of wisdom supernal.
Father of twenty children was he, and more than a hundred
Children's children rode on his knee, and heard his great watch tick.
Four long years in the times of the war had he languished a captive,
Suffering much in an old French fort as the friend of the English.
Now, though warier grown, without all guile or suspicion,
Ripe in wisdom was he, but patient, and simple, and childlike.
He was beloved by all, and most of all by the children;
For he told them tales of the Loup-garou in the forest,
And of the goblin that came in the night to water the horses,

And of the white Letiche, the ghost of a child who unchristened
Died, and was doomed to haunt unseen the chambers of children;
And how on Christmas eve the oxen talked in the stable,
And how the fever was cured by a spider shut up in a nutshell,
And of the marvellous powers of four-leaved clover and horseshoes,
With whatsoever else was writ in the lore of the village.
Then up rose from his seat by the fireside Basil the blacksmith,
Knocked from his pipe the ashes, and slowly extending his right hand,
"Father Leblanc," he exclaimed, "thou hast heard the talk in the village,
And, perchance, canst tell us some news of these ships and their errand."
Then with modest demeanor made answer the notary public,—
"Gossip enough have I heard, in sooth, yet am never the wiser;
And what their errand may be I know not better than others.
Yet am I not of those who imagine some evil intention
Brings them here, for we are at peace; and why then molest us?"
"God's name!" shouted the hasty and somewhat irascible blacksmith;
"Must we in all things look for the how, and the why, and the wherefore?
Daily injustice is done, and might is the right of the strongest!"
But, without heeding his warmth, continued the notary public,—
"Man is unjust, but God is just; and finally justice
Triumphs; and well I remember a story, that often consoled me,
When as a captive I lay in the old French fort at Port Royal."
This was the old man's favorite tale, and he loved to repeat it
When his neighbors complained that any injustice was done them.
"Once in an ancient city, whose name I no longer remember,
Raised aloft on a column, a brazen statue of Justice
Stood in the public square, upholding the scales in its left hand,
And in its right a sword, as an emblem that justice presided
Over the laws of the land, and the hearts and homes of the people.
Even the birds had built their nests in the scales of the balance,
Having no fear of the sword that flashed in the sunshine above them.
But in the course of time the laws of the land were corrupted;
Might took the place of right, and the weak were oppressed, and the mighty
Ruled with an iron rod. Then it chanced in a nobleman's palace
That a necklace of pearls was lost, and erelong a suspicion
Fell on an orphan girl who lived as maid in the household.
She, after form of trial condemned to die on the scaffold,
Patiently met her doom at the foot of the statue of Justice.
As to her Father in heaven her innocent spirit ascended,

Lo! o'er the city a tempest rose; and the bolts of the thunder
Smote the statue of bronze, and hurled in wrath from its left hand
Down on the pavement below the clattering scales of the balance,
And in the hollow thereof was found the nest of a magpie,
Into whose clay-built walls the necklace of pearls was inwoven."
Silenced, but not convinced, when the story was ended, the blacksmith
Stood like a man who fain would speak, but findeth no language;
All his thoughts were congealed into lines on his face, as the vapors
Freeze in fantastic shapes on the window-panes in the winter.

Then Evangeline lighted the brazen lamp on the table,
Filled, till it overflowed, the pewter tankard with home-brewed
Nut-brown ale, that was famed for its strength in the village of Grand-Pré;
While from his pocket the notary drew his papers and inkhorn,
Wrote with a steady hand the date and the age of the parties,
Naming the dower of the bride in flocks of sheep and in cattle.
Orderly all things proceeded, and duly and well were completed,
And the great seal of the law was set like a sun on the margin.
Then from his leathern pouch the farmer threw on the table
Three times the old man's fee in solid pieces of silver;
And the notary rising, and blessing the bride and the bridegroom,
Lifted aloft the tankard of ale and drank to their welfare.
Wiping the foam from his lip, he solemnly bowed and departed,
While in silence the others sat and mused by the fireside,
Till Evangeline brought the draught-board out of its corner.
Soon was the game begun. In friendly contention the old men
Laughed at each lucky hit, or unsuccessful manoeuver,
Laughed when a man was crowned, or a breach was made in the king-row
Meanwhile apart, in the twilight gloom of a window's embrasure,
Sat the lovers, and whispered together, beholding the moon rise
Over the pallid sea and the silvery mist of the meadows.
Silently one by one, in the infinite meadows of heaven,
Blossomed the lovely stars, the forget-me-nots of the angels.

Thus was the evening passed. Anon the bell from the belfry
Rang out the hour of nine, the village curfew, and straightway
Rose the guests and departed; and silence reigned in the household.
Many a farewell word and sweet good-night on the door-step
Lingered long in Evangeline's heart, and filled it with gladness.

Carefully then were covered the embers that glowed on the hearth-stone,
And on the oaken stairs resounded the tread of the farmer.
Soon with a soundless step the foot of Evangeline followed.
Up the staircase moved a luminous space in the darkness,
Lighted less by the lamp than the shining face of the maiden.
Silent she passed the hall, and entered the door of her chamber.
Simple that chamber was, with its curtains of white, and its clothes-press
Ample and high, on whose spacious shelves were carefully folded
Linen and woollen stuffs, by the hand of Evangeline woven.
This was the precious dower she would bring to her husband in marriage,
Better than flocks and herds, being proofs of her skill as a housewife.
Soon she extinguished her lamp, for the mellow and radiant moonlight
Streamed through the windows, and lighted the room, till the heart of the maiden
Swelled and obeyed its power, like the tremulous tides of the ocean.
Ah! she was fair, exceeding fair to behold, as she stood with
Naked snow-white feet on the gleaming floor of her chamber!
Little she dreamed that below, among the trees of the orchard,
Waited her lover and watched for the gleam of her lamp and her shadow.
Yet were her thoughts of him, and at times a feeling of sadness
Passed o'er her soul, as the sailing shade of clouds in the moonlight
Flitted across the floor and darkened the room for a moment.
And, as she gazed from the window, she saw serenely the moon pass
Forth from the folds of a cloud, and one star follow her footsteps,
As out of Abraham's tent young Ishmael wandered with Hagar!

Canto IV

Pleasantly rose next morn the sun on the village of Grand-Pré.
Pleasantly gleamed in the soft, sweet air the Basin of Minas,
the ships, with their wavering shadows, were riding at anchor.
Life had long been astir in the village, and clamorous labor
Knocked with its hundred hands at the golden gates of the morning.
Now from the country around, from the farms and neighboring hamlets,
Came in their holiday dresses the blithe Acadian peasants.
Many a glad good-morrow and jocund laugh from the young folk
Made the bright air brighter, as up from the numerous meadows,
Where no path could be seen but the track of wheels in the greensward,
Group after group appeared, and joined, or passed on the highway.

Long ere noon, in the village all sounds of labor were silenced.
Thronged were the streets with people; and noisy groups at the house-doors
Sat in the cheerful sun, and rejoiced and gossiped together.
Every house was an inn, where all were welcomed and feasted;
For with this simple people, who lived like brothers together,
All things were held in common, and what one had was another's.
Yet under Benedict's roof hospitality seemed more abundant:
For Evangeline stood among the guests of her father;
Bright was her face with smiles, and words of welcome and gladness
Fell from her beautiful lips, and blessed the cup as she gave it.

Under the open sky, in the odorous air of the orchard,
Stript of its golden fruit, was spread the feast of betrothal.
There in the shade of the porch were the priest and the notary seated;
There good Benedict sat, and sturdy Basil the blacksmith.
Not far withdrawn from these, by the cider-press and the beehives,
Michael the fiddler was placed, with the gayest of hearts and of waistcoats.
Shadow and light from the leaves alternately played on his snow-white
Hair, as it waved in the wind; and the jolly face of the fiddler
Glowed like a living coal when the ashes are blown from the embers.
Gayly the old man sang to the vibrant sound of his fiddle,
Tous les Bourgeois de Chartres, and Le Carillon de Dunkerque,
And anon with his wooden shoes beat time to the music.
Merrily, merrily whirled the wheels of the dizzying dances
Under the orchard-trees and down the path to the meadows;
Old folk and young together, and children mingled among them.
Fairest of all the maids was Evangeline, Benedict's daughter!
Noblest of all the youths was Gabriel, son of the blacksmith!

So passed the morning away. And lo! with a summons sonorous
Sounded the bell from its tower, and over the meadows a drum beat.
Thronged erelong was the church with men. Without, in the churchyard,
Waited the women. They stood by the graves, and hung on the headstones
Garlands of autumn-leaves and evergreens fresh from the forest.
Then came the guard from the ships, and marching proudly among them
Entered the sacred portal. With loud and dissonant clangor
Echoed the sound of their brazen drums from ceiling and casement,—
Echoed a moment only, and slowly the ponderous portal
Closed, and in silence the crowd awaited the will of the soldiers.

Then uprose their commander, and spoke from the steps of the altar,
Holding aloft in his hands, with its seals, the royal commission.
"You are convened this day," he said, "by his Majesty's orders.
Clement and kind has he been; but how you have answered his kindness,
Let your own hearts reply! To my natural make and my temper
Painful the task is I do, which to you I know must be grievous.
Yet must I bow and obey, and deliver the will of our monarch;
Namely, that all your lands, and dwellings, and cattle of all kinds
Forfeited be to the crown; and that you yourselves from this province
Be transported to other lands. God grant you may dwell there
Ever as faithful subjects, a happy and peaceable people!
Prisoners now I declare you; for such is his Majesty's pleasure!"
As, when the air is serene in the sultry solstice of summer,
Suddenly gathers a storm, and the deadly sling of the hailstones
Beats down the farmer's corn in the field and shatters his windows,
Hiding the sun, and strewing the ground with thatch from the house-roofs,
Bellowing fly the herds, and seek to break their enclosures;
So on the hearts of the people descended the words of the speaker.
Silent a moment they stood in speechless wonder, and then rose
Louder and ever louder a wail of sorrow and anger,
And, by one impulse moved, they madly rushed to the door-way.
Vain was the hope of escape; and cries and fierce imprecations
Rang through the house of prayer; and high o'er the heads of the others
Rose, with his arms uplifted, the figure of Basil the blacksmith,
As, on a stormy sea, a spar is tossed by the billows.
Flushed was his face and distorted with passion; and wildly he shouted,—
"Down with the tyrants of England! we never have sworn them allegiance!
Death to these foreign soldiers, who seize on our homes and our harvests!"
More he fain would have said, but the merciless hand of a soldier
Smote him upon the mouth, and dragged him down to the pavement.

In the midst of the strife and tumult of angry contention,
Lo! the door of the chancel opened, and Father Felician
Entered, with serious mien, and ascended the steps of the altar.
Raising his reverend hand, with a gesture he awed into silence
All that clamorous throng; and thus he spake to his people;
Deep were his tones and solemn; in accents measured and mournful
Spake he, as, after the tocsin's alarum, distinctly the clock strikes.
"What is this that ye do, my children? what madness has seized you?

Forty years of my life have I labored among you, and taught you,
Not in word alone, but in deed, to love one another!
Is this the fruit of my toils, of my vigils and prayers and privations?
Have you so soon forgotten all lessons of love and forgiveness?
This is the house of the Prince of Peace, and would you profane it
Thus with violent deeds and hearts overflowing with hatred?
Lo! where the crucified Christ from his cross is gazing upon you!
See! in those sorrowful eyes what meekness and holy compassion!
Hark! how those lips still repeat the prayer, 'O Father, forgive them!'
Let us repeat that prayer in the hour when the wicked assail us,
Let us repeat it now, and say, 'O Father, forgive them!'"
Few were his words of rebuke, but deep in the hearts of his people
Sank they, and sobs of contrition succeeded the passionate outbreak,
While they repeated his prayer, and said, "O Father, forgive them!"
Then came the evening service. The tapers gleamed from the altar.
Fervent and deep was the voice of the priest and the people responded,
Not with their lips alone, but their hearts; and the Ave Maria
Sang they, and fell on their knees, and their souls, with devotion translated,
Rose on the ardor of prayer, like Elijah ascending to heaven.

Meanwhile had spread in the village the tidings of ill, and on all sides
Wandered, wailing, from house to house the women and children.
Long at her father's door Evangeline stood, with her right hand
Shielding her eyes from the level rays of the sun, that, descending,
Lighted the village street with mysterious splendor, and roofed each
Peasant's cottage with golden thatch, and emblazoned its windows.
Long within had been spread the snow-white cloth on the table;
There stood the wheaten loaf, and the honey fragrant with wild-flowers;
There stood the tankard of ale, and the cheese fresh brought from the dairy;
And, at the head of the board, the great arm-chair of the farmer.
Thus did Evangeline wait at her father's door, as the sunset
Threw the long shadows of trees o'er the broad ambrosial meadows.
Ah! on her spirit within a deeper shadow had fallen,
And from the fields of her soul a fragrance celestial ascended,—
Charity, meekness, love, and hope, and forgiveness, and patience!
Then, all-forgetful of self, she wandered into the village,
Cheering with looks and words the mournful hearts of the women,
As o'er the darkening fields with lingering steps they departed,
Urged by their household cares, and the weary feet of their children.

Down sank the great red sun, and in golden, glimmering vapors
Veiled the light of his face, like the Prophet descending from Sinai.
Sweetly over the village the bell of the Angelus sounded.

Meanwhile, amid the gloom, by the church Evangeline lingered.
All was silent within; and in vain at the door and the windows
Stood she, and listened and looked, till, overcome by emotion,
"Gabriel!" cried she aloud with tremulous voice; but no answer
Came from the graves of the dead, nor the gloomier grave of the living.
Slowly at length she returned to the tenantless house of her father.
Smouldered the fire on the hearth, on the board was the supper untasted,
Empty and drear was each room, and haunted with phantoms of terror.
Sadly echoed her step on the stair and the floor of her chamber.
In the dead of the night she heard the disconsolate rain fall
Loud on the withered leaves of the sycamore-tree by the window.
Keenly the lightning flashed; and the voice of the echoing thunder
Told her that God was in heaven, and governed the world he created!
Then she remembered the tale she had heard of the justice of Heaven;
Soothed was her troubled soul, and she peacefully slumbered till morning.

Canto V

Four times the sun had risen and set; and now on the fifth day
Cheerily called the cock to the sleeping maids of the farm-house.
Soon o'er the yellow fields, in silent and mournful procession,
Came from the neighboring hamlets and farms the Acadian women,
Driving in ponderous wains their household goods to the sea-shore,
Pausing and looking back to gaze once more on their dwellings,
Ere they were shut from sight by the winding road and the woodland.
Close at their sides their children ran, and urged on the oxen,
While in their little hands they clasped some fragments of playthings.

Thus to the Gaspereau's mouth they hurried; and there on the sea-beach
Piled in confusion lay the household goods of the peasants.
All day long between the shore and the ships did the boats ply;
All day long the wains came laboring down from the village.
Late in the afternoon, when the sun was near to his setting,
Echoed far o'er the fields came the roll of drums from the churchyard.

Thither the women and children thronged. On a sudden the church-doors
Opened, and forth came the guard, and marching in gloomy procession
Followed the long-imprisoned, but patient, Acadian farmers.
Even as pilgrims, who journey afar from their homes and their country,
Sing as they go, and in singing forget they are weary and wayworn,
So with songs on their lips the Acadian peasants descended
Down from the church to the shore, amid their wives and their daughters.
Foremost the young men came; and, raising together their voices,
Sang with tremulous lips a chant of the Catholic Missions:—
"Sacred heart of the Saviour! O inexhaustible fountain!
Fill our hearts this day with strength and submission and patience!"
Then the old men, as they marched, and the women that stood by the wayside
Joined in the sacred psalm, and the birds in the sunshine above them
Mingled their notes therewith, like voices of spirits departed.

Half-way down to the shore Evangeline waited in silence,
Not overcome with grief, but strong in the hour of affliction,—
Calmly and sadly she waited, until the procession approached her,
And she beheld the face of Gabriel pale with emotion.
Tears then filled her eyes, and, eagerly running to meet him,
Clasped she his hands, and laid her head on his shoulder, and whispered,—
"Gabriel! be of good cheer! for if we love one another
Nothing, in truth, can harm us, whatever mischances may happen!"
Smiling she spake these words; then suddenly paused, for her father
Saw she slowly advancing. Alas! how changed was his aspect!
Gone was the glow from his cheek, and the fire from his eye, and his footstep
Heavier seemed with the weight of the heavy heart in his bosom.
But with a smile and a sigh, she clasped his neck and embraced him,
Speaking words of endearment where words of comfort availed not.
Thus to the Gaspereau's mouth moved on that mournful procession.

There disorder prevailed, and the tumult and stir of embarking.
Busily plied the freighted boats; and in the confusion
Wives were torn from their husbands, and mothers, too late, saw their children
Left on the land, extending their arms, with wildest entreaties.
So unto separate ships were Basil and Gabriel carried,
While in despair on the shore Evangeline stood with her father.
Half the task was not done when the sun went down, and the twilight
Deepened and darkened around; and in haste the refluent ocean

Fled away from the shore, and left the line of the sand-beach
Covered with waifs of the tide, with kelp and the slippery sea-weed.
Farther back in the midst of the household goods and the wagons,
Like to a gypsy camp, or a leaguer after a battle,
All escape cut off by the sea, and the sentinels near them,
Lay encamped for the night the houseless Acadian farmers.
Back to its nethermost caves retreated the bellowing ocean,
Dragging adown the beach the rattling pebbles, and leaving
Inland and far up the shore the stranded boats of the sailors.
Then, as the night descended, the herds returned from their pastures;
Sweet was the moist still air with the odor of milk from their udders;
Lowing they waited, and long, at the well-known bars of the farm-yard,—
Waited and looked in vain for the voice and the hand of the milkmaid.
Silence reigned in the streets; from the church no Angelus sounded,
Rose no smoke from the roofs, and gleamed no lights from the windows.

But on the shores meanwhile the evening fires had been kindled,
Built of the drift-wood thrown on the sands from wrecks in the tempest.
Round them shapes of gloom and sorrowful faces were gathered,
Voices of women were heard, and of men, and the crying of children.
Onward from fire to fire, as from hearth to hearth in his parish,
Wandered the faithful priest, consoling and blessing and cheering,
Like unto shipwrecked Paul on Melita's desolate sea-shore.
Thus he approached the place where Evangeline sat with her father,
And in the flickering light beheld the face of the old man,
Haggard and hollow and wan, and without either thought or emotion,
E'en as the face of a clock from which the hands have been taken.
Vainly Evangeline strove with words and caresses to cheer him,
Vainly offered him food; yet he moved not, he looked not, he spake not
But, with a vacant stare, ever gazed at the flickering fire-light.
"Benedicite!" murmured the priest, in tones of compassion.
More he fain would have said, but his heart was full, and his accents
Faltered and paused on his lips, as the feet of a child on a threshold,
Hushed by the scene he beholds, and the awful presence of sorrow.
Silently, therefore, he laid his hand on the head of the maiden,
Raising his tearful eyes to the silent stars that above them
Moved on their way, unperturbed by the wrongs and sorrows of mortals.
Then sat he down at her side, and they wept together in silence.

Suddenly rose from the south a light, as in autumn the blood-red
Moon climbs the crystal walls of heaven, and o'er the horizon
Titan-like stretches its hundred hands upon mountain and meadow,
Seizing the rocks and the rivers, and piling huge shadows together.
Broader and ever broader it gleamed on the roofs of the village,
Gleamed on the sky and the sea, and the ships that lay in the roadstead.
Columns of shining smoke uprose, and flashes of flame were
Thrust through their folds and withdrawn, like the quivering hands of a martyr.
Then as the wind seized the gleeds and the burning thatch, and, uplifting,
Whirled them aloft through the air, at once from a hundred house-tops
Started the sheeted smoke with flashes of flame intermingled.

These things beheld in dismay the crowd on the shore and on shipboard.
Speechless at first they stood, then cried aloud in their anguish,
"We shall behold no more our homes in the village of Grand-Pré!"
Loud on a sudden the cocks began to crow in the farm-yards,
Thinking the day had dawned; and anon the lowing of cattle
Came on the evening breeze, by the barking of dogs interrupted.
Then rose a sound of dread, such as startles the sleeping encampments
Far in the western prairies or forests that skirt the Nebraska,
When the wild horses affrighted sweep by with the speed of the whirlwind,
Or the loud bellowing herds of buffaloes rush to the river.
Such was the sound that arose on the night, as the herds and the horses
Broke through their folds and fences, and madly rushed o'er the meadows.

Overwhelmed with the sight, yet speechless, the priest and the maiden
Gazed on the scene of terror that reddened and widened before them;
And as they turned at length to speak to their silent companion,
Lo! from his seat he had fallen, and stretched abroad on the sea-shore
Motionless lay his form, from which the soul had departed.
Slowly the priest uplifted the lifeless head, and the maiden
Knelt at her father's side, and wailed aloud in her terror.
Then in a swoon she sank, and lay with her head on his bosom.
Through the long night she lay in deep, oblivious slumber;
And when she woke from the trance, she beheld a multitude near her.
Faces of friends she beheld, that were mournfully gazing upon her,
Pallid, with tearful eyes, and looks of saddest compassion.
Still the blaze of the burning village illumined the landscape,
Reddened the sky overhead, and gleamed on the faces around her,

And like the day of doom it seemed to her wavering senses.
Then a familiar voice she heard, as it said to the people,—
"Let us bury him here by the sea. When a happier season
Brings us again to our homes from the unknown land of our exile,
Then shall his sacred dust be piously laid in the churchyard."
Such were the words of the priest. And there in haste by the sea-side,
Having the glare of the burning village for funeral torches,
But without bell or book, they buried the farmer of Grand-Pré.
And as the voice of the priest repeated the service of sorrow,
Lo! with a mournful sound, like the voice of a vast congregation,
Solemnly answered the sea, and mingled its roar with the dirges.
'T was the returning tide, that afar from the waste of the ocean,
With the first dawn of the day, came heaving and hurrying landward.
Then recommenced once more the stir and noise of embarking;
And with the ebb of the tide the ships sailed out of the harbor,
Leaving behind them the dead on the shore, and the village in ruins.

Part the Second

Canto I

Many a weary year had passed since the burning of Grand-Pré,
When on the falling tide the freighted vessels departed,
Bearing a nation, with all its household gods, into exile.
Exile without an end, and without an example in story.
Far asunder, on separate coasts, the Acadians landed;
Scattered were they, like flakes of snow, when the wind from the northeast
Strikes aslant through the fogs that darken the Banks of Newfoundland.
Friendless, homeless, hopeless, they wandered from city to city,
From the cold lakes of the North to sultry Southern savannas,—
From the bleak shores of the sea to the lands where the Father of Waters
Seizes the hills in his hands, and drags them down to the ocean,
Deep in their sands to bury the scattered bones of the mammoth.
Friends they sought and homes; and many, despairing, heart-broken,
Asked of the earth but a grave, and no longer a friend nor a fireside.
Written their history stands on tablets of stone in the churchyards.
Long among them was seen a maiden who waited and wandered,
Lowly and meek in spirit, and patiently suffering all things.
Fair was she and young; but, alas! before her extended,

Dreary and vast and silent, the desert of life, with its pathway
Marked by the graves of those who had sorrowed and suffered before her,
Passions long extinguished, and hopes long dead and abandoned,
As the emigrant's way o'er the Western desert is marked by
Camp-fires long consumed, and bones that bleach in the sunshine.
Something there was in her life incomplete, imperfect, unfinished;
As if a morning of June, with all its music and sunshine,
Suddenly paused in the sky, and, fading, slowly descended
Into the east again, from whence it late had arisen.
Sometimes she lingered in towns, till, urged by the fever within her,
Urged by a restless longing, the hunger and thirst of the spirit,
She would commence again her endless search and endeavor;
Sometimes in churchyards strayed, and gazed on the crosses and tombstones,
Sat by some nameless grave, and thought that perhaps in its bosom
He was already at rest, and she longed to slumber beside him.
Sometimes a rumor, a hearsay, an inarticulate whisper,
Came with its airy hand to point and beckon her forward.
Sometimes she spake with those who had seen her beloved and known him,
But it was long ago, in some far-off place or forgotten.
"Gabriel Lajeunesse!" they said; yes! we have seen him.
He was with Basil the blacksmith, and both have gone to the prairies;
Coureurs-des-Bois are they, and famous hunters and trappers."
"Gabriel Lajeunesse!" said others; "O yes! we have seen him.
He is a Voyageur in the lowlands of Louisiana."
Then would they say,—"Dear child! why dream and wait for him longer?
Are there not other youths as fair as Gabriel? others
Who have hearts as tender and true, and spirits as loyal?
Here is Baptiste Leblanc, the notary's son, who has loved thee
Many a tedious year; come, give him thy hand and be happy!
Thou art too fair to be left to braid St. Catherine's tresses."
Then would Evangeline answer, serenely but sadly, "I cannot!—
Whither my heart has gone, there follows my hand, and not elsewhere.
For when the heart goes before, like a lamp, and illumines the pathway,
Many things are made clear, that else lie hidden in darkness."
Thereupon the priest, her friend and father-confessor,
Said, with a smile,—"O daughter! thy God thus speaketh within thee!
Talk not of wasted affection, affection never was wasted;
If it enrich not the heart of another, its waters, returning
Back to their springs, like the rain, shall fill them full of refreshment;

That which the fountain sends forth returns again to the fountain.
Patience; accomplish thy labor; accomplish thy work of affection!
Sorrow and silence are strong, and patient endurance is godlike.
Therefore accomplish thy labor of love, till the heart is made godlike,
Purified, strengthened, perfected, and rendered more worthy of heaven!"
Cheered by the good man's words, Evangeline labored and waited.
Still in her heart she heard the funeral dirge of the ocean,
But with its sound there was mingled a voice that whispered, "Despair not!"
Thus did that poor soul wander in want and cheerless discomfort
Bleeding, barefooted, over the shards and thorns of existence.
Let me essay, O Muse! to follow the wanderer's footsteps;—
Not through each devious path, each changeful year of existence;
But as a traveller follows a streamlet's course through the valley:
Far from its margin at times, and seeing the gleam of its water
Here and there, in some open space, and at intervals only;
Then drawing nearer its banks, through sylvan glooms that conceal it,
Though he behold it not, he can hear its continuous murmur;
Happy, at length, if he find the spot where it reaches an outlet.

Canto II

It was the month of May. Far down the Beautiful River,
Past the Ohio shore and past the mouth of the Wabash,
Into the golden stream of the broad and swift Mississippi,
Floated a cumbrous boat, that was rowed by Acadian boatmen.
It was a band of exiles: a raft, as it were, from the shipwrecked
Nation, scattered along the coast, now floating together,
Bound by the bonds of a common belief and a common misfortune;
Men and women and children, who, guided by hope or by hearsay,
Sought for their kith and their kin among the few-acred farmers
On the Acadian coast, and the prairies of fair Opelousas.
With them Evangeline went, and her guide, the Father Felician.
Onward o'er sunken sands, through a wilderness sombre with forests,
Day after day they glided adown the turbulent river;
Night after night, by their blazing fires, encamped on its borders.
Now through rushing chutes, among green islands, where plumelike
Cotton-trees nodded their shadowy crests, they swept with the current,
Then emerged into broad lagoons, where silvery sand-bars

Lay in the stream, and along the wimpling waves of their margin,
Shining with snow-white plumes, large flocks of pelicans waded.
Level the landscape grew, and along the shores of the river,
Shaded by china-trees, in the midst of luxuriant gardens,
Stood the houses of planters, with negro-cabins and dove-cots.
They were approaching the region where reigns perpetual summer,
Where through the Golden Coast, and groves of orange and citron,
Sweeps with majestic curve the river away to the eastward.
They, too, swerved from their course; and, entering the Bayou of Plaquemine,
Soon were lost in a maze of sluggish and devious waters,
Which, like a network of steel, extended in every direction.
Over their heads the towering and tenebrous boughs of the cypress
Met in a dusky arch, and trailing mosses in mid-air
Waved like banners that hang on the walls of ancient cathedrals.
Deathlike the silence seemed, and unbroken, save by the herons
Home to their roosts in the cedar-trees returning at sunset,
Or by the owl, as he greeted the moon with demoniac laughter.
Lovely the moonlight was as it glanced and gleamed on the water,
Gleamed on the columns of cypress and cedar sustaining the arches,
Down through whose broken vaults it fell as through chinks in a ruin.
Dreamlike, and indistinct, and strange were all things around them;
And o'er their spirits there came a feeling of wonder and sadness,—
Strange forebodings of ill, unseen and that cannot be compassed.
As, at the tramp of a horse's hoof on the turf of the prairies,
Far in advance are closed the leaves of the shrinking mimosa,
So, at the hoof-beats of fate, with sad forebodings of evil,
Shrinks and closes the heart, ere the stroke of doom has attained it.
But Evangeline's heart was sustained by a vision, that faintly
Floated before her eyes, and beckoned her on through the moonlight.
It was the thought of her brain that assumed the shape of a phantom.
Through those shadowy aisles had Gabriel wandered before her,
And every stroke of the oar now brought him nearer and nearer.

Then in his place, at the prow of the boat, rose one of the oarsmen,
And, as a signal sound, if others like them peradventure
Sailed on those gloomy and midnight streams, blew a blast on his bugle.
Wild through the dark colonnades and corridors leafy the blast rang,
Breaking the seal of silence, and giving tongues to the forest.
Soundless above them the banners of moss just stirred to the music.

Multitudinous echoes awoke and died in the distance,
Over the watery floor, and beneath the reverberant branches;
But not a voice replied; no answer came from the darkness;
And, when the echoes had ceased, like a sense of pain was the silence.
Then Evangeline slept; but the boatmen rowed through the midnight,
Silent at times, then singing familiar Canadian boat-songs,
Such as they sang of old on their own Acadian rivers,
While through the night were heard the mysterious sounds of the desert,
Far off,—indistinct,—as of wave or wind in the forest,
Mixed with the whoop of the crane and the roar of the grim alligator.

Thus ere another noon they emerged from the shades; and before them
Lay, in the golden sun, the lakes of the Atchafalaya.
Water-lilies in myriads rocked on the slight undulations
Made by the passing oars, and, resplendent in beauty, the lotus
Lifted her golden crown above the heads of the boatmen.
Faint was the air with the odorous breath of magnolia blossoms,
And with the heat of noon; and numberless sylvan islands,
Fragrant and thickly embowered with blossoming hedges of roses,
Near to whose shores they glided along, invited to slumber.
Soon by the fairest of these their weary oars were suspended.
Under the boughs of Wachita willows, that grew by the margin,
Safely their boat was moored; and scattered about on the greensward,
Tired with their midnight toil, the weary travellers slumbered.
Over them vast and high extended the cope of a cedar.
Swinging from its great arms, the trumpet-flower and the grapevine
Hung their ladder of ropes aloft like the ladder of Jacob,
On whose pendulous stairs the angels ascending, descending,
Were the swift humming-birds, that flitted from blossom to blossom.
Such was the vision Evangeline saw as she slumbered beneath it.
Filled was her heart with love, and the dawn of an opening heaven
Lighted her soul in sleep with the glory of regions celestial.

Nearer, ever nearer, among the numberless islands,
Darted a light, swift boat, that sped away o'er the water,
Urged on its course by the sinewy arms of hunters and trappers.
Northward its prow was turned, to the land of the bison and beaver.
At the helm sat a youth, with countenance thoughtful and careworn.
Dark and neglected locks overshadowed his brow, and a sadness

Somewhat beyond his years on his face was legibly written.
Gabriel was it, who, weary with waiting, unhappy and restless,
Sought in the Western wilds oblivion of self and of sorrow.
Swiftly they glided along, close under the lee of the island,
But by the opposite bank, and behind a screen of palmettos,
So that they saw not the boat, where it lay concealed in the willows,
All undisturbed by the dash of their oars, and unseen, were the sleepers,
Angel of God was there none to awaken the slumbering maiden.
Swiftly they glided away, like the shade of a cloud on the prairie.
After the sound of their oars on the tholes had died in the distance,
As from a magic trance the sleepers awoke, and the maiden
Said with a sigh to the friendly priest,—"O Father Felician!
Something says in my heart that near me Gabriel wanders.
Is it a foolish dream, an idle and vague superstition?
Or has an angel passed, and revealed the truth to my spirit?"
Then, with a blush, she added,—"Alas for my credulous fancy!
Unto ears like thine such words as these have no meaning."
But made answer the reverend man, and he smiled as he answered,—
"Daughter, thy words are not idle; nor are they to me without meaning.
Feeling is deep and still; and the word that floats on the surface
Is as the tossing buoy, that betrays where the anchor is hidden.
Therefore trust to thy heart, and to what the world calls illusions.
Gabriel truly is near thee; for not far away to the southward,
On the banks of the Teche, are the towns of St. Maur and St. Martin.
There the long-wandering bride shall be given again to her bridegroom,
There the long-absent pastor regain his flock and his sheepfold.
Beautiful is the land, with its prairies and forests of fruit-trees;
Under the feet a garden of flowers, and the bluest of heavens
Bending above, and resting its dome on the walls of the forest.
They who dwell there have named it the Eden of Louisiana."

With these words of cheer they arose and continued their journey.
Softly the evening came. The sun from the western horizon
Like a magician extended his golden wand o'er the landscape;
Twinkling vapors arose; and sky and water and forest
Seemed all on fire at the touch, and melted and mingled together.
Hanging between two skies, a cloud with edges of silver,
Floated the boat, with its dripping oars, on the motionless water.
Filled was Evangeline's heart with inexpressible sweetness.

Touched by the magic spell, the sacred fountains of feeling
Glowed with the light of love, as the skies and waters around her.
Then from a neighboring thicket the mocking-bird, wildest of singers,
Swinging aloft on a willow spray that hung o'er the water,
Shook from his little throat such floods of delirious music,
That the whole air and the woods and the waves seemed silent to listen.
Plaintive at first were the tones and sad; then soaring to madness
Seemed they to follow or guide the revel of frenzied Bacchantes.
Single notes were then heard, in sorrowful, low lamentation;
Till, having gathered them all, he flung them abroad in derision,
As when, after a storm, a gust of wind through the tree-tops
Shakes down the rattling rain in a crystal shower on the branches.
With such a prelude as this, and hearts that throbbed with emotion,
Slowly they entered the Teche, where it flows through the green Opelousas,
And, through the amber air, above the crest of the woodland,
Saw the column of smoke that arose from a neighboring dwelling;—
Sounds of a horn they heard, and the distant lowing of cattle.

Canto III

Near to the bank of the river, o'ershadowed by oaks, from whose branches
Garlands of Spanish moss and of mystic mistletoe flaunted,
Such as the Druids cut down with golden hatchets at Yule-tide,
Stood, secluded and still, the house of the herdsman. A garden
Girded it round about with a belt of luxuriant blossoms,
Filling the air with fragrance. The house itself was of timbers
Hewn from the cypress-tree, and carefully fitted together.
Large and low was the roof; and on slender columns supported,
Rose-wreathed, vine-encircled, a broad and spacious veranda,
Haunt of the humming-bird and the bee, extended around it.
At each end of the house, amid the flowers of the garden,
Stationed the dove-cots were, as love's perpetual symbol,
Scenes of endless wooing, and endless contentions of rivals.
Silence reigned o'er the place. The line of shadow and sunshine
Ran near the tops of the trees; but the house itself was in shadow,
And from its chimney-top, ascending and slowly expanding
Into the evening air, a thin blue column of smoke rose.
In the rear of the house, from the garden gate, ran a pathway

Through the great groves of oak to the skirts of the limitless prairie,
Into whose sea of flowers the sun was slowly descending.
Full in his track of light, like ships with shadowy canvas
Hanging loose from their spars in a motionless calm in the tropics,
Stood a cluster of trees, with tangled cordage of grapevines.

Just where the woodlands met the flowery surf of the prairie,
Mounted upon his horse, with Spanish saddle and stirrups,
Sat a herdsman, arrayed in gaiters and doublet of deerskin.
Broad and brown was the face that from under the Spanish sombrero
Gazed on the peaceful scene, with the lordly look of its master.
Round about him were numberless herds of kine, that were grazing
Quietly in the meadows, and breathing the vapory freshness
That uprose from the river, and spread itself over the landscape.
Slowly lifting the horn that hung at his side, and expanding
Fully his broad, deep chest, he blew a blast, that resounded
Wildly and sweet and far, through the still damp air of the evening.
Suddenly out of the grass the long white horns of the cattle
Rose like flakes of foam on the adverse currents of ocean.
Silent a moment they gazed, then bellowing rushed o'er the prairie,
And the whole mass became a cloud, a shade in the distance.
Then, as the herdsman turned to the house, through the gate of the garden
Saw he the forms of the priest and the maiden advancing to meet him.
Suddenly down from his horse he sprang in amazement, and forward
Rushed with extended arms and exclamations of wonder;
When they beheld his face, they recognized Basil the blacksmith.
Hearty his welcome was, as he led his guests to the garden.
There in an arbor of roses with endless question and answer
Gave they vent to their hearts, and renewed their friendly embraces,
Laughing and weeping by turns, or sitting silent and thoughtful.
Thoughtful, for Gabriel came not; and now dark doubts and misgivings
Stole o'er the maiden's heart; and Basil, somewhat embarrassed,
Broke the silence and said,—"If you came by the Atchafalaya,
How have you nowhere encountered my Gabriel's boat on the bayous?"
Over Evangeline's face at the words of Basil a shade passed.
Tears came into her eyes, and she said, with a tremulous accent,—
"Gone? is Gabriel gone?" and, concealing her face on his shoulder,
All her o'erburdened heart gave way, and she wept and lamented.
Then the good Basil said,—and his voice grew blithe as he said it,—

"Be of good cheer, my child; it is only to-day he departed.
Foolish boy! he has left me alone with my herds and my horses.
Moody and restless grown, and tried and troubled, his spirit
Could no longer endure the calm of this quiet existence.
Thinking ever of thee, uncertain and sorrowful ever,
Ever silent, or speaking only of thee and his troubles,
He at length had become so tedious to men and to maidens,
Tedious even to me, that at length I bethought me, and sent him
Unto the town of Adayes to trade for mules with the Spaniards.
Thence he will follow the Indian trails to the Ozark Mountains,
Hunting for furs in the forests, on rivers trapping the beaver.
Therefore be of good cheer; we will follow the fugitive lover;
He is not far on his way, and the Fates and the streams are against him.
Up and away to-morrow, and through the red dew of the morning
We will follow him fast, and bring him back to his prison."

Then glad voices were heard, and up from the banks of the river,
Borne aloft on his comrades' arms, came Michael the fiddler.
Long under Basil's roof had he lived like a god on Olympus,
Having no other care than dispensing music to mortals.
Far renowned was he for his silver locks and his fiddle.
"Long live Michael," they cried, "our brave Acadian minstrel!"
As they bore him aloft in triumphal procession; and straightway
Father Felician advanced with Evangeline, greeting the old man
Kindly and oft, and recalling the past, while Basil, enraptured,
Hailed with hilarious joy his old companions and gossips,
Laughing loud and long, and embracing mothers and daughters.
Much they marvelled to see the wealth of the cidevant blacksmith,
All his domains and his herds, and his patriarchal demeanor;
Much they marvelled to hear his tales of the soil and the climate,
And of the prairie; whose numberless herds were his who would take them;
Each one thought in his heart, that he, too, would go and do likewise.
Thus they ascended the steps, and, crossing the breezy veranda,
Entered the hall of the house, where already the supper of Basil
Waited his late return; and they rested and feasted together.

Over the joyous feast the sudden darkness descended.
All was silent without, and, illuming the landscape with silver,
Fair rose the dewy moon and the myriad stars; but within doors,

Brighter than these, shone the faces of friends in the glimmering lamplight.
Then from his station aloft, at the head of the table, the herdsman
Poured forth his heart and his wine together in endless profusion.
Lighting his pipe, that was filled with sweet Natchitoches tobacco,
Thus he spake to his guests, who listened, and smiled as they listened:—
"Welcome once more, my friends, who long have been friendless and homeless,
Welcome once more to a home, that is better perchance than the old one!
Here no hungry winter congeals our blood like the rivers;
Here no stony ground provokes the wrath of the farmer.
Smoothly the ploughshare runs through the soil, as a keel through the water.
All the year round the orange-groves are in blossom; and grass grows
More in a single night than a whole Canadian summer.
Here, too, numberless herds run wild and unclaimed in the prairies;
Here, too, lands may be had for the asking, and forests of timber
With a few blows of the axe are hewn and framed into houses.
After your houses are built, and your fields are yellow with harvests,
No King George of England shall drive you away from your homesteads,
Burning your dwellings and barns, and stealing your farms and your cattle."
Speaking these words, he blew a wrathful cloud from his nostrils,
While his huge, brown hand came thundering down on the table,
So that the guests all started; and Father Felician, astounded,
Suddenly paused, with a pinch of snuff half-way to his nostrils.
But the brave Basil resumed, and his words were milder and gayer:—
"Only beware of the fever, my friends, beware of the fever!
For it is not like that of our cold Acadian climate,
Cured by wearing a spider hung round one's neck in a nutshell!"
Then there were voices heard at the door, and footsteps approaching
Sounded upon the stairs and the floor of the breezy veranda.
It was the neighboring Creoles and small Acadian planters,
Who had been summoned all to the house of Basil the Herdsman.
Merry the meeting was of ancient comrades and neighbors:
Friend clasped friend in his arms; and they who before were as strangers,
Meeting in exile, became straightway as friends to each other,
Drawn by the gentle bond of a common country together.
But in the neighboring hall a strain of music, proceeding
From the accordant strings of Michael's melodious fiddle,
Broke up all further speech. Away, like children delighted,
All things forgotten beside, they gave themselves to the maddening

Whirl of the dizzy dance, as it swept and swayed to the music,
Dreamlike, with beaming eyes and the rush of fluttering garments.

Meanwhile, apart, at the head of the hall, the priest and the herdsman
Sat, conversing together of past and present and future;
While Evangeline stood like one entranced, for within her
Olden memories rose, and loud in the midst of the music
Heard she the sound of the sea, and an irrepressible sadness
Came o'er her heart, and unseen she stole forth into the garden.
Beautiful was the night. Behind the black wall of the forest,
Tipping its summit with silver, arose the moon. On the river
Fell here and there through the branches a tremulous gleam of the moonlight,
Like the sweet thoughts of love on a darkened and devious spirit.
Nearer and round about her, the manifold flowers of the garden
Poured out their souls in odors, that were their prayers and confessions
Unto the night, as it went its way, like a silent Carthusian.
Fuller of fragrance than they, and as heavy with shadows and night-dews,
Hung the heart of the maiden. The calm and the magical moonlight
Seemed to inundate her soul with indefinable longing;
As, through the garden gate, and beneath the shade of the oak-trees,
Passed she along the path to the edge of the measureless prairie.
Silent it lay, with a silvery haze upon it, and fire-flies
Gleaming and floating away in mingled and infinite numbers.
Over her head the stars, the thoughts of God in the heavens,
Shone on the eyes of man who had ceased to marvel and worship,
Save when a blazing comet was seen on the walls of that temple,
As if a hand had appeared and written upon them, "Upharsin."
And the soul of the maiden, between the stars and the fire-flies,
Wandered alone, and she cried,—"O Gabriel! O my beloved!
Art thou so near unto me, and yet I cannot behold thee?
Art thou so near unto me, and yet thy voice does not reach me?
Ah! how often thy feet have trod this path to the prairie!
Ah! how often thine eyes have looked on the woodlands around me!
Ah! how often beneath this oak, returning from labor,
Thou hast lain down to rest and to dream of me in thy slumbers!
When shall these eyes behold, these arms be folded about thee?"
Loud and sudden and near the note of a whippoorwill sounded
Like a flute in the woods; and anon, through the neighboring thickets,

Farther and farther away it floated and dropped into silence.
"Patience!" whispered the oaks from oracular caverns of darkness:
And, from the moonlit meadow, a sigh responded, "To-morrow!"

Bright rose the sun next day; and all the flowers of the garden
Bathed his shining feet with their tears, and anointed his tresses
With the delicious balm that they bore in their vases of crystal.
"Farewell!" said the priest, as he stood at the shadowy threshold;
"See that you bring us the Prodigal Son from his fasting and famine,
And, too, the Foolish Virgin, who slept when the bridegroom was coming."
"Farewell!" answered the maiden, and, smiling, with Basil descended
Down to the river's brink, where the boatmen already were waiting.
Thus beginning their journey with morning, and sunshine, and gladness,
Swiftly they followed the flight of him who was speeding before them,
Blown by the blast of fate like a dead leaf over the desert.
Not that day, nor the next, nor yet the day that succeeded,
Found they trace of his course, in lake or forest or river,
Nor, after many days, had they found him; but vague and uncertain
Rumors alone were their guides through a wild and desolate Country;
Till, at the little inn of the Spanish town of Adayes,
Weary and worn, they alighted, and learned from the garrulous landlord,
That on the day before, with horses and guides and companions,
Gabriel left the village, and took the road of the prairies.

Canto IV

Far in the West there lies a desert land, where the mountains
Lift, through perpetual snows, their lofty and luminous summits.
Down from their jagged, deep ravines, where the gorge, like a gateway,
Opens a passage rude to the wheels of the emigrant's wagon,
Westward the Oregon flows and the Walleway and Owyhee.
Eastward, with devious course, among the Wind-river Mountains,
Through the Sweet-water Valley precipitate leaps the Nebraska;
And to the south, from Fontaine-qui-bout and the Spanish sierras,
Fretted with sands and rocks, and swept by the wind of the desert,
Numberless torrents, with ceaseless sound, descend to the ocean,
Like the great chords of a harp, in loud and solemn vibrations.
Spreading between these streams are the wondrous, beautiful prairies,

Billowy bays of grass ever rolling in shadow and sunshine,
Bright with luxuriant clusters of roses and purple amorphas.
Over them wandered the buffalo herds, and the elk and the roebuck;
Over them wandered the wolves, and herds of riderless horses;
Fires that blast and blight, and winds that are weary with travel;
Over them wander the scattered tribes of Ishmael's children,
Staining the desert with blood; and above their terrible war-trails
Circles and sails aloft, on pinions majestic, the vulture,
Like the implacable soul of a chieftain slaughtered in battle,
By invisible stairs ascending and scaling the heavens.
Here and there rise smokes from the camps of these savage marauders;
Here and there rise groves from the margins of swift-running rivers;
And the grim, taciturn bear, the anchorite monk of the desert,
Climbs down their dark ravines to dig for roots by the brook-side,
And over all is the sky, the clear and crystalline heaven,
Like the protecting hand of God inverted above them.

Into this wonderful land, at the base of the Ozark Mountains,
Gabriel far had entered, with hunters and trappers behind him.
Day after day, with their Indian guides, the maiden and Basil
Followed his flying steps, and thought each day to o'ertake him.
Sometimes they saw, or thought they saw, the smoke of his camp-fire
Rise in the morning air from the distant plain; but at nightfall,
When they had reached the place, they found only embers and ashes.
And, though their hearts were sad at times and their bodies were weary,
Hope still guided them on, as the magic Fata Morgana
Showed them her lakes of light, that retreated and vanished before them.

Once, as they sat by their evening fire, there silently entered
Into the little camp an Indian woman, whose features
Wore deep traces of sorrow, and patience as great as her sorrow.
She was a Shawnee woman returning home to her people,
From the far-off hunting-grounds of the cruel Camanches,
Where her Canadian husband, a Coureur-des-Bois, had been murdered.
Touched were their hearts at her story, and warmest and friendliest welcome
Gave they, with words of cheer, and she sat and feasted among them
On the buffalo-meat and the venison cooked on the embers.
But when their meal was done, and Basil and all his companions,
Worn with the long day's march and the chase of the deer and the bison,

Stretched themselves on the ground, and slept where the quivering fire-light
Flashed on their swarthy cheeks, and their forms wrapped up in their blankets
Then at the door of Evangeline's tent she sat and repeated
Slowly, with soft, low voice, and the charm of her Indian accent,
All the tale of her love, with its pleasures, and pains, and reverses.
Much Evangeline wept at the tale, and to know that another
Hapless heart like her own had loved and had been disappointed.
Moved to the depths of her soul by pity and woman's compassion,
Yet in her sorrow pleased that one who had suffered was near her,
She in turn related her love and all its disasters.
Mute with wonder the Shawnee sat, and when she had ended
Still was mute; but at length, as if a mysterious horror
Passed through her brain, she spake, and repeated the tale of the Mowis;
Mowis, the bridegroom of snow, who won and wedded a maiden,
But, when the morning came, arose and passed from the wigwam,
Fading and melting away and dissolving into the sunshine,
Till she beheld him no more, though she followed far into the forest.
Then, in those sweet, low tones, that seemed like a weird incantation,
Told she the tale of the fair Lilinau, who was wooed by a phantom,
That, through the pines o'er her father's lodge, in the hush of the twilight,
Breathed like the evening wind, and whispered love to the maiden,
Till she followed his green and waving plume through the forest,
And nevermore returned, nor was seen again by her people.
Silent with wonder and strange surprise, Evangeline listened
To the soft flow of her magical words, till the region around her
Seemed like enchanted ground, and her swarthy guest the enchantress.
Slowly over the tops of the Ozark Mountains the moon rose,
Lighting the little tent, and with a mysterious splendor
Touching the sombre leaves, and embracing and filling the woodland.
With a delicious sound the brook rushed by, and the branches
Swayed and sighed overhead in scarcely audible whispers.
Filled with the thoughts of love was Evangeline's heart, but a secret,
Subtile sense crept in of pain and indefinite terror,
As the cold, poisonous snake creeps into the nest of the swallow.
It was no earthly fear. A breath from the region of spirits
Seemed to float in the air of night; and she felt for a moment
That, like the Indian maid, she, too, was pursuing a phantom.
With this thought she slept, and the fear and the phantom had vanished.

Early upon the morrow the march was resumed; and the Shawnee
Said, as they journeyed along,—"On the western slope of these mountains
Dwells in his little village the Black Robe chief of the Mission.
Much he teaches the people, and tells them of Mary and Jesus;
Loud laugh their hearts with joy, and weep with pain, as they hear him."
Then, with a sudden and secret emotion, Evangeline answered,—
"Let us go to the Mission, for there good tidings await us!"
Thither they turned their steeds; and behind a spur of the mountains,
Just as the sun went down, they heard a murmur of voices,
And in a meadow green and broad, by the bank of a river,
Saw the tents of the Christians, the tents of the Jesuit Mission.
Under a towering oak, that stood in the midst of the village,
Knelt the Black Robe chief with his children. A crucifix fastened
High on the trunk of the tree, and overshadowed by grapevines,
Looked with its agonized face on the multitude kneeling beneath it.
This was their rural chapel. Aloft, through the intricate arches
Of its aerial roof, arose the chant of their vespers,
Mingling its notes with the soft susurrus and sighs of the branches.
Silent, with heads uncovered, the travellers, nearer approaching,
Knelt on the swarded floor, and joined in the evening devotions.
But when the service was done, and the benediction had fallen
Forth from the hands of the priest, like seed from the hands of the sower,
Slowly the reverend man advanced to the strangers, and bade them
Welcome; and when they replied, he smiled with benignant expression,
Hearing the homelike sounds of his mother-tongue in the forest,
And, with words of kindness, conducted them into his wigwam.
There upon mats and skins they reposed, and on cakes of the maize-ear
Feasted, and slaked their thirst from the water-gourd of the teacher.
Soon was their story told; and the priest with solemnity answered:—
"Not six suns have risen and set since Gabriel, seated
On this mat by my side, where now the maiden reposes,
Told me this same sad tale then arose and continued his journey!"
Soft was the voice of the priest, and he spake with an accent of kindness;
But on Evangeline's heart fell his words as in winter the snow-flakes
Fall into some lone nest from which the birds have departed.
"Far to the north he has gone," continued the priest; "but in autumn,
When the chase is done, will return again to the Mission."
Then Evangeline said, and her voice was meek and submissive,—
"Let me remain with thee, for my soul is sad and afflicted."

So seemed it wise and well unto all; and betimes on the morrow,
Mounting his Mexican steed, with his Indian guides and companions.
Homeward Basil returned, and Evangeline stayed at the Mission.

Slowly, slowly, slowly the days succeeded each other,
Days and weeks and months; and the fields of maize that were springing
Green from the ground when a stranger she came, now waving above her,
Lifted their slender shafts, with leaves interlacing, and forming
Cloisters for mendicant crows and granaries pillaged by squirrels.
Then in the golden weather the maize was husked, and the maidens
Blushed at each blood-red ear, for that betokened a lover,
But at the crooked laughed, and called it a thief in the corn-field.
Even the blood-red ear to Evangeline brought not her lover.
"Patience!" the priest would say; "have faith, and thy prayer will be answered!
Look at this vigorous plant that lifts its head from the meadow,
See how its leaves are turned to the north, as true as the magnet;
This is the compass-flower, that the finger of God has planted
Here in the houseless wild, to direct the traveller's journey
Over the sea-like, pathless, limitless waste of the desert.
Such in the soul of man is faith. The blossoms of passion,
Gay and luxuriant flowers, are brighter and fuller of fragrance,
But they beguile us, and lead us astray, and their odor is deadly.
Only this humble plant can guide us here, and hereafter
Crown us with asphodel flowers, that are wet with the dews of nepenthe."

So came the autumn, and passed, and the winter,—yet Gabriel came not;
Blossomed the opening spring, and the notes of the robin and bluebird
Sounded sweet upon wold and in wood, yet Gabriel came not.
But on the breath of the summer winds a rumor was wafted
Sweeter than song of bird, or hue or odor of blossom.
Far to the north and east, it said, in the Michigan forests,
Gabriel had his lodge by the banks of the Saginaw River,
And, with returning guides, that sought the lakes of St. Lawrence,
Saying a sad farewell, Evangeline went from the Mission.
When over weary ways, by long and perilous marches,
She had attained at length the depths of the Michigan forests,
Found she the hunter's lodge deserted and fallen to ruin!

Thus did the long sad years glide on, and in seasons and places
Divers and distant far was seen the wandering maiden;—
Now in the Tents of Grace of the meek Moravian Missions,
Now in the noisy camps and the battle-fields of the army,
Now in secluded hamlets, in towns and populous cities.
Like a phantom she came, and passed away unremembered.
Fair was she and young, when in hope began the long journey;
Faded was she and old, when in disappointment it ended.
Each succeeding year stole something away from her beauty,
Leaving behind it, broader and deeper, the gloom and the shadow.
Then there appeared and spread faint streaks of gray o'er her forehead,
Dawn of another life, that broke o'er her earthy horizon,
As in the eastern sky the first faint streaks of the morning.

Canto V

In that delightful land which is washed by the Delaware's waters,
Guarding in sylvan shades the name of Penn the apostle,
Stands on the banks of its beautiful stream the city he founded.
There all the air is balm, and the peach is the emblem of beauty,
And the streets still re-echo the names of the trees of the forest,
As if they fain would appease the Dryads whose haunts they molested.
There from the troubled sea had Evangeline landed, an exile,
Finding among the children of Penn a home and a country.
There old Rene Leblanc had died; and when he departed,
Saw at his side only one of all his hundred descendants.
Something at least there was in the friendly streets of the city,
Something that spake to her heart, and made her no longer a stranger;
And her ear was pleased with the Thee and Thou of the Quakers,
For it recalled the past, the old Acadian country,
Where all men were equal, and all were brothers and sisters.
So, when the fruitless search, the disappointed endeavor,
Ended, to recommence no more upon earth, uncomplaining,
Thither, as leaves to the light, were turned her thoughts and her footsteps.
As from a mountain's top the rainy mists of the morning
Roll away, and afar we behold the landscape below us,
Sun-illumined, with shining rivers and cities and hamlets,
So fell the mists from her mind, and she saw the world far below her,

Dark no longer, but all illumined with love; and the pathway
Which she had climbed so far, lying smooth and fair in the distance.
Gabriel was not forgotten. Within her heart was his image,
Clothed in the beauty of love and youth, as last she beheld him,
Only more beautiful made by his deathlike silence and absence.
Into her thoughts of him time entered not, for it was not.
Over him years had no power; he was not changed, but transfigured;
He had become to her heart as one who is dead, and not absent;
Patience and abnegation of self, and devotion to others,
This was the lesson a life of trial and sorrow had taught her.
So was her love diffused, but, like to some odorous spices,
Suffered no waste nor loss, though filling the air with aroma.
Other hope had she none, nor wish in life, but to follow
Meekly, with reverent steps, the sacred feet of her Saviour.
Thus many years she lived as a Sister of Mercy; frequenting
Lonely and wretched roofs in the crowded lanes of the city,
Where distress and want concealed themselves from the sunlight,
Where disease and sorrow in garrets languished neglected.
Night after night, when the world was asleep, as the watchman repeated
Loud, through the gusty streets, that all was well in the city,
High at some lonely window he saw the light of her taper.
Day after day, in the gray of the dawn, as slow through the suburbs
Plodded the German farmer, with flowers and fruits for the market,
Met he that meek, pale face, returning home from its watchings.

Then it came to pass that a pestilence fell on the city,
Presaged by wondrous signs, and mostly by flocks of wild pigeons,
Darkening the sun in their flight, with naught in their craws but an acorn.
And, as the tides of the sea arise in the month of September,
Flooding some silver stream, till it spreads to a lake in the meadow,
So death flooded life, and, o'erflowing its natural margin,
Spread to a brackish lake, the silver stream of existence.
Wealth had no power to bribe, nor beauty to charm, the oppressor;
But all perished alike beneath the scourge of his anger;—
Only, alas! the poor, who had neither friends nor attendants,
Crept away to die in the almshouse, home of the homeless.
Then in the suburbs it stood, in the midst of meadows and woodlands;—
Now the city surrounds it; but still, with its gateway and wicket
Meek, in the midst of splendor, its humble walls seem to echo

Softly the words of the Lord:—"The poor ye always have with you."
Thither, by night and by day, came the Sister of Mercy. The dying
Looked up into her face, and thought, indeed, to behold there
Gleams of celestial light encircle her forehead with splendor,
Such as the artist paints o'er the brows of saints and apostles,
Or such as hangs by night o'er a city seen at a distance.
Unto their eyes it seemed the lamps of the city celestial,
Into whose shining gates erelong their spirits would enter.

Thus, on a Sabbath morn, through the streets, deserted and silent,
Wending her quiet way, she entered the door of the almshouse.
Sweet on the summer air was the odor of flowers in the garden;
And she paused on her way to gather the fairest among them,
That the dying once more might rejoice in their fragrance and beauty.
Then, as she mounted the stairs to the corridors, cooled by the east-wind,
Distant and soft on her ear fell the chimes from the belfry of Christ Church,
While, intermingled with these, across the meadows were wafted
Sounds of psalms, that were sung by the Swedes in their church at Wicaco.
Soft as descending wings fell the calm of the hour on her spirit;
Something within her said,—"At length thy trials are ended";
And, with light in her looks, she entered the chambers of sickness.
Noiselessly moved about the assiduous, careful attendants,
Moistening the feverish lip, and the aching brow, and in silence
Closing the sightless eyes of the dead, and concealing their faces,
Where on their pallets they lay, like drifts of snow by the roadside.
Many a languid head, upraised as Evangeline entered,
Turned on its pillow of pain to gaze while she passed, for her presence
Fell on their hearts like a ray of the sun on the walls of a prison.
And, as she looked around, she saw how Death, the consoler,
Laying his hand upon many a heart, had healed it forever.
Many familiar forms had disappeared in the night time;
Vacant their places were, or filled already by strangers.

Suddenly, as if arrested by fear or a feeling of wonder,
Still she stood, with her colorless lips apart, while a shudder
Ran through her frame, and, forgotten, the flowerets dropped from her fingers,
And from her eyes and cheeks the light and bloom of the morning.
Then there escaped from her lips a cry of such terrible anguish,
That the dying heard it, and started up from their pillows.

On the pallet before her was stretched the form of an old man.
Long, and thin, and gray were the locks that shaded his temples;
But, as he lay in the in morning light, his face for a moment
Seemed to assume once more the forms of its earlier manhood;
So are wont to be changed the faces of those who are dying.
Hot and red on his lips still burned the flush of the fever,
As if life, like the Hebrew, with blood had besprinkled its portals,
That the Angel of Death might see the sign, and pass over.
Motionless, senseless, dying, he lay, and his spirit exhausted
Seemed to be sinking down through infinite depths in the darkness,
Darkness of slumber and death, forever sinking and sinking.
Then through those realms of shade, in multiplied reverberations,
Heard he that cry of pain, and through the hush that succeeded
Whispered a gentle voice, in accents tender and saint-like,
"Gabriel! O my beloved!" and died away into silence.
Then he beheld, in a dream, once more the home of his childhood;
Green Acadian meadows, with sylvan rivers among them,
Village, and mountain, and woodlands; and, walking under their shadow,
As in the days of her youth, Evangeline rose in his vision.
Tears came into his eyes; and as slowly he lifted his eyelids,
Vanished the vision away, but Evangeline knelt by his bedside.
Vainly he strove to whisper her name, for the accents unuttered
Died on his lips, and their motion revealed what his tongue would have spoken.
Vainly he strove to rise; and Evangeline, kneeling beside him,
Kissed his dying lips, and laid his head on her bosom.
Sweet was the light of his eyes; but it suddenly sank into darkness,
As when a lamp is blown out by a gust of wind at a casement.

All was ended now, the hope, and the fear, and the sorrow,
All the aching of heart, the restless, unsatisfied longing,
All the dull, deep pain, and constant anguish of patience!
And, as she pressed once more the lifeless head to her bosom,
Meekly she bowed her own, and murmured, "Father, I thank thee!"

Still stands the forest primeval; but far away from its shadow,
Side by side, in their nameless graves, the lovers are sleeping.
Under the humble walls of the little Catholic churchyard,
In the heart of the city, they lie, unknown and unnoticed.
Daily the tides of life go ebbing and flowing beside them,

Thousands of throbbing hearts, where theirs are at rest and forever,
Thousands of aching brains, where theirs no longer are busy,
Thousands of toiling hands, where theirs have ceased from their labors,
Thousands of weary feet, where theirs have completed their journey!

Still stands the forest primeval; but under the shade of its branches
Dwells another race, with other customs and language.
Only along the shore of the mournful and misty Atlantic
Linger a few Acadian peasants, whose fathers from exile
Wandered back to their native land to die in its bosom.
In the fisherman's cot the wheel and the loom are still busy;
Maidens still wear their Norman caps and their kirtles of homespun,
And by the evening fire repeat Evangeline's story,
While from its rocky caverns the deep-voiced, neighboring ocean
Speaks, and in accents disconsolate answers the wail of the forest.

Bibliography

Any research content where Wikipedia, the Free Encyclopedia was used is under the following license:

Works licensed under Creative Commons Attribution-ShareAlike 3.0 Unported License, cc-by-sa 3.0, https://creativecommons.org/licenses/by-sa/3.0/

Wikipedia contributors. (2021, August 24). Roaring Twenties. In *Wikipedia, The Free Encyclopedia*. Retrieved 13:04, September 5, 2021, from https://en.wikipedia.org/w/index.php?title=Roaring_Twenties&oldid=1040470594

Wikipedia contributors. (2021, November 11). American Dream. In *Wikipedia, The Free Encyclopedia*. Retrieved 22:06, November 21, 2021, from https://en.wikipedia.org/w/index.php?title=American_Dream&oldid=1054601282

Wikipedia contributors. (2021, September 2). Wall Street Crash of 1929. In *Wikipedia, The Free Encyclopedia*. Retrieved 13:13, September 5, 2021, from https://en.wikipedia.org/w/index.php?title=Wall_Street_Crash_of_1929&oldid=1041917307

Wikipedia contributors. (2021, May 18). Dit name. In *Wikipedia, The Free Encyclopedia*. Retrieved 16:27, August 30, 2021, from https://en.wikipedia.org/w/index.php?title=Dit_name&oldid=1023848307

Wikipedia contributors. (2021, August 10). Expulsion of the Acadians. In *Wikipedia, The Free Encyclopedia*. Retrieved 15:41, August 30, 2021, from https://en.wikipedia.org/w/index.php?title=Expulsion_of_the_Acadians&oldid=1038139433

Marsh, James H., "Acadian Expulsion (the Great Upheaval)". In *The Canadian Encyclopedia*. Historica Canada. Article published September 04, 2013; Last Edited July 15, 2015, Retrieved

September 30, 2021. https://www.thecanadianencyclopedia.ca/en/article/the-deportation-of-the-acadians-feature,.

Wikipedia contributors. (2021, August 10). Acadians. In *Wikipedia, The Free Encyclopedia*. Retrieved 15:39, August 30, 2021, from https://en.wikipedia.org/w/index.php?title=Acadians&oldid=1038040070

Wikipedia contributors. (2019, March 14). Violet (ship). In *Wikipedia, The Free Encyclopedia*. Retrieved 15:55, August 30, 2021, from https://en.wikipedia.org/w/index.php?title=Violet_(ship)&oldid=887789190

Wikipedia contributors. (2021, January 17). Duke William (ship). In *Wikipedia, The Free Encyclopedia*. Retrieved 15:57, August 30, 2021, from https://en.wikipedia.org/w/index.php?title=Duke_William_(ship)&oldid=1000970621

Acadian Timeline, https://acadien.novascotia.ca/en/timeline, Acadian Timeline, Nova Scotia Canada, Acadian Affairs and Francophonie, Acadian Timeline, Website developed and maintained by Nova Scotia Communities, Culture and Heritage, Updated Aug 2021, Retrieved 7:25 Aug 24, 2021

Wikipedia contributors. (2021, November 13). Evangeline. In *Wikipedia, The Free Encyclopedia*. Retrieved 06:07, November 22, 2021, from https://en.wikipedia.org/w/index.php?title=Evangeline&oldid=1054982758

Wikipedia contributors. (2021, November 20). Elephant. In *Wikipedia, The Free Encyclopedia*. Retrieved 15:32, November 22, 2021, from https://en.wikipedia.org/w/index.php?title=Elephant&oldid=1056279004

Wikipedia contributors. (2021, November 22). Elephant cognition. In *Wikipedia, The Free Encyclopedia*. Retrieved 16:17, November 22, 2021, from https://en.wikipedia.org/w/index.php?title=Elephant_cognition&oldid=1056500801

Wikipedia contributors. (2021, November 21). Prohibition in the United States. In *Wikipedia, The Free Encyclopedia*. Retrieved 17:14, November 22, 2021, from https://en.wikipedia.org/

w/index.php?title=Prohibition_in_the_United_States&oldid=1056436564

Wikipedia contributors. (2021, November 8). Speakeasy. In *Wikipedia, The Free Encyclopedia.* Retrieved 17:25, November 22, 2021, from https://en.wikipedia.org/w/index.php?title=Speakeasy&oldid=1054218966

Wikipedia contributors. (2022, November 29). Volstead Act. In *Wikipedia, The Free Encyclopedia.* Retrieved 16:12, December 26, 2022, from https://en.wikipedia.org/w/index.php?title=Volstead_Act&oldid=1124519280

Wikipedia contributors. (2021, September 1). Great Depression. In *Wikipedia, The Free Encyclopedia.* Retrieved 14:02, September 5, 2021, from https://en.wikipedia.org/w/index.php?title=Great_Depression&oldid=1041811844

Wikipedia contributors. (2021, August 30). Dust Bowl. In *Wikipedia, The Free Encyclopedia.* Retrieved 14:19, September 5, 2021, from https://en.wikipedia.org/w/index.php?title=Dust_Bowl&oldid=1041478964

Wikipedia contributors. (2021, November 11). Sainte-Anne-de-Bellevue. In *Wikipedia, The Free Encyclopedia.* Retrieved 11:30, November 23, 2021, from https://en.wikipedia.org/w/index.php?title=Sainte-Anne-de-Bellevue&oldid=1054652862

Wikipedia contributors. (2022, October 28). Sainte-Anne-de-Bellevue Canal. In *Wikipedia, The Free Encyclopedia.* Retrieved 20:56, December 28, 2022, from https://en.wikipedia.org/w/index.php?title=Sainte-Anne-de-Bellevue_Canal&oldid=1118766590

Wikipedia contributors. (2021, January 15). Alfred Lépine. In *Wikipedia, The Free Encyclopedia.* Retrieved 11:06, November 23, 2021, from https://en.wikipedia.org/w/index.php?title=Alfred_L%C3%A9pine&oldid=1000448716

Wikipedia contributors. (2021, February 18). Waterloo, Quebec. In *Wikipedia, The Free Encyclopedia.* Retrieved 07:01, November 23, 2021, from https://en.wikipedia.org/w/index.php?title=Waterloo,_Quebec&oldid=1007500575

Wikipedia contributors. (2021, January 13). Asa Belknap Foster. In *Wikipedia, The Free Encyclopedia*. Retrieved 12:38, November 23, 2021, from https://en.wikipedia.org/w/index.php?title=Asa_Belknap_Foster&oldid=1000094804

Wikipedia contributors. (2021, November 2). Marie-Marguerite d'Youville. In *Wikipedia, The Free Encyclopedia*. Retrieved 12:50, November 23, 2021, from https://en.wikipedia.org/w/index.php?title=Marie-Marguerite_d%27Youville&oldid=1053219311

Wikipedia contributors. (2021, November 9). Ohio River flood of 1937. In *Wikipedia, The Free Encyclopedia*. Retrieved 21:51, November 23, 2021, from https://en.wikipedia.org/w/index.php?title=Ohio_River_flood_of_1937&oldid=1054360668

Evangeline: A Tale of Acadie, Henry Wadsworth Longfellow, Retrieved 14:02, September 8, 2023 from https://poets.org/poem/evangeline-tale-acadie, Public Domain

Printed in the USA
CPSIA information can be obtained
at www.ICGtesting.com
JSHW022220231023
50468JS00006B/7